Casper and Jasper and

the Terrible Tyrant

Tilia Klebenov Jacobs

Illustrations by Matt Tames

LINDEN TREE PRESS
—— For Those Who Love to Read ——

LINDEN TREE PRESS
———— For Those Who Love To Read ————

First published 2018 in the United States of America by
Linden Tree Press

Copyright © 2018 Tilia Klebenov Jacobs
All rights reserved.

First edition

ISBN: 978-1949-0480-01 (Linden Tree Press)

To Doug, Nate, and Elwyn
You are my fidelius birds.

Casper and Jasper and

the Terrible Tyrant

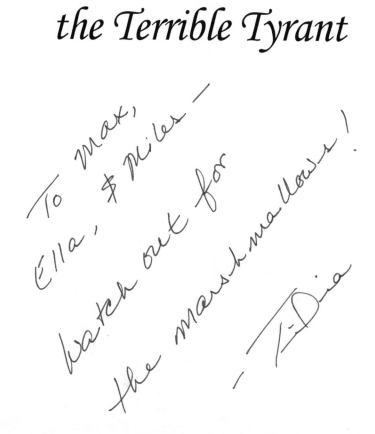

To Max,
Ella, & Miles —
watch out for
the marshmallows!

— T. Dino

This is a tale of wondrous magic and great suffering. You will meet a foul villain and the heroes who battled him. Trolls are involved, and twins. Oh, and a beautiful princess, but not in the way that you might imagine.

Long ago and far away, in the misty, distant Lands of Yonder, farms encircled the villages of Larksong and Nether Wallop, and the twin hamlets of Deasil and Widdershins. The smallest town was called Inglenook; the largest, Middlemost. It is there that we now turn our attention.

Middlemost was a polyglot parcel of neighborhoods. Now, according to *Pilcrow and Inkhorn's Concise Dictionary*, "polyglot" means "many tongues;" but please do not let that revolting image disturb you. What it really means is that Middlemost was home to all manner of people from different backgrounds. Its playground burbled with children and piskies sharing snacks and popular magic spells. If you visited, you might buy clunky mugs at Gargles the Golem's Earthenwares Shoppe, or see a family of horned demons with berets sipping burnt coffee at a café called Charbucks. Two sisters named Scribble and Jot ran Dybbuk's Books, a jolly place to find a novel and a friendly argument. Tree-lined boulevards led to a big, important hospital near a square in the town center.

But that peaceful feeling had shattered six months earlier, when Count Wilhelm Scream arrived and established himself as Supreme Ruler over all the land, holding sway from a mountaintop fortress filled with an army of dangerous creatures who enforced his new laws against almost anything that might be fun. You can only imagine how annoying this was for everyone concerned, except, of course, the count himself. Nowadays Scribble and Jot's big window, previously home to picture books and adventure tales, displayed volumes with titles such as *A Helpful Explanation of Obedience to Count Wilhelm Scream* and *Why Life is So Much Better in a Dictatorship*. They kept the old books in a back room, but one had to know a certain password to be allowed to see them. Otherwise Scribble and Jot would just dust their shelves and talk loudly about how best to organize paperbacks of uneven heights.

Restlessness thrummed through Middlemost. In the schools, on the streets, at the farms and down the alleyways, people grumbled. This was particularly true of young and idealistic people who thought that maybe, just maybe, Count Wilhelm Scream didn't have the right to rule them, especially if said rule involved taking land without asking, levying exorbitant taxes, and maintaining a Special Police force with the disagreeable habit of kicking in doors and dragging off entire families without explanation. This had been happening a lot lately, and the idealists in particular were getting fed up with it.

I trust we have established that Count Wilhelm Scream was not a nice person? Good. It becomes important later on.

Two of the idealists were named Adele and Kale Brandiwygn, and they had been married for about a year and a half. They had red hair and fair skin. So did their babies, twins named Charles and James. The family lived in a cottage on the town square. Its three front steps were decorated with pots of multicolored geraniums, and the door was red with diamond-shaped windows in the upper half. The downstairs held a kitchen and a book-lined living room, and the upstairs had just enough space for two bedrooms tucked under the slanted eaves. It was small but cozy, and they loved it.

On this particular day, the Brandiwygns were hosting a very dangerous, very secret meeting of a brand-new rebel organization. They and many of their friends were teachers who chafed under the new rule. Kale resented having to teach history from *How the Great and Glorious Count Wilhelm Scream Saved Us All,* and Adele was quite sick of being forced to use a blocky textbook called *Science and Other Lies.* Consequently, they had resolved to fight for truth in any way they could. It was brave of them, for if the count or any of his spies heard about it, his police would be on the scene in a heartbeat. As a cover for their meeting, Adele and Kale said they were celebrating the six-month birthday of their twins.

At this point you may find yourself saying, "Six months! Isn't that how long the count has been in power?" This shows what a perceptive reader you are. Indeed, the twins were born the very same day that the count swept down on the Lands of Yonder, drenching them in fear and cruelty.

But back to the main thread. Kale and Adele had hired one of their students to babysit during their meeting. Her name was

Prissy, and she was a lump of a girl, all long, dark hair and sullen eyes, who lived in a local orphanage called Kinderdump. Adele was pleased to note that Prissy handled the twins with the competence of a girl who has been taking care of babies since she was old enough to lift one. And if Prissy's eyes had not exactly lit up at the sight of the swaddled infants, Adele felt it was a small matter. After all, she and Kale would be downstairs in case of emergency.

"They should be ready for their naps in about an hour," said Adele as she showed Prissy the cribs, "Kale's showing them off to our friends, but I'll bring them upstairs when they get tired. And if you get confused about which is which, check their bracelets," she added over her shoulder as she started down the stairs.

Since the twins were identical and parents like to know which child is which, each boy wore a charm fastened securely to his chubby wrist. One was marked with a C, the other with a J. The charms were big enough that the boys couldn't choke on them. Indeed, they were too big to fit into a baby's mouth should either ever find a way to detach it from the bracelet. But they did enjoy pulling on the charms and gnawing on them in a thoughtful manner.

Adele went downstairs, where Kale and the other rebels crowded the living room.

"Let's call ourselves Whisper," suggested a rebel named Bob.

"Why?" said an idealist named Ingrid.

"Because it's the opposite of Scream."

"It's also the opposite of inspiring," said Ingrid. "How about the Ascendant Defenders?"

The discussion went on. Kale held one baby, Adele the other. Kale had made cookies; Adele had made handouts. She distributed them, pausing only to remind people to read them, memorize them, and eat or burn them so they would never be caught with evidence on their persons. A few rebels munched cookies to cleanse their palates. It was precisely noon.

At one minute past noon, the front door smashed off its hinges and a torrent of angry men hurtled in. Their jagged soles tore the carpet. Their black-gloved hands ripped pictures off the walls. Truncheons crashed down on vases, and broken flowers fell to the floor.

The Special Police of Count Wilhelm Scream had arrived.

Prissy ran downstairs. Seeing the mayhem, she smiled.

The rebels screamed. Some tried to eat their handouts. Others threw them in the air. Police grabbed people by the shirts or arms or hair and hauled them outside.

There a terrible sight met them: two windowless wagons painted bright orange and labeled "Prisoners of Count Wilhelm Scream." They seemed to fill the paved square. The Special

Police tossed men into one wagon, women into the other. Black-hooded figures slammed the doors shut as the vehicles filled with frantic victims.

The unhappy fact was this. Thanks to an informant, Count Wilhelm Scream had discovered the rebel movement and ordered a series of raids that very day, targeting every place it lurked: Larksong and Inglenook and Nether Wallop, Widdershins and Deasil—and now, Middlemost.

A crowd gathered. Some shook their fists. Others cried aloud in fear and turned their faces away. Still others merely despaired.

In this crowd was an unhappy couple, Becky and Zach Zuckerman. Their unhappiness had nothing to do with the count or the crowd or the mass arrests of questionable legality that were taking place before their very eyes. In fact, Becky and Zach were so miserable that they scarcely noticed the throng until they were in the thick of it, being jostled to the front by the elbows and shoulders of furious, frightened strangers. Even when they saw the count's wagons, Becky could only pass her hand over her belly and try not to weep. For she and Zach had just come from the important hospital, where an important doctor had very kindly but in no uncertain terms told them that they would never be able to have children.

Becky and Zach wanted children more than anything.

"What's going on?" Becky asked one of the furious, frightened strangers.

"Scream," shouted the man.

"Why?" said Becky.

"Scream," yelled the man. "He's at it again. Look!" He shook his fist as three Special Police dragged a young woman along the sidewalk. She was cramming a sheet of paper in her mouth and chewing vigorously.

Becky looked. So did Zach, who had become separated from her and was in another part of the crowd. The mob roiled. They had seen arrests in the past six months, but never so many at one time. They were so angry they forgot to be scared. A group rushed the wagons, shouting and beating the sides with their fists.

A lieutenant of the Special Police leaped to the roof of a wagon and whipped his sword from its scabbard with a zing. It gleamed like ice in the bright sunshine.

"Quiet," he bellowed. "Unless you want to see the inside of the wagons too."

"Make us," shouted a voice from the mob.

The lieutenant blew a whistle. From behind each wagon stepped a troll. Each carried a club. Each tapped the club in the palm of his huge, hairy hand. And each grinned a gruesome grin, full of jagged, yellow teeth.

"Meet Danegeld and his cousin Skullcleaver," snarled the lieutenant.

At this, some members of the crowd dropped their fists and shoved their hands in their pockets and tried to look as though they held no political opinions of note. Others, however, only became angrier. The crowd seethed. The trolls stomped forward. Becky and Zach were rocked to and fro.

Two Special Police trooped out of the house, pulling Adele and Kale. Kale's vest was askew and Adele's hair was mussed. Each clutched a baby.

Prissy watched from the front door, smiling the smile of someone who has just poisoned ants and is waiting for them to start twitching before they die.

The Special Police heaved the couple toward the wagons. Their doors opened like hungry mouths, and a babble of misery and confusion came from within.

Adele and Kale looked at each other and at the babies and at each other again. And then, in the way that people who know each other very well and love each other very deeply sometimes do, they had the same idea at the same instant.

Adele kicked her Special Policeman in the shin. It bruised her foot, because he was wearing shin guards. She kicked again, harder. He loosened his grip. Adele wrenched free. She drew her arms back and threw her baby into the crowd.

Becky gasped. She held up her hands and bent her knees. The baby landed in her arms, heavy and warm and wide-eyed.

Becky stumbled backwards into the hurly-burly.

At the same moment, Kale elbowed his Special Policeman in the face. It didn't hurt him nearly as much as Kale would have liked, but he dropped Kale's arm so he could say "Hey!" and "Ouch!" and rub his chin.

Kale planted his feet and turned his baby sideways so as to be more aerodynamic. "Go long!" he roared, and threw his baby into another part of the crowd.

Zach leaped into the air and grabbed it.

The baby burped. Zach shouldered his way through the crowd and ran.

With the distinctive bellow of men who realize that they now have to find babies that have been chucked into an angry mob, the Special Police thrust Kale and Adele into the wagons. The doors slammed shut. The engines snarled to life. The wagons lurched forward, into the unknown nightmare of Count Wilhelm Scream's revenge.

Adele slumped on the floor of one darkened vehicle. Kale pressed against the wall of another. They quaked with the horror of knowing they might never see each other again.

But both were thinking, "The babies are safe. At least the babies are safe."

As anyone who has ever gone to pick wildflowers only to stumble across a dragon with seasonal allergies knows, "safe" is a relative term.

By skirting the crowd and ducking down the occasional alleyway, Becky and Zach made their separate ways back to the car they had parked at a meter behind the hospital. The hideous orange wagons full of prisoners blasted past in a scud of dust. A troll trotted alongside, rumbling a victory song deep in his hairy throat. People drifted away in clumps, trembling at what they had seen. Becky and Zach stared at each other and at the babies and at each other again.

"Where did you get that baby?" gasped Becky.

"Where did you get that one?" said Zach.

"Someone threw it, and I—"

"Caught it?"

"Yes."

"Me, too!"

And then, simply because they were frightened and bewildered and overwhelmed, they laughed.

Snuggled in Becky and Zach's arms, the babies looked up at them and at each other and up again at the grownups. They chuckled in the hesitant, gurgly way that babies do.

"What's so funny?" roared a voice.

Becky and Zach whirled around. A Special Policeman loomed over them, gritting his teeth. It was the lieutenant from the square. Behind him stood a grinning troll, his club in his left hand.

Everyone stopped laughing.

Zach held his baby tighter. A dew of sweat broke out on his brow, and the backs of his hands prickled. He had heard, everyone had heard, of the wrath of Wilhelm Scream. Torture, forced confessions, and hard labor were just a few of the possibilities. His arms shook, and without meaning to he squeezed his little bundle.

The infant began to cry. The second one joined him.

"Oh, great," said Becky. She glared at the Special Policeman. "You woke the babies."

The Special Policeman rocked on his heels. It gave the impression that he might jump on them at any moment. "It so happens that we're looking for two babies."

"Two babies," repeated the troll.

"Well, these are spoken for," said Becky.

"Are they yours?" said the Special Policeman.

Zach gave a wheezy chuckle. "Whose else would they be?"

The Special Policeman walked slowly around Zach and Becky so they had to keep turning to keep him in sight. The troll hulked along behind him. "Boys or girls?" he said.

"Boys," said Becky, hoping she was right.

The Special Policeman smiled. The missing babies were boys. Still, lots of people had babies, and half of them would be boys. He pointed at the one in Becky's arms. "What's his name?"

The tot smiled at him, and, seeing the man's finger, reached out to grab it. On his chubby wrist was a bracelet, and from it dangled a gold disk engraved with the letter "C."

"Casper," said Becky.

The Special Policeman whipped toward Zach and pointed a stumpy finger at the baby he held. "And this one?"

The baby in Zach's arms pulled one arm free from his swaddling and waved a tiny fist. On his chubby wrist was a bracelet, and from it dangled a gold disk engraved with the letter "J." At the sight of the gold, the troll's eyes gleamed.

"Jasper," said Zach, pulling the baby close.

"They're twins," said Becky helpfully.

"I can see that," said the Special Policeman in disgust. "Why else would anyone name two boys Casper and Jasper? Why not just call them Pen and Pencil and be done with it?"

Becky turned to Zach in indignation. "See? I told you."

"It seemed like such a good idea at the time," said Zach weakly.

"Don't think either of them will thank you for it in the long run," snapped the Special Policeman. "It's no laughing matter." And he turned his head aside as if to hide his wretchedness.

For this Special Policeman's family name was Dwop; and in a fit of giddiness his parents had named him Wayne. The torments he had endured at school over this had further soured an already rancid personality, so that by the time he was old enough to get a job, Special Policeman was a natural for him.

"There, there." The troll lifted a hairy hand and patted his commanding officer on the shoulder.

Lieutenant Dwop staggered under the buffeting and glared at the troll. "Knock it off, Danegeld."

"Yes, sir." The troll's hand dropped to his side.

"Oh, my," said Becky. She lifted the baby in her arms and sniffed extravagantly at its bottom. "I do believe we have a Brown Alert."

Zach hoisted his baby onto his shoulder and squeezed its behind. "Gosh, yes. I hope it's not one of the goopy ones."

"Either way," said Becky, "we need to get home and change these boys before everything squooshes up their backs. If that's *quite* all right with you, Lieutenant."

Lieutenant Dwop frowned suspiciously. "Do they always, ah, go at the same time?"

"They're twins," said Becky. "They do everything together." She shifted the baby to her other arm. "Perhaps you'd like to come with us, Lieutenant, and make sure they're really boys?"

The troll chortled. It sounded like rocks bouncing down a cliff side. Lieutenant Dwop, whose experience with children was limited to his own miserable youth, shuddered. "These aren't the babies we're looking for," he said. "Move along. Move along."

As Lieutenant Dwop and the troll stomped away, Becky and Zach looked at each other and quaked with relief and fear.

"This," said Zach, "has to be the best worst day ever." He looked down at the baby snuggled into the crook of his arm. It blew a bubble at him and hiccupped in a satisfied way.

"I wonder if they really are twins," said Becky. Both had round blue eyes and pink skin and fuzzy hair tinged with orange.

"I wonder if they really are boys," said Zach.

"Guess we'll find out soon enough," said Becky.

"They're beautiful," said Zach.

"Yes," said Becky. "They are." She glanced at the shop that overlooked the sidewalk where they stood, and her eyes lit up. "Yarn!"

"Yarn?" said Zach.

"They're going to need booties," said Becky blissfully, "and little caps, and darling wee sweaters. What colors do you think?"

"No idea," said Zach, handing her the baby he already thought of as Jasper. "But the meter's run out. I'll join you in a minute."

Smiling and holding a baby in each arm, Becky sauntered into the shop. Zach clinked a coin into the meter. Footsteps ran up behind him. He jumped, expecting to see Lieutenant Dwop or the troll or more Special Police. Instead, a pudgy girl with long, dark hair tumbled to a stop before him, gripping her side with one hand.

"Prison wagons," she panted. "Where?"

"There." Zach pointed.

A look of rage crossed the girl's face. She tore up the street in the direction Zach had indicated.

"Don't!" cried Zach. "It's too dangerous." But the girl, if she heard, did not respond and was soon out of sight. Zach shuddered.

Becky came out of the shop, still holding the babies. A bag hung from her elbow, bulging with multicolored balls of yarn. A pair of fancy, gold-tone knitting needles stuck out of one of the balls, and Zach could see part of a book called *The Knit Wit's Guide to Easy Patterns for Beginners.*

"What's wrong?" said Becky.

Zach gestured up the street. "A girl—chasing the vans. I thought maybe her family—maybe she was trying to rescue them."

"She can't," said Becky quietly.

"No."

"Not from him."

"No," agreed Zach again.

Becky handed him one of the boys, and they looked down at them.

"I wonder who they were," said Becky. "The ones who had these."

"Good parents, by the look of it," said Zach. The babies were clean and obviously well fed, and seemed to know no fear.

"With good throwing arms," agreed Becky.

They were silent. Finally Zach said, "What now?"

"Right," said Becky briskly. "We can't afford to be sentimental. Whoever the boys'—babies'—parents are, they won't be coming back, that's for sure. So it looks like we have kids, Zach."

"Step one is to buy diapers," said Zach. "I bet you don't want to knit those."

"Step two is to leave town," said Becky.

Zach blinked. "Why?"

"Don't you think the neighbors might find it odd if we suddenly turned up with two babies?"

"Well, sure, but—"

"People talk," said Becky. "And the count doesn't like loose ends."

The baby in Zach's arms wiggled. So did the one Becky was holding. "I see what you mean," said Zach. "So where do we go?"

"I was thinking Inglenook. My sister was telling me just last week she needs help at the shop."

Inglenook stood in the shadow of Count Wilhelm Scream's Mountain, which the locals now called "Mount Count." The town's walls were so thick that in places homes and businesses had been built into them. They held back a bleak forest and an extensive quagmire. A sign at the town gate read, "Inglenook: Last Corner of Charm before the Desolation Begins."

Zach stifled a screech. "You want to move *closer* to Scream?"

"Not particularly," said Becky. "But I do want a roof over my head, and a job, and," she shifted the baby, who was growing wigglesome and heavy, to her other hip, "neighbors who won't wonder why we suddenly have kids."

The wagons lurched up Mount Count. At a fork in the road, the men's went one way, and the women's went the other. Presently the women's wagon jolted to a halt. The doors screeched open. "Out!" shouted a harsh voice.

Adele and her friends stumbled out to find themselves before a tower of yellow and brown fieldstone dotted with chips of mica that glittered like broken mirrors. It was built into the mountainside, and had windows only at the very top, under its conical slate roof. "One of the count's new prisons," Adele thought as armed guards hustled them through a door of studded oak.

Inside, the guards made them hand over their shoes and clothes and all their jewelry, except for wedding rings, which they were allowed to keep to remind them how much they missed their husbands. They were issued Highly Efficient and Appropriate Work Attire, which was what Count Wilhelm Scream called denim overalls covered with flour and chaff, and shoes so heavy that the women felt as though they had tortoises on their feet. The overseer, a nasty woman with a body like a sack of flour and a head like a potato, explained that this was so their feet would be protected from the heat and bone-crushing gears of the prison's machinery, and was proof of how much

Count Scream loved them even though they had been very wicked and needed to be punished for the rest of their lives.

This was not true, of course. The shoes were heavy to prevent the prisoners from escaping, because they could not run in them. Plus, no one believed for a moment that Count Scream loved anyone, and certainly not them.

Without further ado, the overseer, whose name was Spudd, set Adele and her friends to work alongside newly arrested rebels from other towns, lifting heavy bags of grain and pouring it into the grindstones that shrieked in the center of the Food Mills. The bags were heavy and the mill was hot and the prisoners were scared and miserable. Adele suspected this would be their lot for a long time.

She was correct. It would be weeks before they even saw the sky again.

Meanwhile, Kale and his friends stumbled from their wagon into a large, dirt circle enclosed by tangles of wire studded with razor-sharp blades. It held a barracks and a few other buildings. The forest pressed against the fence, its fingers dripping with shadows. Kale wondered how far from home he was.

Inside the barracks, the men were also issued Highly Efficient and Appropriate Work Attire and heavy boots; and they too were allowed to keep their wedding rings to remind them that the count was holding their wives prisoner and that they had better behave. Dozens of rebels from other towns were already there, looking frightened and miserable. Their overseer was a man with a dark, formless body and a head like a lump of coal. His name was Plotz, and he smiled as he told them that Count Wilhelm Scream had decided to be merciful and not kill them. Instead, out of the greatness of his heart he would allow them to work in his Ice Mine prison camp, digging out chunks of ice until they died.

Kale and the other men did not feel that this was particularly merciful of the count, but no one said so.

"Rainbow Ice goes in the carts," said Plotz. "Black Ice in the warehouse. And boys—watch out for that stuff."

"Why?" said Bob.

Plotz laughed raucously and flung open the doors of the barracks. Kale squared his shoulders and led the way outside. What else could he do?

Grinning guards with truncheons poked and herded the prisoners into a big, wire-cage elevator. Kale found himself jammed into a corner with Bob's elbow in his ear. The door slammed shut and the elevator descended into the darkness of the mine. As the black, airless atmosphere of the shaft gripped them, the men felt their hearts shake.

Bob eased his elbow down. "What's with the Black Ice?"

Kale stared ahead bleakly. "If you touch it, you die."

Bob swallowed. "How long does that take?"

"A second. Maybe."

The men groaned and wondered what other horrors awaited them.

The answer was, a great many. The elevator bumped to a halt, and the doors opened with a yowl. "Out. Now!" barked a voice. The men stepped out.

A tunnel stretched before them, its black walls glistening with ice in every color: green as springtime, red as sunsets, and blue as the sky they could no longer see. Every yard or so lanterns hung from chains drilled into the ceiling, but between them shadows shifted like evil spirits. It was so cold Kale's breath frosted before him.

A guard smacked a helmet onto Kale's head, and thrust gloves and a rock hammer into his hands. "Start digging. You too. Move!"

The men bent to their work, chipping ice and loading it onto carts and hoping it would not kill them with its touch.

Kale almost tripped on something. He bent and picked up a little hammer, half the size of the one he was using. The floor was littered with similar tools: tiny pickaxes, shovels, and mallets with broken handles. Kale squatted for a better look. Near the floor the wall was scribbled over with strange words, like "gevalt" and "shmendrick" and "nu." The writing was small, and Kale wondered if the count had enslaved children in the mines. This made him think of his sons, and he almost cried as he straightened up and began hacking at the cold, hard walls.

Atop Mount Count stood Castle Mirkstone, the stronghold of Count Wilhelm Scream. It was a jumble of ramparts and towers around a courtyard guarded by a fanged portcullis. The throne room was designed to frighten visitors. Its windowless walls were blue-white ice, and they rose so high you would have to crane your neck to see where they met overhead in a frosted arch. A carpet ran like a streak of blood from the door to the room's sole item of furniture, a throne that gleamed wickedly in the pale light of the rimy room. The count sat there now. He was tall, and his hair was thin. As you might expect, he wore black, and a cape hung down his back straight as a waterfall. He was cloudy of visage, which is a poetic way of saying the skin of his face was dark. His cheeks were scarred by a childhood illness, his nose curved like a hawk's beak, and his mouth was a grim line.

Now, much nonsense has been written about the throne of Count Wilhelm Scream: that it was made of the frozen bones of his enemies, that anyone who looked at it would die, that if one touched it one would be transformed into a zombie and stagger about with one's arms outstretched, having developed a sudden predilection for brains. None of this is true. For one thing, no throne can kill you with its mere appearance. That is the job of a basilisk, or Medusa's face. Furthermore, one does not become a zombie by touching a throne any more than one becomes a werewolf by patting a husky. It is easy to see how such rumors get started, but it should be our job always to strive for the truth.

In reality, the throne was made of Black Ice, the very substance that now threatened Kale and his companions. Unlike them, however, the count could touch it and not die; so he saw himself as marvelously strong, and despised the weakness of others.

The throne was the source of much of the count's power. It gave him his ability to kill with a touch, and it made his darkest desires reality. If he wanted dungeon doors locked or his enemies shackled; if he wanted hope to die in prisoners languishing in the cells deep below his throne; if he desired anything cruel or evil or petty, then it would be so, thanks to the throne of Black Ice. But the throne's power only extended to the walls of Mirkstone. Outside was a different matter. Outside people could think and plan and dream. This, the count felt, was dangerous; and so he was expressionless as he listened to Lieutenant Wayne Dwop of the Special Police describe the raid on Middlemost.

"A triumph," said Lieutenant Dwop. "We have quashed the uprising." The officer was doing his best to sound breezy and confident, but the architecture of the room, plus his frankly rather terrifying boss, were having their intended effect. His voice squeaked at unexpected times, and his nose was sweating, which happened whenever he felt ill at ease.

The count's voice did not squeak. "The rebels are captured?"

"Yes, sir."

"And imprisoned?"

"Yes, sir."

The count leaned forward. "And?"

"Sir?" Dwop twitched.

The count's mouth thinned. "We are just beginning to help this unruly land."

"Yes, sir." Dwop felt drops of sweat gathering on his nose.

"Yet rebellion murmurs in every town and village. If we allow disobedience, others will spring up."

"Yes, sir."

"We must make an example of this group."

"Yes, sir." Dwop's nose tickled. He dared not swipe at it.

"Have you?"

"Sir?" The droplets meandered toward Dwop's cavernous nostrils. Soon they would form a rivulet. He sweated harder.

The count looked down at him with bleak menace. "Did you learn their plans and thwart them? Have you destroyed their pamphlets, booklets, posters, or other materials that promote disobedience? Have you paid the loyal subjects who assisted you in today's campaign? And are you certain that none escaped?"

Dwop gulped. Sweat dribbled onto his uniform jacket. "The fliers are destroyed, sir." This was true, since the rebels had eaten them.

"And the plans?"

"Thwarted." The plans, such as they were, amounted to meeting again next Thursday, so here Lieutenant Dwop felt he could speak with confidence.

The count looked in disgust at Dwop, whose face was frozen in a ghastly rictus of a smile that he meant to be ingratiating. The lieutenant's eyes quaked in their sockets, and his uniform was spattered with sweat. Slowly, the count peeled off a glove and let it fall.

The count turned his hand. The bones stood out under the skin. "How did this traitorous cabal escape your notice till now?"

"Ah." Dwop swallowed. "Of course, sir—intelligence operations—even in the best conditions—"

The count glided down from the throne. He held his bare hand next to the lieutenant's cheek. Cold stung Dwop's skin. He gasped. The Count smiled.

"You are sworn to obey me, Lieutenant."

"Yes, your grace," whispered the miserable man.

"Do you know what happens to those who are not obedient to me?"

"Well—um—"

The count towered over him. "What is obedience, Lieutenant?"

Dwop struggled. He had never been good in school, and this sounded suspiciously like an essay question. "It means—doing as one is told—always." He gulped. "Right?"

"Only partly." The count waved his bloodless hand before Dwop's face, and the lieutenant felt a crinkling sensation as the sweat on his nose turned to ice. "Obedience—true obedience—is peace. My greatest gift."

"Of course, sir," whimpered Dwop.

"But rebellion is disobedience and discord and unhappiness," said the count. "You permitted this."

"Sir, I never disobey!"

The door to the throne room scraped open, and a girl with long, dark hair stormed down the blood-red carpet, breathing heavily.

"Liar," gasped Prissy, and dropped to her knees before the count.

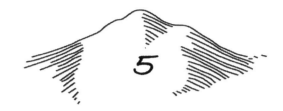

The count surveyed the girl from head to toe. Her clothes were plain and ill-fitting, her hair stringy, her shoes ragged. Although she was out of breath, she did not tremble. Instead, she looked directly at him, as though they were equals; and behind her dark eyes, he caught a glimpse of something cold and monstrous.

"Who are you?" he said. "And how dare you enter my throne room?" But his voice was mild, and he settled back on his throne to hear her answer.

The girl took a deep breath and glared at Dwop, who was swabbing ice chips from his nose with a handkerchief. "He said he'd pay me." Her voice was nasal and uncultured, and threaded with rage. "Then he didn't. Ain't that disobedience?"

"I will," said Dwop patiently, "on the third Tuesday of the month. That's when informants are paid. Yesterday was Wednesday—that's for saboteurs." With a light chuckle he folded his handkerchief and placed it in his pocket in a way that he hoped indicated the conversation was over.

The girl snorted. "Third Tuesday my left shoe."

"Have you filled out the proper forms?" said Dwop. He glanced nervously at the count. "Little girl, this is a place for grownups. If there's a problem, you need to ask your mommy or daddy to—"

Prissy rocketed to her feet, fists clenched, trembling to every hair on her head. "I did what you said, and I ain't waiting three Tuesdays for a decent meal," she snarled.

A shudder of delight hummed through the count's thin frame. "Young lady," he said. She turned to face him, still glaring. "What is your name?"

The girl, who had always hated the name Prissy, hesitated. "Princess."

One corner of the count's mouth curved upward. "And your last name?"

It was Anders, but she hated that too. "Abattoir." She had seen the word on a sign partway up the mountain, and felt strangely drawn to it.

"Where are you from, Princess Abattoir?"

"Middlemost." She folded her arms.

"And your parents?"

"Dead."

"I see," said the count. "What happened to your father?"

"He got sick. It was real slow." Her lip curled in contempt.

"And your mother?"

The girl snorted. "Dropped dead in the kitchen. Heart attack, they said. "

The count clasped his hands on his knees. "When did this happen?"

"Six years ago. I was six."

"And you live in Middlemost now."

"They don't feed us enough at the orphanage," she said. "I need the money he said he'd give me."

"I see," said the count again. "How did you get here?"

"Followed the wagons."

"Followed the wagons?" One of the count's elegant eyebrows lifted.

"From Middlemost. After the raid. When he ran out without paying me."

"You can't have," burst out Dwop. "It's too far. You're just a kid."

Lieutenant Dwop was not entirely wrong. Princess Abattoir, as she now styled herself, was indeed just a kid; and it really was too far. She had had to walk from Middlemost to the mountain. She had picked her way around a perilous swamp and stumbled through a dark and deadly forest pocked with frozen clearings that stayed cold all year long, all the while focusing on the castle of Count Wilhelm Scream, or at least as much of it as she could see while making her way over the mangled landscape. Small wonder, then, that even as she glared at the count she swayed, as though her tired legs and bloody, tattered feet would no longer hold her up. But she did not fall, and at this the count was pleased.

"How did you get past my guards?" he said.

"I told 'em there was a bunch of rebels gonna rescue their friends and they was starting a fire down the hill to burn the castle and harm yer august personage," she said.

"And they believed you?"

"Dunno. But they run off to put out the fire."

"What fire?" said Dwop.

Slowly Princess Abattoir turned her head to bestow upon him a look of acid contempt. "The one I set down the hill so I could get in the castle. *Sir.*"

Dwop goggled. The count tented his fingers. "Lieutenant."

Dwop jumped. "Your Grace?"

"Once the guards have put out the fire, have them shot for deserting their posts."

"Yes, sir."

"Replace them with trolls. I expect they will be more reliable."

"Yes, sir."

The count turned back to the girl. "So it was you who informed the lieutenant about the rebels."

"Yeah."

"And," he coughed delicately, "uncovered a certain weakness in my castle's security system."

"Yeah."

"How did you find out about the rebels?"

"At school. I heard the teachers talking about the meeting," replied the girl. "They all hate yer most honorable lordfulship."

"Do they?"

"Yeah. Said they was glad there's people like them everywhere 'cos you'd be wrecked in, like, two weeks, three tops. So I says, 'Can I babysit?' 'Cos I knew they had kids. So they said yes, and I went and told *him,*" she jerked her head at Dwop, "about the meeting, and the other rebels, and he said he'd give me lots of money for being loyal to your Grace and blah blah blah, but then him and his guys just broke up the meeting and so the teachers never paid me for the babies and he never paid me for the snitch. And now what am I supposed to do?" She folded her arms and scowled first at Dwop, then at the count as though certain he would sympathize.

The count shifted his gaze to his officer. "Lieutenant. We do not wish to discourage such obedience among our young citizens."

"No, sir," agreed Dwop, whose nose had begun to sweat again.

"No waiting till the third Tuesday for Princess Abattoir," said the count.

"No, sir."

"And no paperwork."

"No, sir."

"Bring her reward immediately."

"Yes, sir." Dwop turned and strode out of the room as fast as he could without cantering. He noticed that the count had not asked any questions about Kale and Adele's babies, and he had no wish to be around if the conversation took that turn.

The door shut behind him. The count contemplated the girl. She looked back at him.

"Princess Abattoir," he said. "Would you care to work for me?"

"Why?"

"Why?"

"Yeah."

The count's eyes were black and beckoning. "Because, Princess, I have powers you cannot imagine. Because you are in my world now, not that shambles of an orphanage. And if I choose to raise some lowborn nothing of a girl who can be of service to me, I can do that. Or I can destroy her with a touch." He leaned forward, and his shadow cloaked her in cold.

She glared. "The hags at the orphanage says stuff like that too."

The count almost laughed. "Would you like to know what makes me different from them?"

Princess Abattoir found, as many people did, that there was something magnetic about the count. "Sure. Yer grace."

"I have power."

"I just got past yer guard."

"I don't mean them. I mean me." He stood, tall and black against the pale walls of his chamber, and his voice was icy. "I can move stone and chill the air. I can kill with a touch or grant life with a word. Follow me, be my help, and I can place your most dizzying desires between your thumb and forefinger. Can anyone else do that?"

"No," she was forced to admit.

The walls of the throne room crackled as crystals grew within them. The count's teeth glittered like icicles. "There is one requirement."

"What's that?"

"Obedience," he said. "You will find that obedience is peace."

Slowly, Princess Abattoir nodded. "Okay." The count leaned back in his throne. "One final question, Princess. Have you ever heard of a wyvern?"

One night a few weeks later, Kale pulled himself onto his bunk in the prisoners' barracks. His muscles felt like bricks, and he imagined he could hear his bones grinding against each other. He was cold through and through. He looked at his wedding ring and wondered what Adele was doing.

Bob lay on the bunk next to his and stared past him with glassy eyes. "I'm done," he mumbled.

Kale turned his heavy head. He felt responsible for Bob, who would not be there if Kale had not invited him to the rebel meeting. "What do you mean?"

"I found some Black Ice. Tomorrow I'm going to grab it."

Kale jerked upright. "You can't."

"I will."

"No!" cried Kale. "If you kill yourself, the count has won!"

"He already has," said the exhausted fellow.

Kale ran his hands through his hair. "Bob," he said, "what's your address?"

"Huh?"

"Your address," repeated Kale. "What is it?"

Bob moaned. He was covered with grit from the mines, and his body ached. Tonelessly he recited, "123 Leafy Bough Way, Middlemost. Who cares?"

"What color is your door?" said Kale.

"Go away."

"What color is your door?" Kale reached over and shook Bob by the shoulder. "I can't go away and you know it, so you might as well answer."

"Green," said Bob. "With a brass knob. And the carpet in the hallway is blue. Why?"

"Jerry," called Kale. "Why did you and Stella name your dog Snowball?"

"Because we found him in the snow," sighed the man named Jerry. "Who cares?"

"Don't you see?" said Kale. "As long as we remember all this, we're still us. The count can work us and beat us and take us away from our homes, but as long as we know who we are and where we came from, we're still the same people we were before—this."

"So what?" said Jerry. "So I know my dog's name, and Bob knows what color he painted his front door. How does that help? We're still stuck here."

Kale rested his head in his hands. His brain was foggy from too much work and not enough food or rest, but an idea was squirming through it. "Who here knows about the mountains?" he said. "And the roads, and—and everything about this land?"

"I know Middlemost pretty good," said Bob, interested in spite of himself. "My family's lived there forever."

"My grandparents were farmers outside the city, near the mountain," said Jerry. "I used to explore the woods and stuff when I visited them."

"Whoopee," said a rebel named Norbert, from Nether Wallop. "So now I guess we can just open the gates and drive home."

"This is great," said Kale, ignoring Norbert and rubbing his hands together. "Gather round, lads! We're going to see what we know—what we *all* know—about where we are."

"Why?" said Bob and Jerry at the same time.

"We're getting out of here," said Kale.

"What?" said Jerry.

"How?" said Bob.

"When?" said Jerry.

"I don't know," said Kale. "But it'll happen. We'll get a break. We'll know it when we see it, and when we do, we'll be prepared."

"For what?" said Bob.

"I don't *know,*" said Kale. "But look. Failing to prepare is preparing to fail. We need to be as ready as we can for whatever it is. So come on, all. Who's an expert in what?"

"Kale, stop it," said Jerry. "This isn't an Ascendant Defenders meeting, for crying out loud."

Kale winced. "I deserve that. Look, guys, it's my fault you're—we're—here. I don't know how Scream found out about the meeting, but he did. So now I owe you."

"Got that right," muttered a tired, dusty man at the back of the room.

"I can't win against these guys by myself," said Kale. "But guess what? I don't have to." He spread his hands in a way that included every exhausted, frightened, dirty man in the room. "We've got each other. It's all we've got. And maybe it's not enough. Okay, sure—maybe we've got inches when we need miles. But if I've got an inch and Jerry's got an inch and Bob has three, we can put together those inches and you know what? They add up to miles. The miles we need to get shut of this place. You, me, all of us. It'll work if we work together. It'll fail if we don't. So which is it going to be—fight together, or give up alone?"

"Fight," whispered Jerry. He looked surprised at the sound of his own voice.

"You got it," said Kale. "Now, c'mon—it's sharing time. No one of us is as smart as all of us. And if we're going to get out of here, we need to know what we've got against the count and Plotz."

There was silence. Finally Bob said, "I really hate that guy Plotz."

"Yeah," said Kale. "Me too."

Slowly and wearily, but with the beginnings of their old enthusiasm, the men gathered around Kale. It turned out, as is always the case, that each was indeed an expert in something. One knew about constellations; another, model train engines. Some understood how physics worked. One could make seeds grow into luscious, healthy plants, even when the soil was poor.

"How about you, Kale?" said Norbert. "What's your expert knowledge?"

"History," said Kale briskly. "I can tell you about every failed or successful revolt, and what the rebels did right and wrong."

"Maybe we should call you Commander Brandiwygn."

Kale grinned. "Maybe you should."

"How about home?" said a Widdershins man, who had just recited the middle names of every goldfish he had owned since he was eight. "What are your kids called?"

Kale bowed his head. "Charles," he managed finally, "and James." He lifted his head and looked each man in the eye. "We're doing this for them," he said. "And for your kids, and our wives, and for Snowball, and Bob's green door, and—and a pile of dead goldfish someone loved enough to give middle names."

"Doing what? I don't get it," said Jerry.

"Don't worry," said Kale. "You will."

By the end of the evening, Kale had organized a series of classes, to be led by each prisoner in turn while lookouts watched for the guards. They would be held in secret, after work was done and before Count Wilhelm Scream's Beneficent and Completely Mandatory Lights-Out.

"I never liked school," griped Bob.

"You'll like this," said Kale.

He was right. The classes started the next night, and continued every evening that the prisoners were not visited by Plotz or one of his minions. The secret students found that even when they were trembling with exhaustion and sick with fear and longing for their homes and families, they somehow found reserves within themselves that kept them awake and alert through the covert meetings.

Part of the appeal, of course, was that the meetings *were* secret. When people are oppressed and watched and controlled every moment of their lives, they delight in invisible rebellion. It gives them something to be proud of.

Furthermore, as the men were surprised to discover, the life of the mind confers a peculiar kind of liberty. When one's entire existence is circumscribed by coils of barbed wire around a patch of dirt in the midst of a gnarled and foreboding forest just down the hill from the castle fortress of a vicious tyrant, the ability to spend even a few stolen minutes letting one's imagination leap to freedom means that suddenly everything is fascinating. Sonnets; cooking; legends about magic spells; how to darn socks—all these and more did the men of Count Wilhelm Scream's Ice Mines learn in the dusky hours snatched from their tormentors.

Spudd hurled open the door to the dormitory. "Get up, you lazy louts!"

"What's happening?" asked Adele as they struggled to their feet and put on their dusty, gritty overalls.

"Shut up," suggested Spudd. "Put on these boots. Line up."

Wondering what new torments the day would bring, the prisoners selected heavy boots from a pile Spudd had dumped on the floor of the mill room. Guards marched them downstairs and out through the double doors of the mill.

It had been weeks since any of them had seen open air and sunlight. They lifted their faces to the sky and breathed in great lungfuls of forest-scented breezes. The air was cool and damp and lively, and they could hear birds singing.

"Somebody shoot that bird," said Spudd. "March!"

Just outside stood several wagons distressingly similar to the one that had brought them from Middlemost. Guards held open the doors, and the prisoners reluctantly stepped inside and sat on hard benches bolted to the sides. The doors slammed shut. The wagons began to move. A woman named Stella whimpered. Adele put a hand on her friend's shaking shoulder.

The wagon had no windows, but the prisoners could tell that they were going downhill. They could also tell that the road was in serious need of repair. The wagon bucked, hitting holes and humps so hard the rebels were thrown off the benches. They suspected the driver, who unlike them had a cushioned seat, was doing it on purpose. Eventually they gave up and sat on the floor.

The wagon lurched to a stop. The doors opened. "Get out," said Spudd.

They got out. So did the prisoners in the other wagons. They stared.

Before them lay an expanse of muddy water broken up by clumps of floating weeds that looked and smelled like vomit. Hummocks pocked the surface, tangled with spiky creepers. Logs lay in the water next to shattered stumps. Trees slanted drunkenly, their half-drowned roots sucking into the mud, their trunks furred with dripping moss. Ropy vines dangled from branches, and eyeless things on leathery wings flapped through the shadows.

"Welcome to the Slough of Despond," sniggered Spudd. "Get to work."

"Work?" said Adele blankly.

"Work," said Spudd. "See that?"

They looked. A clump of fibrous green shafts stood in the muck, swaying despite the windless air. Some were as thick as elephant's legs and as tall as houses; others were thinner and shorter. All were topped with gloppy white balls that gleamed faintly in the gloaming.

Adele's eyes grew wide. "Carnivorous Marshmallows."

"That's right," cackled Spudd. "Cauldrons are in the second wagon. Get cracking."

And Adele knew what horrid task awaited them.

Marshmallow was a key ingredient in any number of sweets and delicacies in the count's realm, and the chief source of marshmallow was, well, marshmallow—the very plants in the dank waters before the prisoners. The blobs crowning each stalk were sweet and squishy and good to eat, especially when boiled down. But as Adele knew, and her fellow prisoners suspected from the name "Carnivorous Marshmallow," these particular plants ate meat.

Live meat.

The mallows could feel vibrations with millions of tiny, hair-like roots that spread out under their stalks. If anything wandered too close, the blob would whip down and engulf it. Once the marshmallow had its prey, it released fluids called "digestive juices" which turned the victim into a sort of soup, suitable for slurping.

"Just in case you get any funny ideas, we have extra guards, all armed," said Spudd. She waved at a stack of cordwood near the mallows. "Get the fires going, Shorty. Fatso and Stinky Pants, unload the cauldrons. You three, get in the water and cut down those mallows. And as for you—"

"No," said Adele.

The women gasped. Spudd gawked. "*What* did you say?"

"Not those," said Adele. "We'll do the stand further back in the woods, behind that dead tree that looks like a troll with a wart condition."

Spudd scowled till her eyebrows tickled the end of her nose. She was not used to being crossed, and although she fully planned to make Adele pay for her insolence, she was curious. "Why?"

Adele gestured at the water. "See those circles between us and the marshmallows? Venom Clutch."

Venom Clutch was another carnivorous swamp plant, a predatory vine whose tendrils were dotted with crystalline spheres that paralyzed whatever they touched. Like the Carnivorous Marshmallow, Venom Clutch melted its prey with digestive juices. On rare occasions one might see a slow plant battle over an animal whose front end was frozen by Venom Clutch and whose rear end was being sucked up by a Carnivorous Marshmallow. However, this was not as common as you might think, for Venom Clutch seeded in deep water, whereas Carnivorous Marshmallow preferred shallows and damp ground. However, the Slough of Despond was full of sunken spots creating invisible pools. Knowing this, Adele had taken a quick scope of the slop between the marshmallows and the dry land. Now that everyone knew where to look, they could clearly see the vines snaking just under the surface, waiting for their next meal.

"I knew that," said Spudd.

"So did I," said Adele.

Spudd put her hands on her hips. "What makes you so dang smart?"

Adele stood straight. "I'm a science teacher."

"You *were*," sneered Spudd.

"If we go into that water, most of us will be injured and some will die," said Adele. "And there goes your quota for the rendering."

Spudd stepped unpleasantly close to Adele. "I make the decisions here."

Spudd was a big woman, and often angry. Adele swallowed and tried not to blink. "Yes, ma'am."

"You'll do as I say."

"Yes, ma'am."

Spudd raised her voice. "Harvest the stand back in the woods, behind that dead tree that looks like a troll with a wart condition."

"Yes, ma'am," said the prisoners.

"Now shut up and get to work."

"Yes, ma'—oh, right."

The guards handed out machetes and other tools. Adele tromped to the marshmallow stand with Stella and the others. She worried that Spudd would punish her later. But for now, no one could be quite as afraid of the overseer.

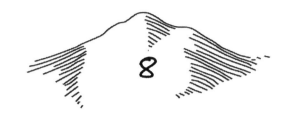

All morning the prisoners cut down marshmallows, doing their best not to get eaten, and sliced the sticky white balls into slabs, which they loaded into cauldrons. Adele's friend Ingrid maintained the fires and set the marshmallow to simmer. Clouds of sweet-scented steam drifted off the cauldrons, but the prisoners were not allowed to taste their own cooking.

"Yarf!" yelled Spudd. A dazzle of green and gold flashed through the dead trees.

"Fidelius bird," said Sergeant Bram, who was in charge of the guards. He puffed on a cigar that smelled like burning rubber.

The fidelius bird was the most beautiful creature in the Lands of Yonder. Its green and gold feathers glistened like a forest drenched in sunshine. Its song was an ascending scale of pure notes that mended broken hearts and gave hope to the sick and weary. People who caught a glimpse of one thought of that day as lucky forever afterwards.

"I hate those things," said Spudd.

"Why?"

"That noise they make."

"But everyone likes—"

"Well, maybe I'm special," screamed Spudd.

"No kidding," muttered the sergeant.

"What was that?"

"Ever had one of their eggs?"

"Hah!"

"What 'hah'?"

"Nobody's had one of their eggs. It's an expression, like, 'brave as a dragon rider,' or 'Go punch a manticore.'"

"I got one at home."

"No, you don't."

"Yeah, I do."

"How?"

"Got it off a troll from another unit. Dummy didn't know what it was worth." Bram grinned. "Traded my sandwich for it."

Spudd's eyes gleamed. She pulled a deck of cards from her baggy pants. "You a gambling man?"

"Nope."

"What's the matter? Scared?"

"Nope."

Spudd tried again. "You win, I cover your guard duty for a week."

"Nope and nope."

"Two weeks."

"Well." The sergeant wavered.

"In the forest. And the swamp." Spudd fanned the cards.

Bram bit down on his cigar. "Nights too."

Spudd scowled. "How often is that?"

"Two, three times a week."

"Fine. Nights too."

"You're on." They sat down. The other guards gathered around them. Soon they were absorbed in the sounds of cards shuffling, and mutterings of "Too rich for my blood," and "Go fish."

"Psst," said Adele.

"What?" said Stella.

"Come on." She waved to Ingrid, who followed them.

Casting frequent glances over her shoulder at the guards hunched around the card game, Adele led her friends to some bushes that were thick with spines and clusters of bright red berries. Sliding her hand through the thorns, she broke off a bunch of berries and popped one into her mouth. "Eat." She passed the rest around.

The skins were so crisp they snapped when Ingrid and Stella bit into them. The juice was sweet as honey. It slid down their throats and made their fingertips tingle. They stuffed their pockets with the fruit, electric with the joy of their first fresh food in weeks.

"Ouch." Stella jerked her hand away from the bush.

"What is it?" said Adele.

Stella showed her an oozing red line on the back of her hand. "Thorn."

"Wait here." Adele walked to the water's edge and plucked leaves from a low, green plant with glassy stalks. She mashed the leaves between her fingers, making a poultice that she pressed into the scrape. "How's that?"

"Oh—it doesn't hurt any more," marveled Stella, keeping her voice low.

"It stops the bleeding too," whispered Adele. "It's called diamond weed, or mother's helper."

"Let's take some," said Ingrid. They crammed their socks with the leaves, for they were forever getting small injuries at the mill.

Next, Adele broke a long piece from a marshmallow stalk. "It's a tube, but there's fiber in it," she said, holding it so they could see. Sure enough, the inside looked as though it were full of cobwebs.

"So?" said Ingrid.

"So watch this." Adele knelt on a rock, put the end of the tube into the water, and drank. Stella and Ingrid gasped, for it was well known that the water of the Slough of Despond contained enough parasites to give a mastodon purple pustules. Adele swallowed, smiled, and showed them the tube. The inside was gunked with debris. "See? It's a natural filter. Drink away." So they did; and when they were done, they shoved straws into their sleeves to share with the others.

"Hold it right there!" screamed Spudd.

They jumped. Spudd stood over the circle of guards, meaty fists shaking. "Lousy cheater."

"Watch who you're calling names, you old fleabag," growled Bram.

A prisoner named Abigail looked at Adele in panic. Spudd was sure to see the little group by the thorn bushes. "Oh, ma'am," she cried, "Did the sergeant gentleman drop that extra ace I see?"

With a howl, Spudd launched herself at Bram. The guards leaped to their feet. The air filled with grunts and blows and the sharp scent of crushed swamp weeds.

Adele and Stella dashed back to the marshmallows. Ingrid sprinted to her cauldron. Everyone was hard at work by the time the melee ended with Spudd in a half-nelson assuring the sergeant that he was no cheat and that she would happily take on a third week of his guard duty.

Although the sergeant was pleased at the outcome of the card game, Spudd did not share his sunny outlook. As soon as she regained feeling in her arms, she stomped among the prisoners, randomly punching them. Then she sat down for a lunch of stew, fresh fruit, and pastries, smacking her lips with gusto. Only when she had finished burping over the last crumbs did she allow the women their meal of grey bread and black bananas. They huddled together, eating with their heads ducked as though in defeat. This gave Spudd the kind of bliss that most people get from seeing a delicate sunrise or a baby troll doll wrapped in pink ribbons.

Unbeknownst to Spudd, however, the prisoners were sharing the berries that Adele, Ingrid, and Stella had collected, and pressing diamond weed mash into their scrapes. They hid the marshmallow-tube filters in their pockets as Adele explained under her breath that these would allow them to drink as much fresh water as they wanted, provided they did so in secret.

As the sky grew dim and the shadows thickened, Spudd barked orders and flicked pebbles at anyone who was working too slowly or too fast. The prisoners used enormous paddles to scrape the boiled marshmallow into flats the size of dining room tables. Ingrid's crew banked the fires. Adele and Stella and their group scrubbed the cauldrons clean. Everyone clambered wearily back into the wagons.

"Get used to it, ladies," sneered Spudd. "We're here all season."

The women tried to look sad. The guards locked the doors, and the wagon bumped back up the rutted road. The overseer never suspected her prisoners were full of delicious, forbidden food and knowledge.

"We can do more tomorrow," said Adele. "The swamp is full of useful plants."

"I can't wait," said Stella.

"Same here," said Ingrid.

In the darkness everyone smiled, because each scrap of secret knowledge made them freer, healthier, and more alive. As the wagons jounced up the mountain, they felt more hopeful and rebellious than they had since their unjust arrests.

However, I hope you were not expecting a quick end to Kale and Adele's imprisonment, because the unhappy truth is they stayed where they were for many years and suffered greatly. Indeed, the count's prisons filled as he tightened his grip on his lands. Most prisoners were eventually released so they could cripple home and relate the horrors they had endured. This policy, one of Princess Abattoir's early innovations, was designed to terrify the populace and, in the words of her boss, turn them to the delights of obedience. But the Ascendant Defenders was the first group to rebel against the count, and therefore, he felt, the most dangerous. He resolved never to set them free. Their work was hard, their clothes were scratchy, and their food tasted like paste. They were not allowed entertainment of any kind, so their chief occupation was worry. The women wondered if their men were alive, and the men were sick with fear whenever they thought about what might have befallen their wives.

How did they endure for so long? Well you may ask. The fact is that time moves differently for adults. For a girl or boy, a school year might seem an eternity. To an adult, it is a few months. Thus it was that for the rebels, long years of imprisonment became a series of days punctuated by tiny, gleeful moments snatched from their overseers.

At the Ice Mines, Plotz found himself bedeviled by a flurry of strange occurrences. Food disappeared from the kitchen, the lights in the shaft blinked on and off in giddy patterns, and insulting graffiti appeared low on the walls of the buildings. Occasionally Plotz's motor vehicle got topped off with sherry from the officers' mess, and it would spend hours charging around the camp shouting "Yoiks!" and "Tally ho!" before collapsing sobbing and telling Plotz that it loved him. One dreary fall day, someone altered the barracks' life-sized portrait of Count Scream, painting big ears and a clown nose on his dark face, and baggy underwear with hearts over his elegant black trousers. Although the men felt this was a vast improvement, Plotz did not agree; and when he was done yipping and tearing out his hair, he decided to make an example of someone. Princess Abattoir was due for a visit, and punishing prisoners always made him look good. So Plotz sentenced Bob to twenty-four hours in the Cold Box, a windowless shed attached to the warehouse where the Black Ice was stored. Upon Bob's release the guards dumped him unceremoniously at the door to the barracks. Hearing the noise, Kale opened the door and discovered his friend lying on the ground, cold to the touch and struggling to breathe.

Kale pulled Bob to his feet. "Stoke that fire," he called. He and Jerry half-carried their friend to the hearth where the other men were hastily building up the small blaze they were allowed. "Got a stool? OK, then—"

"*Oy!*" yelled a voice at Kale's knees. "Doya mind? I was usen dis, *if* dat's okay wit you."

Kale almost dropped Bob's cold wrist. A scowling blue figure stood on the stool between him and the fireplace, arms crossed. It wore brown boots and a red wool jacket cinched at the waist with a scarred leather belt. The jacket was buttoned up wrong, and holes in the elbows had been inexpertly darned. His broad-brimmed hat sported a broken feather. "What—who the heck are you?"

The little creature's eyes snapped like black sparks. "I'll tell you vat I'm not," he said. "I'm no *farshtunkener Gonif* takin' over honest kobolds' home, dat's what. I'm no *Dumkopf* tinkin' he knows *das Frözenshaften* better dan de people who bin dere for—for—a long time. I'm—"

"Cold," moaned Bob.

"Hold him for a minute, will you?" Kale let go of Bob's arm and squatted so he could look the angry blue man in the eye. Slowly he extended his hand. "Hi. I'm Kale."

The creature glared. "You wid de Count?"

Kale almost laughed. "We're his prisoners."

The creature hesitated, then shook Kale's hand. "Wulfgrim."

"Kale Brandiwygn." The tiny hand was cool and dusty. "It's a pleasure to meet you, Wulfgrim. What are you doing here?"

"Dis is my home."

"It is?" Privately, Kale thought he was welcome to it.

"Yah. Us kobolds, we is de Mineshaft *Gemeinschaft*."

"I've never seen you before."

"I bin livin' under de varehouse fer some time. Got too noisy last night so I left."

"Noisy?"

"Yah, someone moanin' in de Cold Box like dere's no tomorrow."

"Well excuse *me*," muttered Bob.

Kale glanced at his friend and back to the little blue man. "Well, Wulfgrim, perhaps while we get to know each other better you could lend my friend this—your—stool. He needs the fire badly."

Wulfgrim hesitated, then hopped down from the stool. Bob sat, half-falling, and held his quaking hands to the warmth. The little man examined him. "You part kobold, *mein Chum?* 'Cos blue don' look so good on you."

"It was so cold," moaned Bob.

Wulfgrim grinned, showing teeth that would have been at home in a bear trap. "Refreshing, yah?"

"Horrible," said Bob. "Even being close to it is hard."

"Except for *him*." Jerry gestured at the clown-faced picture of the count. "He can touch it. They say."

Wulfgrim chuckled at the defaced portrait. "Some of my best work, I tink."

Bob almost fell off the stool. "You did that?"

"Now don' be jealous," said Wulfgrim, backing up.

"Jealous?" screamed Bob. "You almost got me frozen to death."

"Oy gevalt," said Wulfgrim in genuine distress. "I din' know dat."

"Now you do." Bob turned back to the fire, still shaking. Shadows flickered across his face. "I don't think I'll ever be warm again."

"Don' be such a moaner, *Herr Coldilocks.*" Wulfgrim patted Bob's quaking knee. "A nice hot drink, dat's what you need."

Bob rolled his eyes. "Yeah. Sounds great."

"Hokey-dokey." Wulfgrim turned on his heels and disappeared through the crowd of legs.

"Where'd he go?" said Kale.

"Who cares?" said Bob.

A few minutes later Wulfgrim trotted up to the stool with a steaming mug. From the aroma wafting off it, everyone could tell it was hot chocolate. Everyone's mouth watered. "Drink dis."

Bob eyed it suspiciously. "Where did you get it?"

"De kitchen."

"The kitchen?"

"Yah."

"They'll skin you alive."

"Only if dey catch me."

Bob sipped the hot chocolate. His shaking stopped and color returned to his cheeks. "This is amazing."

"De secret is a little Rainbow Ice melted in," said Wulfgrim. "An' a nip of brandy."

Bob hiccupped and handed back the empty mug. "Thank you, Mr., um, Wulfgroan."

"Call me Herschel."

"Bob." They shook hands.

"Wan' some fire peppers? We puts dem between de kids' toes when dey gets frosty. Works like a charm iffen it don' burn de skin off."

"I really need to sleep," said Bob. "Thanks, Herschel. I mean it." He walked unsteadily but without help to his bunk, and pulled the threadbare covers over his head.

Kale squatted again. "You have performed a great service here tonight, Mr. Wulfgrim."

Herschel twisted a toe in the floorboards. "Ah, *shucksen*."

"Why have we never seen you before?"

Herschel sighed. "De only times I seen people like you it was dat count and de guards an' such. I thought you was helpin' him steal de ice."

"Hardly. He makes us do it."

"Dat's funny. He won' let us do it."

"Why would you want to?"

"Dis is our *Frözenshaften, yah?* An' he trew us out."

Kale almost laughed. "He threw us in. If only there were a way to reverse our situations."

"My folks, dey tell me stay here an' keep de place tidy for when dey gets back."

Kale scratched his head. "By any chance did they also tell you to make life very unpleasant for everyone else?"

"Yah."

"So it's been you stealing food, killing the lights in the mineshaft—"

"An' puttin' garlic powder in the guards' toothpaste, you bet."

"That time Plotz got stuck in the washing machine?"

"Yer welcome."

"The welts were all colors." Kale and Herschel Wulfgrim smiled at the memory.

A klaxon blared the one-minute warning before lights out. The men scrambled for their beds. Kale stood. "You're a kobold?"

"Yah. We live here till dat *Poopipantsen* showed up." Wulfgrim spat at the portrait of Wilhelm Scream.

Kale settled himself in his bunk with his head on the lumpy pillow. "Mr. Wulfgrim, I think we're going to be good friends."

One afternoon in late fall while Spudd was yelling at the prisoners to work harder, she noticed a bird on the windowsill above the food mill, flashing green and gold in the sunlight. She turned on Adele, to whom she always gave the most dangerous and unpleasant tasks. "Get a ladder," she snarled.

"Why?" asked Adele, wiping her hands on her overalls.

"There's a fidelius bird up there. Get me its eggs."

Some birds lay eggs in the fall. The fidelius is one of them. Spudd had been obsessed with fidelius eggs since losing her card game to Sergeant Bram years before. Because the birds nested on cliff sides and other high structures, almost no one had ever tasted one of their eggs, and Bram had assured her, with more than a bit of gloat, that the yolks tasted like custard, and the whites whipped up to meringues the size of cumulus clouds. Spudd hoped to find out firsthand how much of his report was true, and perhaps win Princess Abattoir's favor by giving her an egg. If there were enough to go around.

Soon a wobbly ladder was produced and propped against the wall with its top rung just under the windowsill; and Adele, who was not crazy about heights and who knew perfectly well that if she fell Spudd would respond only by yelling at someone to get a spatula, gripped the rungs and carefully ascended.

At the summit of the ladder, Adele slid the window up. She was higher than the treetops of Gloamwoods. Perhaps more to the point, she was nose to beak with a gleaming, eagle-sized bird that stared at her, unblinking.

Adele caught her breath. The fidelius bird was the most beautiful thing she had seen in years. Its eyes glittered like obsidian, and its breast gleamed like liquid gold. Even though she was close enough to touch it, Adele could not make out individual feathers, any more than she could see separate drops of water in the Slough of Despond. It was smooth, perfect.

And yet, its stillness frightened her. The bird seemed to radiate danger from its dark eyes and curved, blade-like beak.

"Hello," said Adele, hoping she sounded more confident than she felt.

The bird beat the air with its wings. Dust and leaf fragments burst up in an angry cloud.

"Easy. I'm not going to hurt you." Adele slid her hand into the nest, under the creature's brightly colored breast. Its feathers were warm and soft.

The bird lashed out with its beak. Adele yanked her hand back. Blood gushed from her wrist. Red droplets spattered on the sill. The bird hissed. A crimson drop fell from its beak.

"Where's that egg?" yelled Spudd.

"Checking now," called Adele. Scowling, she reached into the pocket of her overalls and pulled out a bunch of diamond weed leaves. She mushed them with her fingers and pressed them to her wrist until the bleeding stopped. The bird glared at her over the blade of its beak.

"Nothing personal." Adele raised her hand as if to seize the bird's head. It lunged for her. She grabbed its throat. The creature screamed and flapped. Air pounded Adele's ears like waves in a storm. She reached under the bird. Its scrabbling talons scratched her wedding ring. Her fingers closed over hard, warm eggs.

Two of them.

Adele let go of the bird's throat. It opened its beak and rasped at her.

"You poor, sweet thing," Adele whispered. "How brave you are." She descended the ladder empty-handed, pulling down her sleeve to hide the blood.

"Well?" snapped Spudd. "Where are the eggs?"

"There weren't any," said Adele.

"Then go back tomorrow." Spudd stomped off, leaving Adele to soothe her torn wrist and get back to work.

The next day, Adele again climbed the rickety ladder and opened the window. The fidelius bird hissed and beat its wings. Slowly, Adele reached into her pocket and pulled out a bread crust. She put it on the ledge between them.

The fidelius bird looked at it. She looked at Adele. Then, quick as a snake, she shot her beak out and swallowed the crust whole.

"Hurry up," yelled Spudd.

"Yes ma'am," said Adele.

A screech of machinery slashed the air. "What's that?" Spudd howled.

"The pulverizer caught one of my boots," came Stella's voice faintly. The screech grew louder.

"You idiot!"

"I was only—"

"You break that and Princess Abattoir will break me." Spudd's voice grew fainter, and Adele knew the overseer was lumbering toward the wailing gears. She pulled out another crust, then another, pausing only to throw harried glances down at the floor. Sharing food and showing kindness were strictly prohibited in the prisons of Count Wilhelm Scream.

Adele the science teacher was interested in the bird for two reasons. First, it had two eggs. The usual number was one. That meant the bird had had to work hard to produce the second egg, and was probably exhausted.

Second, it seemed to have no mate. Usually a nesting fidelius had a small, dark companion that brought it food while it kept the eggs warm. But no insect shells littered the windowsill, and no crushed berries stained the dark stones of the tower. This meant he was either dead or captured.

Fidelius birds mated for life. They did not find a new love if their first one died. A brooding, widowed fidelius was almost certainly doomed: she would not get off the eggs, and there was no one to bring her food and drink all winter.

Adele slid her hand under the bird's breast again. This time the creature kept a wary eye on her but did not stop her. The eggs were bigger than hen's eggs, and wide at one end. This was to prevent them from falling off the cliff side nests the fidelius bird favored: if they got nudged, they would simply spin in small circles and return to where they had started, more or less. These were warm, and Adele imagined she could feel the chicks growing inside them, thumping on the shells, impatient to get out into the world. She shuddered with a mix of loss and joy. But she could not cry, because Spudd would see the tears, and she could not laugh, because Spudd would hear the peals. She kept her voice low. "Twins, huh? You're going to love it."

The bird cocked her head and fixed Adele with a glistering eye.

"I'll be back when I can." Adele brushed the crumbs off her fingers and went back down.

"Well?" The machinery was humming at its usual rate, and Spudd had returned to the base of the ladder.

"Well what?"

"Don't get smart with me," yelled the overseer. "Where are the eggs?"

"I can't make her lay if she's not ready," said Adele. "And it's really frightening going up there. I don't know if I can do it again."

"Oh, is that so?" snarled Spudd. "Well, you can just go up that ladder every day till that bird lays. Now get to work!" And she stormed off.

Adele adjusted her overalls and joined Stella at their workstation.

"How'd it go?" mouthed Stella.

"Great," whispered Adele. "Can you do it again tomorrow?"

"You bet."

So every day Adele went up the ladder, bringing scraps from the kitchen—never the prisoners' food, which she was afraid might kill it, but crumbs and insects and once even half a strawberry. The hungry bird ate everything. Down below, the prisoners distracted Spudd, sometimes by creating problems with the machinery, sometimes by asking her questions they already knew the answers to, and sometimes by loudly wondering if they should go to the bathroom in alphabetical order or by largest to smallest shoe size. Annoying Spudd was one of their few reliable pleasures, so no one begrudged Adele her time at the window.

11

Once the men made friends with Herschel Wulfgrim, conditions improved considerably. A miner who had a sniffle found an extra blanket on his bunk; pranks on the guards occurred only while the prisoners were below ground and could not be blamed; and extra food sometimes found its way onto their plates, easing the hunger that gnawed at their guts.

Over games of cards and dice he had stolen from the guards, Herschel explained his sad history. Early in his reign, Count Scream had expelled the kobolds from the mines. The departing sprites had named Herschel Karetaker Eccentrikkus and told him to stay, charging him with tidying the mineshaft and keeping fresh flowers in the vases until they could return.

"I've never seen any flowers down there," said Bob. He and Herschel were playing checkers on a board that the kobold had produced one winter evening. It was inscribed, "To Plotzikins on your birthday. Love, Mummie."

"Scream broke all de vases." Herschel moved a piece to the center of the board.

"Your folks must think a lot of you to trust you with the mineshaft."

"Or maybe dey said, 'Hey, dat Herschel is scared of his own hat. Better leave him.'" The kobold scowled.

Bob picked up a piece and double-jumped Herschel. "Gotcha!"

"Keep it down," said Jerry from his bunk.

Kale stood watch at the window. "All clear."

Herschel moved his piece into the empty spot left by Bob's double-jump. "King me."

"*Vey is mir,*" sighed Bob, who had been spending a lot of time with the kobold. He half-dropped a piece onto Herschel's.

Herschel glanced at Bob's fingers. "What's wid yer hand?"

"Still a little frozen." He showed Herschel his fingers, which were stiff in the joints and blue under the nails.

Herschel clucked sympathetically. "Next time, I move de ice away from de Cold Box, yah? Make tings not so chilly inside."

"It would kill you."

"Nah."

"Nah?"

"Black Ice is fine fer kobolds. My bubbe sleep on it. She say to me, 'Helps you keep a cool head.' 'Course, her head never cool. I remember de time dat *Schnorrer* Balkan come 'roun' askin' her for a few more gold dragons. Hah! She *shlogg* him one on de *Kopf* wid a brick an' dat guy decide preddy quick he can live widout her gold."

"Did you sell it back then?" said Bob. "The Black Ice?"

"Nah. Chust de Rainbow Ice."

"Does anyone?"

"Nah."

Bob frowned. "What does he want with it?"

"Who?" said Kale.

"The count. I mean, I guess it's the count."

"What do you mean?"

Bob put down his piece. "We've been stockpiling Black Ice since we got here. The warehouse is almost full."

"So?"

"So what's it for? He can't make money on it. Everyone's scared to death of the stuff."

Kale rubbed his chin. "I never thought of that."

"I thought about it plenty in the Cold Box." Bob pushed another piece. Herschel jumped him and crowed.

"No need to gloat, *Porkenschnoz.*"

Herschel pouted. "I gonna stop teaching you kobold insults."

"Too late. I learn fast."

"Den I is definitely not gonna tell you what de count wants wid de Black Ice." Herschel slid a piece into a safe spot behind Bob's.

Bob glanced at Kale. "You don't have to tell me."

"Good, 'cos I won't."

"Fine then."

"Fine."

Bob moved his piece. Herschel moved his. Bob moved another. Herschel looked up at Bob, eyes bulging.

Kale left the window and sat by the board. "Bob," he said, "don't you want to know the plan for the Black Ice?"

"No."

Herschel twisted in his seat.

"I'd hate to see that stuff fall into the wrong hands."

"As long as it stays away from my hands, I don't care." Bob bent his stiff fingers.

"But the count's plan? It might be something really awful."

"True."

Herschel drummed on the legs of the stool with his heels.

"We've got to find out," said Kale.

"I don't see how."

"Another win for the count, then."

Herschel made a sound like air coming out of a balloon.

"I hate to see that guy win again," said Bob. "He just wins and wins and—"

Herschel Wulfgrim rocketed to his feet. "De count is making a wiggle-dragon!"

"A what?" said Kale.

"Princess Abattoir was talkin' to Plotz about it when I stole hot chocolate for him." Herschel gestured at Bob. "Dey gonna cross-breed a dragon wid a wyvern."

Bob looked at Kale. "Wiggle-dragon?"

"Dat's what she said. Said dey is caught a wyvern an' he in love so dey is close."

"What's a wyvern?" said Bob.

"Like a dragon but with only two legs," said Kale. "They come from cold places. But what's a wiggle-dragon?"

"No such thing," said Jerry. He moved to the window to take Kale's place.

"Not yet," said Herschel.

"What do you mean, not yet?"

"Dragons is hot and wyverns is cold, so dey never meet. But Princess Abattoir an' de count got one of each an' dey made eggs. An' she say iffen you put dose eggs on Black Ice, you gets wiggle-dragons when dey hatches. An' den—*oy gevalt!*"

"Why *oy gevalt?*" Bob knew that meant bad news.

"Instead of fire, dey breathes ice."

Kale blinked. "Ice?"

"You betcha."

"How much ice?"

"Dunno. But Princess say dis way de count make everytink obedient."

And Kale understood.

This was why he and his friends were forced to mine Black Ice at daily peril to their lives: so Count Wilhelm Scream could create a monster that would give him what he had always wanted more than anything else—complete control. Not just over the towns and villages, but over nature itself.

If the course of a river displeased him, he could turn it to ice.

He could congeal forests and meadows to terrify his people.

If he felt a farm was not producing enough wheat or a bakery was not making enough bread, he could freeze them solid.

If new rebels arose, he could set his dreadful creature upon them. A giant, flying lizard, spewing a vapor of Black Ice.

How many people would die? How many farms and cities and woodlands and meadows would freeze because of the count's tantrums?

Kale touched his wedding ring. Adele might still be alive. What if the count chose to make an example of the women of the rebellion?

And what of their sons? Kale had dreamed of them a thousand times in the years since his arrest. They were possibly—no, he told himself, *probably*—still alive as well. But what if they ran afoul of the count? The best throwing arm in the world couldn't save them from this new horror.

"Oh, hey, lookit dat," said Herschel cheerfully as he maneuvered his last piece into the final row on Bob's end of the board. "King me."

"How close are they?" said Kale.

"How close is who?"

"How much more ice do they need?"

"Oh, dat. Well, not too much I reckon."

"You sound awfully cheerful about it," said Bob.

"Yah, well, I figgur he won' be ice-blitzin' de mines, right? Got plenny of ways of killin' folks here awreddy. So we is safest from de wiggle-dragon right where we is. You gonna king me or not?"

Bob's numb fingers dropped a piece onto Herschel's. The little blue man giggled and hopped up and down on his seat.

"Herschel." Kale's voice was low. "Can you help us?"

"T'ought dat was what I bin doin'."

"You have. And we're grateful. But look—if the count gets that—that wiggle-dragon up and running, we'll all be in danger, in prison or out."

"How come?"

"There's never been anything like it before. Who knows if they can control it?"

"I can't do *Bupkis* 'bout dat."

Kale ran his hands through his hair. "Well, then—what about your people?"

"What about dem?"

"Can you find them? Get them back here?"

"Nah."

"Why not?"

"Dey won' listen to me."

"Why?"

Herschel's eyes grew mournful. "After my bubbe mops up de floor wid Balkan, I laugh at him. So he tell everyone I wouldn' help him fight. He say I afraid of my own bubbe."

"What nonsense!"

"Nah, it's true. Anybody not fearing of her is whacko. But dis is right around de time de count out-kick us. So de others, dey says dey gots no use fer a kobold koward. 'Take care of de place, Herschel,' dey says. An' den dey leaves." His eyes trembled with tears.

Kale brought his fist down on the table. The board and all the pieces jumped. "Coward?" he shouted.

"Quiet," hissed Jerry from the window.

"Coward?" whispered Kale. "Herschel Wulfgrim, man of true blue, a coward? Never!"

Herschel's face grew purple. "Dat's what I said."

"Say it again. And tell your people the time has come to reclaim their ancestral homeland, *dos*—um—*Freezy-shifty!*"

"*Das Frözenshaften,*" corrected Herschel. "Dey won' listen."

"Make them."

"How?"

"Tell them we're here." Kale gestured at the room of tired, dirty prisoners longing for home. "We're a fifth column."

"What's dat?"

"It means we're on the inside and we can help you."

Herschel scowled. "If you guys is de fifth column, who is de other four?"

"You and your people. Together we can stop the count."

"Will it be dangerous?"

"Terribly."

"Well." Herschel considered this tempting tidbit.

"And if you succeed," went on Kale, "you will no longer be thought of as Karetaker Eccentrikkus. No, Herschel—to us you will be Karetaker Gloriosus."

Herschel jumped to his feet. "I do it!" He barreled out the door. It slammed behind him.

"There he goes." Jerry peered through the dirty glass. "How did you know he wanted to be a hero?"

Kale joined him. "He already is."

"Huh?"

"How long has he been taking care of the mines by himself?" said Kale. "Plus tormenting the guards and stealing them blind. Imagine what they'd do if they ever caught him."

Jerry shuddered.

"He's always been brave," said Kale. "He just didn't know it."

As winter drifted over the Lands of Yonder, Adele began to enjoy her daily trips to the nest. The view from the window was immense. Gloamwoods and the Slough of Despond were covered with snow, and there, just where the shadow of the castle brushed the base of the mountain, was a small town that might be Inglenook.

One day Adele reached the top of the ladder and smiled at the bird. But when she put out her hand to feel the eggs, two bald, grey heads popped out of the mother bird's feathers. Their eyes were wide, their skin was wrinkled, and when they opened their beaks to squawk they sounded exactly like bedsprings. Adele laughed. It felt like using a muscle she had forgotten existed.

"What was that?" roared Spudd.

Adele gave a yelp. "Oh, no—this is terrible!" She reached under the bird and pulled out the broken eggshells. She emptied her pockets (breadcrumbs, part of a cookie she had baked at midnight, and a mildewed prune), and crushed the speckled, oblong shells before putting them in her pocket.

At the base of the ladder, Spudd paced in a tight, angry circle. "Well?" she demanded. "Don't tell me that bird's not brooding yet."

Adele wrung her hands. "Please don't beat me. It's not my fault." Shaking all over, she pulled the crushed shells out of her pocket. "She must have laid them last night."

"Do you think I'm stupid?" snapped Spudd. "They take longer than that to hatch."

"These never hatched," said Adele (who did think Spudd was stupid). "A snake must have eaten them."

"A snake?"

"Egg-eating snakes. They swallow the eggs whole and spit out the shells."

Spudd tore at her thinning hair. "Where's the snake that did this to me?"

"Probably near the nest," said Adele, thinking fast. "You know, to be close to the eggs."

Spudd stopped tearing her hair. "Can it get in here?"

"Oh, yes," said Adele. "They slither through very small spaces, and then they drop down onto whoever's beneath."

"What?"

"Wonderful droppers, these snakes."

Spudd gnashed her teeth. "Get back up there and kill that snake. Now!"

"Oh, please no. I'm terrified of snakes!"

Spudd lifted her hand as though to strike Adele, who shrieked and ran back up the ladder. She had gotten used to the height and the ricketiness, so the hardest part now was trying not to laugh.

By the time she got back up again, the mother bird was gone and the babies were staggering around the nest like small, bedraggled drunkards. Adele did not touch them, for they looked too delicate; but she marveled at the folds of their grey skin and the bright white down on their backs and wings. Their eyes were as dark as their mother's, but their feet seemed comically large and their wings were little flesh-covered Vs that would be useless for flying for some time to come.

"Guess your mom went out for a bite, huh?" she said to the twins. "Can't say I blame her. She's been cooped up a long time."

Just then the fidelius bird swooped back, landing on the windowsill and flapping her wings to keep her balance. She waddled over to the baby birds. They stuck their necks up straight as little daisies, opening their beaks. Their mother dipped her head and made a noise that sounded like "Flarharghghg!" Out of her mouth poured a warm mix of insects, winterberries, and water that she had swallowed and regurgitated. (For a baby bird, this is a really delightful way to eat dinner.)

"Well," said Adele after a few moments of watching the family have its first meal, "I'll let you eat in peace. See you tomorrow." And she started to descend the ladder.

At this, the mother bird yapped, as if to say, "Hang on! Don't go just yet." And she held out one foot, which clutched a small but perfectly ripe sparkleberry.

Sparkleberries were a plum-like fruit with orange flesh, juicy and sweet. Their skin, though thick, was chewy and delicious. They were cultivated by hand in the gardens and greenhouses of the wealthy and powerful. A single fruit was worth several gold dragons.

Adele's eyes widened. "For me?"

The bird placed the fruit on the sill and nudged it toward Adele with her beak. Its skin glistened in the sunlight, and its sweet scent filled the air.

Adele, whose fresh food had for years been limited to what she could steal from the swamp, shook with happiness. She lifted the fruit to her lips, breathing in its perfume. "Thanks."

She wanted to eat the sparkleberry slowly to make it last, but the first bite was so fantastic she gobbled it down in seconds. She wiped the juice off her chin and went back down the ladder, lest Spudd become suspicious.

From then on, the fidelius bird brought sparkleberries and other gifts every day; and every day Adele pretended to search for snakes. She would take a big stick with her and thump the end of the windowsill opposite the nest, yelling, "Eeek!" or "Get away from me, you horrid thing!" or "Agh! I'm scared of snakes! And there are so *many*." Spudd chose to supervise the hunt from the floor of the mill.

All the while, the chicks grew plumper. Their skin smoothed out and their feathers came in. They were not the same brilliant green and gold as their mother; that would not happen for a few years, when they were full-grown. Instead they were soft grey and brown, colors that would keep them hidden in the forest when it came time to leave the nest.

Then one day the fidelius bird dropped its daily offering on the sill with a *clink*.

Clink? Thought Adele. Food does not usually go "clink." She picked up the object.

It was a wedding ring.

Adele laughed softly. "But sweetheart, I'm already married. See?" And she showed it the simple gold band on her ring finger. It was engraved with a design of two intertwined hearts.

So was the other one.

Adele choked and almost fell off the ladder. With shaking fingers, she picked up the ring and looked at the inside. There was an inscription.

I am my beloved's and my beloved is mine. Kale and Adele.

"Where did you get this?" she whisper-screamed at the bird.

The bird blinked and backed toward the ledge, as if ready to fly away.

"Wait." Adele slid the new ring, which was much too big for her finger, onto her thumb. She yanked off her own ring, and with trembling fingers slipped it over the bird's foot and above the joint in its leg. "Take this to him. If he's alive, *take this to him.*" She gasped. "Please."

The fidelius bird looked at the ring and shook her leg. It looked at Adele as if to say, "Oh, well—if you insist," and flew away.

Adele rubbed the too-big ring and thought about the inscription inside. Hers was almost identical. It said, *"I am my beloved's and my beloved is mine. Adele and Kale."*

If Kale were alive, he would know her ring immediately.

If he wasn't...she had his ring to remember him by.

13

The next day, the bird was waiting for Adele. It opened its talons and dropped something on the wide stone ledge.

Clink.

It was Adele's ring. The bird hadn't been able to deliver it.

Kale must be dead.

Adele dared not cry. With heavy fingers, she reached for the small gold circle, determined to wear it every day for the rest of her life to remember her husband and keep him in her heart.

One of the baby birds nosed at the ring, flipping it over, revealing a tiny scroll of paper rolled up tight inside the band.

Adele jerked. The baby bird's eyes gleamed, and it reached for the ring with its beak. Gently, Adele pushed it away. The bird lost its balance and landed on its bottom, feet in the air, squawking.

"Sorry," whispered Adele as she picked up the ring. Carefully, so as not to tear it, she pulled the scroll out.

One word was written on it.

Adele?

Adele slipped the ring over her finger and shoved the paper into her pocket. She climbed back down the ladder.

"Kill any snakes?" asked Spudd.

"Oh, yes," she gasped. "Loads." And she went back to work.

That night, when everyone else was asleep, Adele crept to the fireplace. In the moonlight from the high window, she could see where the stones were blackened with soot. She scraped some into a cup, mixed it with oil she had stolen from that night's meal, and dipped in a straw from the lumpy pallet she slept on. The dark liquid crept up the shaft. She pulled the curled-up paper from her pocket and, slowly and carefully so as not to drop a blot, wrote one word.

Yes.

The next day she handed Kale's ring and the scroll to the fidelius bird and watched it fly away. From then on, she and Kale exchanged daily messages on scraps of paper or cloth stolen from dusty corners or torn from disused prison uniforms. Kale's ink was iridescent, and changed color in the sunlight. Adele treasured each loop of the familiar handwriting.

Thank heavens. I was afraid you were dead, wrote Kale.

When I saw your message, I stopped breathing, replied Adele.

Really?

Well, obviously I started again, wrote Adele. *How are you?*

Alive.

How did you know to give the bird your ring? Adele wanted to know.

I didn't! The little creep stole it. (I hope birds can't read.)

Stole it how?

Princess Abattoir was visiting. She has a troll guard, and you know how they are about gold. So I hid my ring under a rock to keep it safe. Next thing I knew our friend here was flying away with it. I thought it was gone for good.

Are you well? Adele asked.

There was a long pause at this point, and Adele was terribly afraid that someone had caught Kale sending messages. But it turned out he was just writing a detailed reply, and as he had to do this in secret it took a few days and several scraps of paper.

I am all right. I have been working in the mines since we were captured. Sometimes other people come here for a while and get sent home if they don't die first. But the rebels are here for good, or so we've been told.

Adele shuddered and read the second piece of paper.

We go down the shaft every day and hack out lumps of ice. When I tell you that our breath freezes on the walls, you will understand how cold it is. We fear the Black Ice because its touch is death.

How awful, thought Adele. And how very like Count Wilhelm Scream.

When the Rainbow Ice melts, it stains, and that's what I'm using for ink. Pretty, isn't it? But the work is exhausting and the food stinks. We used to have a friend who brought us treats but he had to leave so we are all pretty hungry. In short, I am alive and as well as can be expected. But I miss you and I miss the boys.

The next day, Adele brought the fidelius bird a cookie she had baked in the embers as she sat by the fireplace writing to Kale. She had stamped letters into the dough. The message said, "Eat. Love, A."

The fidelius bird rolled a sparkleberry at her and sat back. It was a big one, and the bird looked proud. The baby birds lunged at it, their beaks agape. The mother whipped her wings open, knocking them flat. The twins picked themselves up with great dignity and waddled back to the nest. They sank down in its depths but each kept one eye above the rim, fixed on the sparkleberry.

Adele laughed and stroked her friend's feathers, scratching a special spot between its wings that she knew it liked. "That looks delicious," she said. "If it's not too much to carry, can you take it to him along with this?"

The fidelius bird cocked its head at Adele in an attitude that said, "You're nuts." But she grasped the cookie in one clawed foot and the fruit in the other and flew away on gleaming wings.

That afternoon as the sun was sinking and Adele was whacking at imaginary snakes, the fidelius bird came flapping back slowly. She landed on the windowsill and unclenched her talons from a rag bundle. Adele unwrapped it.

A lump of ice clunked to the windowsill. Colors leaped from its depths and splashed onto the stones: red like poppies, orange and yellow that reminded Adele of autumn leaves, and green, blue, indigo, violet that made her think of spring flowers pushing through a crust of snow.

Carefully, Adele put Kale's gift to one side of the window where no one but she and the birds would see it. She almost hated to turn away from the brilliant display, but she picked up the rag to read her husband's message.

My darling Adele, I can't tell you how much that cookie and the fruit meant to me. I can't send you food but I can send you beauty. The colors of the rainbow ice are like hope—they shine even in our darkness. So every time you look at this, know that I love you.

Adele looked at the fidelius bird. "You know," she said, "I may just get through this after all."

"Flarharghghg," replied the mother bird, and dipped her head to feed her fast-growing babies.

That night, emboldened by Kale's message of hope, Adele told her friends about the messages.

"Why didn't tell us before?" said Abigail indignantly.

Adele sighed. "Remember that time Princess Abattoir found out a new prisoner had smuggled in a letter from her mother?"

Stella shuddered. "Do I ever. Abattoir dipped the paper in acid and made the girl eat it. It burned through her tongue, and she whistled when she talked after that."

"Exactly," said Adele. "Believe me, I wanted to tell you. But I didn't dare."

"So now we're all in danger?" squawked a rebel from Larkspur.

"I'm afraid so," said Adele.

"Never mind that," said Stella. "What did Kale say about the others? Is Jerry there?"

"Did he say anything about my husband?" asked Ingrid.

"Or my brother?" said Abigail.

"I'll find out." The next day Adele asked Kale to send a list of the names of the surviving members of their band. His reply was one word.

Everyone.

Glowing with joy, Adele could barely wait till lights-out to share the news.

The next day, the other women began sending food and messages too. Some smiled. A few even hummed jolly tunes as they toiled. This irritated Spudd, who felt it reflected poorly on her; so she worked them extra hard to cultivate the proper attitude. Unbeknownst to her, this just created opportunities for them to bake tidbits and scrounge medicine to send to their husbands.

At the mines, the fact that Kale and his friends were suddenly cheerful and even appeared to be better fed was most annoying to Plotz, who responded by adding new work details; but the men remained bafflingly healthy.

Adele was glad that she could go up the ladder only once a day, for she feared her friends' enthusiasm would otherwise exhaust the fidelius bird, which, after all, still had a family to feed. But the bird seemed not to mind. She dropped off messages almost every time she came back from Gloamwoods and the Slough of Despond to feed her babies, who grew fat and contented under her care. Adele was there the day in spring when they took their first flights into the woodlands. For weeks afterwards she would occasionally spot the three birds from a distance, the mother squawking encouragement as the twins learned to fly faster and better, soaring above Gloamwoods and swooping among the branches.

One day the birds did not reappear. The nest fell apart in a storm, and Adele ran out of excuses to climb the ladder. She climbed down, sick with misery. Since fidelius birds do not remarry, this one would never raise another family on the window ledge. Adele would never see her friend again, and her means of contacting Kale was as dead as if it had touched Black Ice.

But what of the boys? What happened to them after Zach and Becky Zuckerman caught them that dreadful day as Kale and Adele were arrested?

At this point you will have to bear with me as we glide over a large stretch of time in a short stretch of words—specifically, about twelve years.

As Kale and Adele eked out their existences in prison, their sons grew up. The boys' eyes darkened from blue to green, and their hair deepened to an unambiguous orange. Becky and Zach, who both had brown hair and dark eyes, knew that no one would believe that they had produced such red-headed wonders; so they told everyone, including Casper and Jasper, that they were the boys' aunt and uncle, and that the parents had died in an accident that was too tragic to discuss. This suited everyone just fine—except, that is, for Casper and Jasper. The boys were bright as comets and tough as tungsten, and their curiosity was a carnivorous creature.

"What was our mother like?" Casper asked Aunt Becky one day when he was five and Count Wilhelm Scream was erecting a monument to himself on Inglenook's green.

"She was a very brave woman," said Aunt Becky. "She would have done anything for you." This was true, and had the advantage of being the only thing Becky actually knew about her. Casper wanted to know more, but Aunt Becky suddenly became very busy in the bakery where she now worked.

"What was our father like?" Jasper asked Uncle Zach one day when he was nine and Count Wilhelm Scream had just released new coins with pictures of Princess Abattoir on them.

"A strong fellow who did what he thought was right," said Uncle Zach, who had given this answer many times over the years.

"What was our father's name?" said Jasper. But Uncle Zach suddenly became very busy in the ice cream part of the store where he and Aunt Becky now worked.

For Aunt Becky's plan had worked out perfectly, and the entire family now lived in a cozy apartment above the Inglenook Bakery and Sweet Shop. Becky's sister had handed the day-to-day aspects of business over to the Zuckermans while she managed boring grown-up stuff such as advertising and receipts and invoices and a mysterious something called "marketing." Her name was Matilda, and she was so happy moving bits of paper around in her office that she almost never came out, so she does not enter into our story much at all.

The bakery was a pleasant, grey stone building with thick walls and a slate roof. Flowering vines framed the doorway, and a big shop window overlooked the sidewalk and displayed cookies and cakes and canisters of freshly churned ice cream. A laborer named Bunny brought regular shipments of marshmallow and Rainbow Ice, which the family used to make these delectable treats. Inside the shop was a small area for people to eat and chat in squooshy armchairs draped with afghans Becky had knitted, and decorated with cushions she had crocheted.

As Casper and Jasper grew, they became even more identical-looking than they had been the day they fell into Zach and Becky's arms as warm, squirmy bundles, and so the medallions were essential to telling them apart. Eventually Zach and Becky cut off the bracelets and hung the medallions on smooth, gold chains around the boys' necks. They had had to save up for the necklaces, but this was about the time the boys were starting school, and the adults feared that bracelets might seem odd.

"The other kids might make fun of them," said Aunt Becky.

"I would have," said Uncle Zach. And so it was agreed.

So each boy always felt the secure weight of the disk hanging on his chest, sometimes under his shirt, sometimes bouncing over it, but always there with its C or its J so that Uncle Zach and Aunt Becky knew exactly whom to yell at when Jasper forgot to clear the table after dinner or Casper left a dead raccoon in the freezer.

Casper and Jasper attended the Count Wilhelm Scream Elementary School for Rigorous and Orthodox Education, a square, cement building seemingly run by a headmaster with pasty skin and a square, cement head. In reality, of course, Count Wilhelm Scream ran it. He had taken to heart Princess Abattoir's offhand remark many years earlier that teachers hated him: he had burned all the books from the area schools in a massive bonfire, and made the teachers watch. Anyone who cried was fired. Anyone who smiled stayed. Thus, the schools were now staffed with teachers who hated books but were very fond of obedience. To promote this principle, the headmaster at the twins' school used what he called the "proctor system," which meant that the oldest and meanest kids were issued blue uniforms and Thwacking Sticks. They kept order by hitting younger kids who had annoyed them by, for example, giggling at jokes or reading anything other than textbooks.

The twins did not agree with the headmaster's philosophy. Thus, several days in any given week would find them in the headmaster's office for beating up schoolyard bullies, usually someone who had been too free with a Thwacking Stick. If this happened often enough, they would be suspended. This annoyed them because they rather enjoyed beating up schoolyard bullies. At home, they worked at the shop alongside their supposed aunt and uncle, baking cookies, creating new ice cream flavors (nutmeg-butterscotch was Jasper's favorite; apricot cream was Casper's), and helping unload Bunny's deliveries from Count Wilhelm Scream's Highly Efficient Centralized Food Distribution Center.

The proctors were also in charge of Count Wilhelm Scream's League of the Crocodile, which all children were required to attend. Twice a week they gathered after school for meetings where grownups told them how wonderful Count Scream was. Twice a month they went camping and learned how to build fires and shelter while trying not to get hit by proctors. This was supposed to make them hearty and obedient.

Casper and Jasper hated the meetings but enjoyed the camping. The proctors in the twins' group discovered fairly early that their Thwacking Sticks tended to end up in the kindling, so they kept them discreetly sheathed.

One sunshiny, summertimey day, the boys pulled open the shop's sliding wooden doors to admit Bunny's delivery cart. The back of the shop was an open area with doors to the kitchen and storerooms full of flour, sugar, and other necessities. In the middle of the room stood a waist-high chopping block. The floor was rutted where delivery carts had rolled on it for years. The stone walls had only a few small windows, but the doors let in plenty of light. Bunny had been bringing ice and other supplies to the sweet shop for a few months. Her face was not old, but her hair was pure white and so soft that it drifted in the breeze when she turned her head, and her eyes were pink-rimmed as though from crying. Hammers and chisels hung from her belt, and she wore a multi-pocketed vest for her many tools. The boys liked her.

"You're late," said Jasper.

"Smacks of rebellion, disobedience, and lack of personal integrity," said Casper. "Well done."

"How are the birds?" said Jasper. He knew she often sprinkled broken crackers at the town green on her way to the shop as a treat for the birds. Bunny smiled shyly. Casper grabbed a bag of flour. A youngster who was not used to managing these sacks would have staggered under its shifting weight, but Casper and Jasper knew all the tricks to hoisting and hefting a delivery from the Food Distribution Center. With his free hand Casper opened the door to the storage room and set the bag down with a soft *whump*. A poof of flour settled on his hair and the smock he wore over his clothes.

Bunny applauded. Then she took a pocket watch out of her vest and opened it, frowning. "Oh, dear."

Jasper grabbed the handles of her cart and maneuvered it next to the chopping block. "Are you wondering why we're not in school?" he said as she dropped the watch back into her pocket.

"We got suspended again," said Casper, trying not to sound as though he were bragging.

"Oh, my." Bunny's fingertips quaked on the handle of the ice cart. It was a funny thing about her. She always seemed so frail, as though the slightest breeze could knock her flat; and yet she chucked fifty-pound bags of flour about and pushed a fully loaded ice cart with ease. As Casper said, you wouldn't want to throw her a surprise party; it might kill her. But as Jasper pointed out, she always got the job done, no matter what it was.

"I think we may have disappointed her," said Casper to Jasper.

"She may feel school is important," agreed Jasper.

Rolling her eyes, Bunny hefted a bag of flour onto her slender shoulders and staggered to the storage room.

"We're not sure school is a good fit for us," Casper called after her. Bunny set her bag down and came out, brushing her hands on her pants. It set her tool belt pealing like wind chimes.

"We question whether the institution has anything to offer us," said Jasper.

"But—" began Bunny.

"Oh, we'll go back," said Casper.

"Aunt Becky and Uncle Zach have been pretty clear about that," said Jasper. "And really, parts of school are fine."

"Recess especially," said Casper.

"But we feel our destiny lies elsewhere."

"Outside Inglenook, we reckon," said Casper. "But not today."

"Got ice to chip," agreed Jasper. He positioned a vat next to the chopping block. "Aunt Becky said twenty pounds should be enough."

"*You load twenty pounds, and what do you get?*" sang Bunny. It was a popular song by a local singer named Flora, and Casper and Jasper knew all the words.

"*Another day colder and tons of regret,*" they sang.

> *I do all the work and the count gets all the pay.*
> *Keeping him happy takes up my whole day.*
> *The man in the castle says I'm living a dream,*
> *But sometimes all I can do is Scream.*

They all giggled and glanced at the open doorway in case a spy strolled past. The song was prohibited, so everyone sang it. But quietly.

"Very bright today," said Casper, peering into Bunny's cart. "Look at those colors."

Bunny examined her gloves as if searching for holes before putting them on. She was very particular about them. Next she grabbed her tongs and lifted a chunk of ice. The size of a small suitcase, it shimmered and glimmered red and orange and green and gold and blue. New colors formed and swirled where the tints touched each other. Rainbow Ice was the key ingredient for Uncle Zach's ice cream. Unlike regular ice, it stayed cold and solid for days, sometimes weeks at a time. So did the ice cream made from it. And when even a tiny bit of it was ground up and mixed into Zach's confections, the colors disappeared but the most marvelous flavor infused any recipe. The chocolate tasted darker and more mysterious; lemons sang with clear, tart voices; and the cherries in cherry-vanilla simply tasted more cherry-ish than any that had not been frosted with the magic ice.

The only problem was, it stained. This was why Casper and Jasper wore smocks while working. As for Bunny, her work clothes were dotted with so many colors that she looked like a tragic victim of an explosion in a paint factory.

Bunny patted her belt for the right-sized chisel. She settled it into a crack in the ice and struck it with her hammer. With a *tchink,* a chunk fell off, and another. Dots of blue and gold and red flew through the air as Jasper pulled on gloves and placed the chunks in the vat.

"Darn!" exclaimed Casper. He held up his necklace. A colored droplet from the Rainbow Ice had landed on it, tarnishing the disk and obscuring the letter C.

"Same thing happened to mine last week," said Jasper. "Vinegar and viper snot takes care of most of it." He took off his glove and held up his hand. "Here."

Casper slipped his head out of the necklace and tossed it to his brother. But Jasper's fingers were cold and he fumbled, dropping it onto the ice. Bunny had just raised her hammer and chisel to crack another chunk free, and the blade fell squarely on the medallion.

Tchinkkkkrack!

It split in two.

"My necklace!" Casper jumped at the chopping block and grabbed the disk he had worn every day of his life.

They stared at it.

It was not a disk. It was a locket, and one half held a drawing of a nice-looking lady and a nice-looking man. The lady cuddled a baby in her arms. On the other half of the locket was an inscription: "For dearest Charles."

Casper showed Jasper. Bunny looked too. Her pink eyes widened, and she dropped the chisel.

"Thanks," said Jasper. He slipped off his own necklace and brought the chisel down on it. It popped open. They crowded around.

Jasper's locket showed the same nice-looking lady and man. In this drawing the man was holding a baby and smiling with great pride. On the other half of the locket an inscription read, "For dearest James."

"Who's Charles?" said Casper.

"Who's James?" said Jasper.

A shadow fell across the doorway.

"We heard a shout," said Uncle Zach. "Are you—?"

Aunt Becky and Uncle Zach looked at the boys and the lockets. The words died on Uncle Zach's lips.

"Uh oh," said Aunt Becky. Uncle Zach clenched his fists.

Bunny looked around wildly. "Oh, dear," she said. "Oh, dear." She yanked her watch out of her vest and shoved it back in. "I'm going to be late." She threw her tools into her cart and hurtled through the open doorway in a cloud of flour and glittering, rainbow-colored mist.

Uncle Zach locked the door to the shop and hung the "Closed" sign in the window. The League of the Crocodile was parading through Inglenook with marching bands to celebrate Princess Abattoir's birthday, and he hoped the excitement would be enough to keep anyone from wondering why they were not open for business. He and Aunt Becky hustled the boys downstairs to the basement, a cool room with earthen walls and a dusty floor, and sat them at a small wooden table. Aunt Becky lit a lantern. Its mustard-colored light only made the shadows seem darker.

Casper and Jasper sat in stunned silence as for the first time they heard the story Aunt Becky and Uncle Zach had long feared to tell them: of that awful day in Middlemost when Count Wilhelm Scream had descended like a wolf on the fold and Casper and Jasper's parents had used the last seconds of their freedom to save their little boys.

"Stunned" and "silent" were not two ways Casper and Jasper were going to stay for long. "Silent" went first.

"So you've known this for—" began Jasper.

"Twelve years," finished Casper.

"And you never *told* us?" said Jasper.

"Obviously not," said Uncle Zach. Overhead, they could hear the faint sounds of the marching band playing "Perfect Princess," a standard on such occasions.

"You said our parents died in an accident," said Casper in outrage.

"Sometimes we said 'tragedy,'" said Aunt Becky.

"So where are they now?" said Casper.

Uncle Zach sighed and looked uneasily at his wife. "No idea," he admitted.

"The thing you have to realize," said Aunt Becky, "is that no one escapes from the count."

"Are they dead?" demanded Jasper.

"Probably," said Aunt Becky.

Uncle Zach cleared his throat. "Maybe not."

All eyes turned to him.

Uncle Zach's fingers twitched a loose thread on his sweater, which Aunt Becky had knit for him to wear while he worked with ice cream. Like the twins' smocks, it was dotted with rainbow-colored spatters. "Boys, we only saw your parents once, and it was brief. But they were young and healthy. My guess is the count put them to work."

Aunt Becky put her hand over his. "He may have," she said. "Or they might be—I'm not sure which is the worse fate."

"So they were just—*lost*—and you never told us?" said Jasper.

"No one you love is ever truly lost," said Aunt Becky.

"Spiffy," said Jasper. "Absolutely sporking. But there's one small glitch."

"We've never met our parents," said Casper. "Not really."

"I don't think drooling on them counts," agreed Jasper.

"So we have no idea if we love them or not."

"Or vice-versa."

"Plus, it turns out they're not lost at all," said Casper. "They're in some horrible prison—"

"Or being worked to death—"

"—up on that mountain."

"Maybe," said Aunt Becky. "Maybe." Her voice was almost lost in the sounds of marching overhead. Attendance at parades was mandatory, as was enthusiasm, and she prayed no one would notice their absence.

"Which you forgot to mention," said Jasper.

"For twelve years," said Casper.

Aunt Becky clenched her jaw.

"We're grateful," said Jasper. "Really. *So* grateful that you lied to us—"

Uncle Zach slammed his palm down on the table. They all jumped. "Darn right we did," he snapped. "Want to know why?"

"Not really," said Casper.

"It was to save you," said Aunt Becky. Her voice was thin and tight.

"From what?" said Jasper. "Our imprisoned parents?"

"From the people who took them from you," Uncle Zach almost shouted. "If you had known anything, *anything* about them, someone could have guessed it or tortured it out of you." He leaned back in his chair, surveying the boys and breathing hard, as though he had been running. The loose thread had pulled out of the sweater, leaving a small hole.

"And now Bunny's seen those pictures," said Aunt Becky. "Let's hope she doesn't tell anyone."

Casper snorted. "It took three weeks for her to say good morning to us. I think she'll keep quiet."

"Either way, she's fired," said Uncle Zach.

"What?" cried Casper and Jasper.

"Shush," said Aunt Becky.

"You can't," said Casper.

"What if she can't find another job?" said Jasper.

Uncle Zach kept his voice low. "I'm sorry, but we can't risk having her around anymore."

The crowd in the streets above emitted desultory cheers. The bands played louder.

"Sounds like Princess Abattoir just arrived," said Uncle Zach.

"Never mind her," said Jasper. "What about Bunny? And our parents?"

Aunt Becky snapped around to Jasper. "Your parents."

"Our real parents," supplied Casper. "The ones who—"

"The ones who what?" shouted Aunt Becky. The boys gawked. Aunt Becky never shouted. "What makes them so real?"

"They—" began Casper.

"Gave birth to you," said Aunt Becky. "Threw you into the crowd. Yes, I know, Casper. I'm the one who caught you. And took you home and fed you and burped you and stayed up all night with you when you were sick, and knit sweaters and hats and socks till my fingers stung. Uncle Zach and I are the ones who get called to your school two or three times a week when you make trouble, and let you get away with it because we're not crazy about Scream ourselves. And I'm not saying your—

your *other* parents are bad people. I don't know a thing about them. But since you don't either, I'm not sure what makes them so real and us so fake." She blinked hard, and if she drew a sobbing breath the sound was lost in the strains of triumphant music from the street.

"Sorry," whispered Casper.

"Me too," said Jasper.

"There's more than one kind of real," said Casper.

Uncle Zach squeezed his wife's shoulder. "Yes," he said. "Yes, there is."

"The count must really hate them," said Jasper.

Uncle Zach sighed. "I can only tell you two things about that, boys. First, they loved you enough to risk death to save you. And second—" He stopped and drew a deep breath before reaching out to touch the boys, Casper on the shoulder and Jasper on the hand. He swallowed.

"Second?" said Jasper.

Uncle Zach shook his head. "Count Wilhelm Scream doesn't like loose ends."

In the street above, the crowd sang "Oh, How I Love Obedience," a favorite of the count's that concluded many of his public rallies. They did not sound terribly enthusiastic.

Casper and Jasper knew how they felt.

Later that evening, after dinner and dessert and homework—the dessert had been larger than usual, and the homework smaller, because Aunt Becky and Uncle Zach felt guilty about their deception—Casper and Jasper lay on their beds, staring at the ceiling. Finally, Casper spoke.

"My name's Charles," he said, trying it out.

"James," said Jasper. He flipped open the locket and gazed at the man and the woman and the baby. "Pleased to meet you."

Now that they knew the disks were lockets, they could see a faint line where the two sides met in a hinge on one side and a lock on the other. The locket was so finely crafted that these features blended with the designs etched into the gold. Aunt Becky had surmised that it was a kind of goblin-crafted workmanship that had been very popular in the area about twelve years earlier.

"I wonder what they were like," said Casper.

Jasper thought about this. "Brave."

"Quick-thinking. Chucking us into the crowd like that."

"Wouldn't have occurred to a lot of people," agreed Jasper.

Casper looked at the picture inside his locket, then turned onto his stomach so he could see his brother. "Do you think they're dead?"

Jasper mulled this over. "No," he said finally. "I don't."

"Why not?"

Jasper sighed and put his hands behind his head, staring at the ceiling. "I don't know. I just think they're still alive."

"Aunt Becky and Uncle Zach kept us alive."

"Yes. That's one way to fight the count."

Casper opened his locket to look at the drawing. "We look a little like them."

"A lot." Jasper had already memorized the kindly features of the man and woman.

"Wonder what they're like."

"Me too."

"I don't mean tall or short," said Casper.

"Course not," said Jasper.

"I mean to talk to."

"And be with."

"I mean, which do they like best, puppies or kittens?"

"Exactly. Chocolate or vanilla? Serious or funny? These are the real questions."

Jasper gazed past the ceiling. Casper crossed his ankles and waved his feet slowly from side to side. "I guess it's up to us, then."

Jasper looked out the window. Their bedroom had originally been intended for storage, so it had high ceilings and tall windows. The walls were so thick that the windows were recessed almost three feet, and the boys could comfortably sit on the sill. Casper got off his bed and sat there now.

Inglenook was all twisted, cobblestone streets and crooked houses half-cloaked with vines that burst with pink and purple flowers and glossy, green leaves in summer. Families planted gardens in the central green, and every fall the ground was full of pumpkins and squashes, their skins orange and yellow and striped and spotted or sometimes bubbling like witches' brew; and the air hung heavy with the perfume of grapes and apples. After the harvest, the leaves fell and the town looked sad and bewildered, especially when it rained; but as soon as the snow came, the townspeople hung lights in the streets and froze colored water in balloons which they then peeled off, making ice globes of red and green and blue which they placed randomly along walls and sidewalks, just for pretty, and lit candles behind them; and Inglenook glittered all through the darkest months.

From where he sat Jasper could see, halfway under his bed, a cement-colored textbook entitled *Count Wilhelm Scream's Wholesome and Uplifting Narrative of the Lands of Yonder, Inglenook Edition*. The cover showed hearty, scrubbed-looking children clustered around a beaming Count. Girls presented him with bouquets of flowers, and boys showed him pictures of Inglenook, Gloamwoods, and Castle Mirkstone to indicate how very pleased they all were to be under his iron-fisted subjugation. Casper and Jasper had blacked out several of the count's teeth, and given him spiky hair that sprang out over his ears.

This official history explained that at Inglenook's time of bleakest poverty and despair, Count Scream had arrived, trailing clouds of glory. He instituted order, making sure everyone was fed and clothed and cared for, thereby allowing them all sorts of free time to thank him; and they bathed themselves in gratitude and obedience, which *Count Wilhelm*

Scream's Dictionary of Correct Word Meanings defined as "doing everything a tall, dark person of authority says."

The unofficial version was not in the book. It was what is called "oral history," which means it was murmured behind locked doors late at night, or under umbrellas tilting toward each other in rainstorms that drowned the sound of conversation. According to this account, Inglenook had been built when a group of elderly knights who still did a bit of questing on weekends had discovered this land of green meadows fed by spring water as clear as glass, and settled on it as the perfect location for a retirement community. Realizing that nearby loomed a dark, tree-girt mountain pocked with treacherous swamps and swarming with magical creatures of dubious repute, they raised fortifications. They built houses. Merchants came, and farmers and teachers and others. Inglenook flourished.

Then Count Wilhelm Scream arrived.

Gossip said he had started life as an angry infant abandoned near a cleft in the mountain, his body dusted with black powder that burned to the touch. Many supposed the powder to be rime from Black Ice, which explained why he could touch the wicked substance and not die. Some said he was born of trolls. Others said that was a rotten thing to say about trolls.

A hunter found the baby and took him to Kinderdump, where he became a sallow boy with dead eyes. When he was sixteen he announced that his name was Count Wilhelm Scream, and counts did not live in orphanages. Then he left.

He came back years later, announcing that he would save the Lands of Yonder from its enemies. This puzzled a great many people who had not known they had enemies; but those who were angry and nervous believed him, and soon he had a following. They built Castle Mirkstone on the mountain whose shadow brushed the gates of Inglenook. The count moved in. The land around Mirkstone, though untamed, was rich: the swamps teemed with plants for food and medicine; the mountain held shafts of magical ice. The count asked the little blue creatures who lived there to build him an ice throne. As soon as it was completed he took it to Mirkstone.

The next day he announced that the mine-dwellers had threatened his lands. He attacked them with an army of trolls and other horrid, withered creatures. In the face of this overwhelming force, the mine folk departed, screaming in protest and saying very rude things about the count. In his victory speech, he called them "vermin" and "toxic monsters." He distributed posters showing grinning little blue men stealing toys from babies and kicking puppies. His followers clung closer to him.

Next, he erected mills on the mountain to grind his special flour. He knew that if he controlled the source of everyone's food, they would have to obey him. But no one wanted to work in the Ice Mines, and the farmers had always ground their own flour or sent it to Middlemost.

When the count heard about the rebels, he knew his most vicious dreams had come true.

As soon as the unfortunate prisoners had the mills and the mines producing, the count announced that from now on, the people would buy ice and flour only from him. Those who objected were free to make their case to the count himself, and he would gravely and wisely hear them.

A dozen concerned citizens from the various towns went to plead with Scream. They never came back. But a few days later, twelve new clearings appeared in the dense forest around Mirkstone, icy patches where the ground was frozen, trees shattered like ice, and no plant would grow.

At about this time, the citizens the Lands of Yonder decided that there were worse things than buying flour and ice from Count Wilhelm Scream's Highly Efficient Centralized Food Distribution Center. They also agreed to refer to him as His Most Cuddly and Beneficent Highnessness, and to celebrate his birthday with timbrels and dancing and gifts of gold and silver to be determined by Count Scream's Most Efficient Accountants and given freely and in gratitude for his ever-present mercies.

The count was a man of his word. As long as the townsfolk bought their materials from him and were loudly and publicly grateful and fomented no rebellion, life in the Lands of Yonder was largely peaceful.

And yet.

Casper and Jasper and people like them chafed at the daily indignities of life under Count Wilhelm Scream: the way they had to step off the sidewalk to make room for any Special Police walking past; the prohibition against flying flags that did not bear the silhouette of Princess Abattoir; the requirement that they accompany Aunt Becky and Uncle Zach when they went to vote in state elections, which invariably resulted in a landslide victory for the count, and the mysterious disappearance of whoever ran against him.

The twins realized their parents must have felt the same way. It made them want to know them.

Jasper joined his brother at the window. They sat facing each other, their backs against the rough stone. Jasper gazed at their room. Almost everything in it was on Count Wilhelm Scream's List of Unwholesome and Therefore Prohibited Items, which made Aunt Becky nervous. The beds and bureaus were scattered with comic books, adventure stories, and tales of dragon-slayers. Many featured battles against an evil villain who lived in a mountain fortress. On one wall, Jasper had put up a poster of Flora, the singer. She had long, straight, blonde hair and a dazzling white smile. Looking at it always gave him a giggly feeling in his stomach. Aunt Becky hated it, because she knew the Special Police would not approve of a singer who had penned such tunes as *Don't Count on the Count* and *Obedience is Overrated*.

Jasper pushed his feet against Casper's, and Casper pushed back. They rocked back and forth until their feet slipped and their heels bumped on the windowsill.

"So now what?" said Casper.

He meant, "What do we do now that we know our parents might, just might, be alive but imprisoned by an evil and unfortunately efficient villain?"

Jasper understood. "Uncle Zach said not to do anything."

"True," said Casper.

Which meant, as Jasper also knew, "So what?"

Jasper cracked his knuckles. "Our parents saved us from Wilhelm Scream," he said. "Isn't it about time we returned the favor?"

"That's about how I had it sussed out too," said Casper. "Wonder where we start."

"No idea," said Jasper. "But that never stopped us before."

Casper fingered his locket. "Did you see the look on Bunny's face when these opened?"

"No."

"She looked like she'd been hit with a sock full of wet sand."

"She always looks like she's been hit with a sock full of wet sand."

"This time she looked like she'd been socked harder than usual."

"Do you think she knew about the lockets?" said Jasper.

"No," said Casper thoughtfully. "I don't think anyone knew these things opened. But when she saw the pictures—"

"You're right," said Jasper. "She jumped."

"She bolted."

"And went haring out of here."

"Which means," said Casper, "she might know something about Charles and James and their parents."

"We could ask her."

"I'm not sure where she lives."

"Finding out might involve missing school."

"Shucky darn."

"Tomorrow, then?"

"Tomorrow."

They stared out the window. Jasper flexed his toes. "Can I ask a stupid question?"

"Better than anyone I know," said Casper brightly.

"How badly do we want to do this?"

"What do you mean?"

"Let's say we succeed," said Jasper.

"We often do."

"We'd have two sets of parents," said Jasper. "Effectively."

"Ah," said Casper.

"It's been hard enough raising an uncle and aunt," said Jasper. "Breaking them of their bad habits."

"The way they do insist on school," agreed Casper.

"And homework." The boys' school assigned hours of meaningless busywork every night. This was because the grown-ups who ran the school reasoned, quite correctly, that children who spend all their time doing homework have no opportunity to play, or create imaginary worlds, or read for fun. Children who do such things tend to learn how to think for themselves, and this, the grown-ups felt, was dangerous.

"And only one dessert per meal," said Casper. "Usually."

"If we bring home this second set, we'd be outnumbered," said Jasper. "Making beds might become a standard part of the day. Or even wearing matching socks."

Casper sighed. "You're right. You're absolutely right. But it's a risk we'll have to take."

"Because?"

"Like you said," said Casper. "Our parents saved us from Wilhelm Scream. It's time we returned the favor."

The next day marked the end of Casper and Jasper's suspension. They returned to school and ate lunch in the cafeteria under a mural of Count Wilhelm Scream beaming at proctors in League of the Crocodile uniforms saluting him with their Thwacking Sticks. Students generally avoided sitting there, as the nausea produced by this vignette made lunching difficult, so the boys had the privacy they needed.

"First things first," said Jasper. "Where does Bunny live?"

"Lookit." Casper pulled a thick, yellow book from his backpack and balanced it on his knee under the table. "Town directory."

"Impressive," said Jasper. "Where did you get it?"

"Head's office," said Casper. "We were discussing a minor infraction that I was pretty sure would land me there."

"What infraction was this?"

"I felt Blagden Coalblort was being excessively generous with his Thwacking Stick, especially as regards kids half his size."

"Did Headmaster Slab agree?"

"He did not."

"What did you tell him?"

"I said Blagden would come down from the tree when he got hungry enough, and there was an excellent chance the limp was only temporary."

"Grand." Jasper opened the book and ran his finger down columns of addresses. He shook his head. "I don't even know her last name. Do you?"

"I heard Uncle Zach say she lived on Warren Street," said Casper.

Still keeping the book under the table, Jasper opened to the map in the middle. Warren Street was in the corner of town farthest from the Inglenook Sweet Shoppe.

"It's a start." Jasper closed the directory, and Casper slid it back into his pack. "After school?"

"After school."

Warren Street was not easy to find. The streets around it were narrow and unmarked, and so crooked one couldn't see more than half a block in any given direction. Urchins in bandit caps slouched on street corners, whistling off-key. Houses tilted; cars parked half-on, half-off the sidewalks. Some had wheels.

After several fruitless hours of poking down backstreets and byways, Casper inhaled sharply and touched Jasper on the arm. He pointed. In front of a ramshackle hut, Bunny was pulling cabbages and carrots from a green garden and piling them in a wheelbarrow. A trowel poked from a pocket in her rainbow-spattered vest. The boys strolled nonchalantly toward her.

Bunny glanced up. Her pink eyes flew open. "Oh, dear—it's getting late!" She bolted into the hut and slammed the door.

Casper wheeled the barrow to the door. He knocked. "Vegetable delivery."

No answer.

"Bunny," he said loudly. "We know you're in there."

Casper and Jasper waited. But she did not answer, and even as the sky dusked over and the air grew damp and chilly, no lights came on inside.

"That went well," remarked Jasper as they turned to go.

"We need a Plan B," said Casper.

"Are we only up to B?"

"We need to track Bunny without her seeing us." Casper stepped around a pink-and-white car in front of the house.

"And then what?"

"I'm not sure. But we need to find her someplace where she can't run away."

"We can't do any worse than we have so far," said Jasper, and with this encouraging thought the boys walked home.

Because so many things were banned in the prisons of Count Wilhelm Scream, the prisoners had a wealth of forbidden activities to pursue in secret. Needless to say, the mill prisoners' favorite rebellion was writing notes to their husbands; but there were other things as well. Because they were not allowed to read, they recited stories to each other. If they were caught, they hastily inserted Count Wilhelm Scream into the tale as its hero. Because they were not allowed to have jewelry other than their wedding rings, they made earrings and necklaces out of broken cogs and bits of machinery. If Spudd noticed, they said they loved their work so much they wanted to wear it. The overseer always scowled and stomped away. But somewhere deep in the recesses of her potato-shaped head she sensed the prisoners were getting away with something, and she vowed to catch one of them.

One day during a break, she found Stella sitting on the floor, decorating her work boots. Spudd shot across the room and yanked the poor creature to her feet. "Aha," she screamed. "Princess Abattoir has been wanting to make an example of someone. It's the end for you, my sweet."

Stella cried out and tried to pull free, but Spudd only gripped her harder. With her free hand she raised a whistle to her lips and blew a short blast. Guards appeared in the doors. "Take her away."

But as the guards stepped forward and seized the sobbing woman, and as the other prisoners gasped in dread, a quiet voice spoke.

"Excuse me," said Adele.

"Shut up," said Spudd.

"I believe there's been a misunderstanding."

"Get back to work." Spudd gave a nasty grin. "Unless you want to join her."

This was a dreadful threat, for the prisoners had met Princess Abattoir many times on her visits to the mills. Her delight in torture was well known.

Adele picked up the boot and turned it over in her hands. Her fingers shook, but her voice was calm. "Is this the problem, ma'am?"

"Problem? Not at all," gloated Spudd. "The Princess will be delighted to show what happens to rule-breakers."

"But this isn't rule-breaking at all, ma'am." Adele sounded as serene as a summer Sunday.

"Oh, it isn't, isn't it?"

"We code our boots to tell whose is whose." Adele put it on the floor next to her own foot. They matched almost exactly. Boldly she turned her ankle so that the overseer could see the designs she had engraved on her own boot. "So we don't lose time finding them."

"Decorating, altering, or mutilating the Count's Highly Efficient and Appropriate Work Attire is strictly prohibited and punishable by punishment," barked the overseer.

"But it's only so we can spend as much time as possible doing the work the count has so graciously given us," said Adele. "Because we love him so dearly."

"Oh, is that so?"

"Also, we find it has increased productivity by sixteen to twenty-one percent."

Spudd gritted her teeth. She thought about how much she disliked Adele and her friends. The guards tightened their grip. Stella made the kind of small noises in her throat that people make when they are trying not to cry. Spudd thought about being able to brag that she had improved production by sixteen to twenty-one percent. Her face turned aubergine. She whirled on Stella. "What are you lazing around for?" she demanded. "Get back to work!"

The guards released Stella. She almost collapsed, but caught herself in time. The machinery, which had been silenced for break, started up again. The drudgery of life in the Food Mills recommenced.

Spudd grabbed Adele's sleeve and yanked her close. "I've got my eye on you," she snarled.

As this was almost literally true, Adele said only, "Yes, ma'am."

"You're smart," said Spudd.

"Thank you, ma'am."

"Smart people make trouble." Spudd's meaty fingers dug into Adele's arm.

Adele said nothing, and after a moment Spudd continued. "Next week is rendering."

"Yes, ma'am."

"I better see that sixteen to twenty-one percent improvement."

"Yes, ma'am."

The overseer dropped Adele's arm as though she were throwing away something that had gone bad. With a final, manic glare she clomped away. Stella rubbed her own arms where the guards had left marks. "Thanks," she said. "How did you ever think of that stuff about increasing productivity?"

"The calendar," said Adele. "Next week is the Feast of Cypher Mendatius."

"So what?"

"He taught the art of lying with statistics." Adele chuckled. "Let's hope he watches over us while we try for that sixteen to twenty-one percent improvement." And they went back to their work.

Not everything Adele had said was a lie. Decorating the boots really did help, though perhaps not in the way Spudd would have liked. The designs made the prisoners happy. Stella had been etching stars and moons onto her boots. Ingrid liked to draw houses and tall buildings on hers. And Adele? Her right boot showed a bunch of kale growing as if in a garden; and her left had a design of two intertwined hearts around the letters C and J.

The next day, Casper and Jasper returned to Warren Street to lurk in a recessed doorway a few houses down from Bunny's hut. Hours passed, but the thrill of breaking so many rules all at once kept them from getting bored. Finally, just as they were thinking they would have to come back another time, Bunny tiptoed out. She turned keys in three locks on the door and dropped each key into a different pocket on her vest. Casper and Jasper straightened their tired joints and prepared to follow.

Bunny got into the pink-and-white car in front of her house and drove off.

"Dang it!" said Casper.

"Did not plan for that," said Jasper as the car disappeared around a corner.

"We should have known it was hers," said Casper.

"Parked right out front," said Jasper.

"And parallel to the curb." Tidiness was rare in this neighborhood. "Did you get the license plate?"

"No. But it was colorful."

"Easy to spot. Tomorrow?"

"Tomorrow."

The next day they waited at an apothecary on the corner where they had last seen Bunny's car. They stood at the big front window and pretended to read state-approved pamphlets about children who ate nutritious food. A pink-and-white car went past. It went two blocks and turned again.

The day after that, Casper and Jasper waited at the end of the second block, playing marbles in front of a pub called The Greasy Lapel. They wore baseball caps for Inglenook's softball team, the Puissant Knights, pulled low on their brows. Handwritten posters for an upcoming concert half-covered the pub's mural, which showed Count Wilhelm Scream and Princess Abattoir heralding the harvest as local farmers brought them their crops. Casper and Jasper thought the farmers in the painting looked far happier about this arrangement than any they knew in real life.

A troll with a large, misshapen head emerged from the pub bearing a truncheon and a scowl. "No loitering."

"Littering?" said Casper in surprise.

"Nothing of the sort," said Jasper.

"We plan to take our marbles with us when we depart."

The figure stepped closer. He wore boots and a black vest with a badge that said HELLO MY NAME IS THORFIN SKULLCLEAVER. "I am the bouncer. Scram."

"No, thank you," said Jasper.

"Not at the moment," said Casper.

"But soon, my good fellow."

"If nothing else, out of deference to our elders."

"And tallers."

"And hairiers."

The figure swung his club over his head. The pink-and-white car drove into sight. Casper and Jasper bolted. The club crashed into the sidewalk. The bouncer's curses followed them as they ran.

The car went three blocks before turning at a yarn shoppe called Purls of Wisdom near Inglenook's high walls.

"She can't go much further," said Casper. "There's not much further to go."

"And we can use some of that," said Jasper, pointing at the shoppe.

"Yarn?"

"Wisdom. But we'll say we're there for yarn."

"I hope we catch up with her tomorrow," said Casper.

"Me too," said Jasper. "Me too."

According to tradition, fog on the Feast of Cypher Mendatius was good luck. If so, reflected Adele, they should be fantastically lucky that day. The weather was drizzly, and a sulky mist obscured the tops of the marshmallow stalks. One-eyed creatures huddled under rusty mushrooms, winking balefully. Adele walked among the prisoners, making sure their work went smoothly. Technically this was Spudd's job, but she had long ago realized that letting Adele do it had advantages, in that it let Spudd smoke and play cards all day with the guards.

Mist dampened the workers' clothes, and chilled their cheeks and hands. The trays for rendered marshmallow got so wet that everything stuck to them. Ingrid stirred a cauldron over a sullen fire giving out clouds of stinging smoke. "How's it going?" said Adele.

Ingrid uttered a few choice words to indicate that it was going poorly.

"Let's see." Adele leaned over the cauldron to inspect its contents, which were brown and gloppy instead of white and smooth. "We can fix this. A few drops of—"

Something heavy knocked her to her knees. She tried to stand but couldn't. A pale blob covered her leg. Her skin blistered at its touch. She screamed.

"Mallow attack!" yelled Ingrid.

Workers rushed in. Some whacked the marshmallow with their tools, or kicked it with their heavy boots. Others grabbed Adele's arms and pulled her from the sucking embrace of the hungry plant. She came loose with a squelching sound. Her overalls hung in tatters, and her foot was bare.

Freed of her weight, the marshmallow swung back up into the fog. Insolently, it spat out her boot, which splashed into the water.

"You're lucky it was young," panted Stella. "Full-sized—can you imagine?"

Adele winced and flexed her toes. Her skin was covered in white bumps ringed in red and purple. "Immature mallows have stronger venom," she said. "It's more concentrated."

Spudd stormed into the group as Ingrid and Stella helped Adele to her feet. The words, "Get back to work, you lazy louts" died on her lips as she saw Adele's ragged clothing and the sores on her leg.

She gestured to the guards. "Take her to the infirmary," she said. "Looks like she finally found a way to get out of work."

Shortly thereafter, Adele was delighted to find herself in the Healing Center of the Ever Beneficent Count Who Cares for You Even Though You Are Scum. She wore a burlap nightgown, which, though coarse, was clean and dry. Her injury was what the prisoners called a "lucky break," meaning it was nonlethal but severe enough that she would be laid up for a while. This meant she could take that rarest of all things, a rest, until she was deemed healthy enough to return to her life of slave labor.

As soon as the nurse departed to attend to her other patients, Adele was alone. This was supposed to be a punishment, for Spudd feared she might make friends with other patients or spread the message of rebellion. But since Adele had not been by herself since her arrest, she actually enjoyed the peace and quiet. She regretted only the loss of her boots, with their designs that reminded her of her husband and sons. One boot lay in the squelch of the slough; the other had been thrown away as soon as she reached the infirmary. Maybe Stella or Ingrid would get the first one for her. They had chopped down the mallow that attacked her, more for revenge than logic. The muddy splash it made when it hit the water had been Adele's last sight of the swamp as she was hustled away.

She half-sat in bed, her leg wrapped in gauze bandages and covered with slimy but effective medicine. Idly, she looked out the window. The fog had lifted, and some distance away she could see a clearing in the woods. It was ringed with sparkling coils of wire atop a tall fence, and contained a dark, shed-like building plus several other structures.

Adele raised her head. She remembered the descriptions Kale had sent her of his prison camp.

Were these the Ice Mines?

She could see helmeted men loading blocks into carts. Was one of them Kale?

He must be. He hadn't been anywhere else since their arrest.

With a jolt that made the hairs on her arms stand up, Adele realized that she was closer to her husband than she had been in twelve years.

The Feast of Cypher Mendatius dawned damp and cold in Inglenook. Everything dripped, and the mountaintop hulked under a bank of fog as thick as flannel. The Count Wilhelm Scream Elementary School for Rigorous and Orthodox Education observed the holiday by adding several hours of math classes, which Casper and Jasper felt would have been reason enough to skip school even without their urgent mission; and so they had gone directly to the spot where they had last seen Bunny. Soon enough mist lifted, shops opened, and merchants arrived to set up stalls, but Bunny did not appear.

By late afternoon, crowds danced in the streets and the sidewalks were thick with vendors selling trick slide rules and oblong Pi Pies they claimed were round. The boys lurked in Purls of Wisdom, where baskets of yarn were stacked floor-to-ceiling. Jasper bought a purple skein, extra soft, for Aunt Becky while Casper watched at the window.

"Hist!" said Casper. Jasper jammed the yarn into his pocket and left his change on the counter as he bounded to meet his brother.

A pink-and-white car bumped slowly along the cobblestones, avoiding the revelers. Casper and Jasper dashed out of the store, backpacks bouncing on their shoulders. People thronged the narrow avenue, laughing and tossing coins at the feet of ragged children dancing the Rhombus Rumba or the Primetime Swing.

"Where could she be going?" said Casper as they dodged through the crowd.

"Math games!" bellowed a vendor at a cart stacked with boxes and scrolls. "Guaranteed to make you feel stupid!"

"Probably," gasped Jasper, nipping around the cart, "wherever—she goes—every—day."

Vaudevillians in baggy pants pranced in a circle, shouting to the crowd. "What did the zero say to the eight?" yelled the first.

"Nice belt!" yelled the second. "Why was the math book so sad?"

"It had too many problems!"

People roared with laughter. Coins flew into the performers' hats, silver stags and bronze eagles, and even a gold dragon or two glinting in the honey-colored sunlight. The twins sprinted past.

"No running," hollered a juggler tossing compasses and protractors from hand to hand.

"Of course not," called Jasper over his shoulder.

"That's how accidents happen," agreed Casper, vaulting over a group of small children eating candy abacuses. "See her?"

"There!" Jasper pointed, and they slowed to a walk, trying to breathe normally.

The car, now empty, sat by an open door set into the stones of the town wall. A troll stood at the doorway, holding a club the size of a dinosaur leg. Just above its head hung a sign reading, "The Tone-Deaf Troubadour." Cautiously, Casper and Jasper approached. A raucous crowd of wenches, adventure-seekers, and ne'er do-wells filled the tavern, almost obscuring their view of a diminutive figure with soft, white hair bobbing through the throng.

"Good evening," said Casper, and stepped past the troll.

THONK.

One end of the club landed hard on the ground between Casper and the doorway. The other end was gripped in the troll's hand, which was hairy and so muscled that it appeared to be made of enormous, shaggy stones.

"Stop," said a deep voice. It sounded thick, as though the speaker's throat were made of oatmeal.

Casper and Jasper looked up, past the hand to the hairy, hard-looking arm that it was attached to, and to the face above that.

Trolls are, generally speaking, not pretty. This one was no exception. Its close-set eyes were small and piggy, and glittered above a nose the size of an eggplant. Its dark, stringy hair hung almost to its waist, and it wore baggy leather boots laced up its ankles. Its chest and stomach were covered with necklaces of colored beads. More beads and the skulls of small animals were braided into its voluminous beard. It was half again as tall as the tallest man Casper and Jasper had ever seen, and easily twice as broad in the chest and shoulders. It smelled like wet rocks.

"How do you do?" said Jasper.

"Stop," repeated the troll.

"We've stopped," pointed out Casper.

The troll thought about this for a moment. He lifted his club to his shoulder.

"You can not go in there," he said in his thick voice.

"Why not?" said Jasper, for he and Casper could not imagine being unwelcome anywhere.

"No kids." The troll shook his head, and the beads and skulls in his beard rattled.

"Why not?" said Casper, who had a question for every answer.

"Grownups only." The troll gripped his club. A line began to form behind the boys.

"That's a mighty impressive Thwacking Stick you have there," said Jasper.

The troll glared. "This is no Thwacking Stick."

"It's not?"

The troll displayed the club lovingly in both hands. "It is a shillelagh," he said.

"And a fine specimen at that," said Casper.

"I'm not sure I've ever seen one close up," said Jasper.

"You don't often see such a fine grain in the handle," said Casper.

"And the grips—they seem to be spaced exactly right for your generously sized digits," said Jasper. "Mr. Troll, sir, I believe this is a custom-made shillelagh."

The troll beamed. "You boys know your thumpers," he said.

"No, no," said Casper modestly. "Such high-quality workmanship speaks for itself."

"It is not a custom job," confided the troll. "I modified it."

"Not really!" exclaimed Jasper. "I didn't think an ordinary shillelagh owner could do such a thing."

"I thought you needed special tools," said Casper.

"And training."

The troll drew himself up straight. "I learned at school." He did not wish to brag, but he was a graduate of the School of Hard Knocks, where he had concentrated in General Thuggery. This had led directly to his present occupation at the Tone-Deaf Troubadour. "Also," he went on, "I had to do it."

"Why?" said Casper.

The people in line began to shift from one foot to the other. The troll sighed deeply and extended his left hand. "I am Guthrum Danegeld. They call me Danegeld the Sinister."

"Who does?" said Casper indignantly. "You seem to be a sterling fellow. Cheerful, thrifty, brave—"

Jasper nudged him. "No, you twit. He means he's left-handed. Isn't that right, Mr. Danegeld?"

Guthrum Danegeld, aka Danegeld the Sinister, nodded as his beady eyes filled with tears. "And would you believe," he said, "Sig Sour does not make a left-handed shillelagh?"

"No!" gasped Jasper.

"Shocking," said Casper.

"Can we get in, please?" said a voice from the line.

Danegeld wiped his eyes on a hairy forearm. Casper and Jasper took the opportunity to stand on tiptoe and peer into the tavern. An unseen band thumped a familiar tune, and dancers stomped in time. The boys could not see Bunny.

"Just for our edification," said Jasper when Danegeld had collected himself, "could you remind us who Sig Sour is?"

A coven of witches with nametags on their robes joined the line, chatting eagerly and comparing hats.

"He is the millionaire lemon magnate who went into the cudgel business when the Cuddly and Good-Hearted Count

Scream created such a market for them," said Danegeld. "Mr. Sour makes all the best thumpers: clubs, bats, sticks, truncheons...."

"But only for the right-handed," guessed Casper. He glanced sideways through the door. Was that Bunny?

Danegeld nodded sadly.

"This is appalling," said Jasper.

"The tyranny of the majority," agreed Casper. "The very idea that a hard-working fellow like you, slubbering away at his job evening and day, morning and night—"

"Only evening," said Danegeld. "I have another job the rest of the time."

"Even worse," said Jasper. "Here you are, slaving at two jobs—"

"Of course, I am young," said Danegeld. "I am not even a hundred and fifty yet."

"That helps, naturally," said Casper.

"—and deprived of the basic tools of your trade," said Jasper. "Forced to modify your own shillelagh."

"Ahem," said a witch.

"Could there be any further degradation?" said Casper.

"Yes!" bellowed Danegeld. Casper and Jasper jumped. The troll leaned in close to them. "Can you imagine," he rumbled, "Sig Sour does not even make a left-handed shillelagh holster?"

"I'll be zonkered," said Jasper.

"I'll be late for our meeting," said the witch. "Mind stepping aside?"

"So I have to carry my shillelagh instead. The other trolls laugh at me." He gave a loud sniff. "They call me...Guthrum the Shillelagh Carrier."

"Give me strength," muttered the witch.

But Casper and Jasper could only look at Guthrum in a muteness of horror and sympathy. "Kids can be so cruel," said Casper finally.

With effort, Danegeld collected himself. He stroked his shillelagh fondly, running his fingers over the indentations that perfectly fit his left hand.

"Is there anything we can do to help?" said Jasper.

Danegeld sighed. "I am saving up for a custom holster," he said. "They are expensive. You would be surprised."

Jasper shook his head. "After this conversation, nothing would surprise me."

"You and me both," grumbled the witch. The line had lengthened to include several warlocks and a snake charmer with boa constrictors twining around her arms. Several people tapped their feet; others glanced pointedly at their watches.

"I think," said Casper, "that if you let us in we could help."

"Why?" said Danegeld. "How?"

"Our friend inside has untold riches," said Casper, which was sort of true, for Bunny had never told him of any riches. "We might be able to persuade her to make a donation."

"If I let you in?" said Danegeld.

"Yes."

"No."

"No?" said Jasper.

"My job is to guard this door," said Danegeld. He tapped the ground between them with his modified left-handed shillelagh. "No kids."

"So shove the kids aside and let us in," hissed the snake charmer.

Casper looked at Jasper. Jasper looked at Casper. They both looked at Guthrum Danegeld, aka Danegeld the Sinister, and his whacking big shillelagh.

"Is there anything we can do to change your mind?" said Casper.

"Yes," said Danegeld.

"And that would be?"

"Bribe me."

Jasper blinked. "Excuse me?"

"Bribe me," repeated Danegeld. "I am a professional."

"And be quick about it," said the witch.

"Well, then," said Casper. "What's your price?"

"Gold," said Guthrum Danegeld. "I like gold."

"We don't have any gold," said Jasper.

Danegeld jabbed his club at Jasper's chest. "What is that, then?"

Jasper's locket gleamed on its gold chain. The locket marked with the letter J, the locket that held the key to...well, everything.

Jasper stuffed it under his shirt. His fingers felt cold. "It's not for sale," he said.

"Do you have one?" said Danegeld, turning to Casper and poking the shillelagh at him.

"No," said Casper. "And it's not for sale either."

Danegeld planted his feet firmly in the dust and clasped his shillelagh. "No kids."

Casper rocked on his heels. Jasper jammed his hands in his pockets. His face brightened. He turned to his brother. "You know," he said, "gold's not the only thing."

"Yes it is," said Danegeld.

"Sometimes," said Jasper, "a really clever fellow recognizes the value of, well, other kinds of treasure."

Casper nodded sagely. "But only a truly clever one," he said. "You can't expect ordinary people to be that discerning."

"Naturally not," said Jasper. He dropped his voice. "An ordinary bouncer, now—not to name names or anything—"

"Don't tell me you're thinking about that pumpkin head at the Greasy Lapel," exclaimed Casper.

"What?" said Danegeld.

"Shhhhh," said Jasper. "Yes, I was thinking about him, in a general way."

"He is my cousin," said Danegeld.

"Oops," said Casper.

"He is dumber than a brick."

Jasper sighed and looked up at the troll. "Mr. Danegeld," he said reproachfully. "Were you eavesdropping on our conversation?"

"Certainly not," said Danegeld.

"It must be conceded," said Casper, "that our friend Guthrum—may I call you Guthrum? Thanks—raises an excellent point. His pumpkin-headed cousin is, in fact, dumber than a brick. Which explains everything, doesn't it?"

"I'm really not following this," called a warlock from the end of the line. "But if you boys could just—"

Jasper tossed off a light laugh. "Does it ever. Can you believe he turned down—well, never mind."

"Never mind what?" said Danegeld.

"I don't wish to insult your family," said Jasper.

Danegeld's piggy little eyes flashed. "He calls me Lumpy Lefty."

"Egad," said Casper.

"When really he is the lumpy one."

"As last week's porridge," agreed Jasper. "And his is precisely the attitude you could expect from someone who would refuse a bargain such as the one I offered him only yesterday."

"What bargain?" said Danegeld.

"I demand to see the manager," shouted the warlock.

"He refused—*this.*" Jasper withdrew the skein of yarn from his pocket.

Danegeld squinted. "What is it?"

"This," said Jasper solemnly, "is some of the most powerful magic you will ever see."

"It is yarn."

"Magic yarn," said Jasper. "Plant it in your back yard, and astonishing things will happen."

Several of the witches whipped off their hats and guffawed into them.

"Yarn is not like beans," said Danegeld. "It does not grow into anything."

Jasper stuffed the skein back into his pocket and looked helplessly at Casper. "That's exactly what old Pumpkin Head said too," he said.

Casper surveyed the troll in disappointment. "Guthrum, are you going to be the second person in your family to walk away from this opportunity?"

Guthrum shifted his feet and gripped his shillelagh first in one hand, then the other. The crowd murmured impatiently. Finally he said, "How much?"

"It's not for sale any more," said Jasper.

Danegeld's mouth dropped open. "But it is in your pocket. You can take it out and sell it to me."

"He's right, you know," said the warlock.

"No," said Jasper. "You hurt my feelings." He turned his back and crossed his arms.

"Well, now you've done it," said Casper.

"I did not mean to hurt his feelings," said Danegeld.

"But you did it anyway, didn't you?" said Casper. "And forget the magic yarn. That ship has sailed."

Guthrum Danegeld stomped his feet. "I want the yarn! I want the yarn!"

Jasper looked over his shoulder. "No deal."

The troll threw back his head and howled. It sounded like an ostrich trying to dislodge a tuba from its windpipe.

"Really, Mr. Danegeld," said Jasper. "A grown troll like you? Shameful."

Guthrum's eyes filled with tears, and his fingers trembled on his shillelagh. Casper laid a consoling hand on his brother's arm. "Jasper, I think we can work this out."

"How?" said the troll.

"I'm listening," said Jasper.

"You say it's not for sale," said Casper. "Well, what if our friend Guthrum traded us something for it instead?"

Jasper rubbed his chin. "Well...."

"Yes!" shouted Danegeld. "I will trade. Trade! Trade! Trade!"

"The thing is," said Jasper, "I'm not sure Mr. Danegeld has anything we want."

"Hmm," said Casper. He closed his eyes for a moment, then opened them with a delighted smile. "Jasper, I think I have it."

"About time," said the snake charmer.

"Have what?" said Danegeld.

"If our sinister friend here lets us into the tavern, can you give him the yarn?"

Jasper wrinkled his mouth. "I don't know."

"Yes!" shouted Danegeld again. He brought his left-handed shillelagh down into the dirt again with a loud *paff*. "Give me the yarn. Give it to me! And I will let you in."

Jasper's hand hovered over his pocket. "Well, it goes against my principles."

"Oh, come on," urged Casper. "It's just this once."

"If you really think it's okay," said Jasper.

"I do."

"I second that," called the warlock. The witches scowled and flexed their knobby fingers.

"My shift is over soon anyway," said Danegeld. "I will be at my other job and I will not care that I let you in."

Jasper sighed deeply. "In that case." He reached into his pocket and pulled out the soft bundle, placing it in Danegeld's eager, upturned hand.

Danegeld bowed and stepped to one side, gesturing the queue through the open door with his shillelagh. And Casper and Jasper stepped over the threshold into the light and music and ale-scented air of the Tone-Deaf Troubadour.

At first, Adele's leg was too badly burned to support her weight. The nurse, a gargoyle of a woman with a crisp apron and cardboard eyelashes, elevated the injured limb in a sling and iced it, giving Adele strict instructions to stay in bed. Adele spent those hours planning.

Later in the day, the nurse removed Adele's injured leg from the sling and laid it on pillows. "We can probably send you back to work tomorrow," she said.

"All right," said Adele, deliberately not looking at the window.

Adele's can-do attitude puzzled the nurse, for usually patients who were in the infirmary with a lucky break assured her that they were nowhere near cured, and needed weeks if not months to recover fully in order to serve His Beneficence, Count Wilhelm Scream, who was so very good to them. But all she said was, "You can try walking this afternoon."

"Yes, nurse," said Adele.

"Wear the orthopedic shoes," said the nurse, putting them at the foot of the bed.

"Yes, nurse."

"They keep your feet from swelling."

"Yes, nurse."

"Don't walk till I say you can."

"Yes, nurse."

As soon as the nurse had left, Adele sat up and gingerly put weight on her hurt leg.

The pain was intense. The burns seemed to glow with heat, and the skin on her leg felt as if it were vibrating. Putting on the orthopedic shoes, which were heavy and ugly, was almost too much to bear. But once she had tied the laces, Adele stood up and hurried to the window as fast as she could limp.

Her room was on the top floor of a squat, stone tower, so Adele had a good view of her surroundings. She could see Castle Mirkstone. She could see a road twisting through Gloamwoods. And she could see the Mining Camp of Count Wilhelm Scream.

Adele watched for hours. Carts rolled in and out of the clearing. The elevator doors opened and closed, taking workers up and down. She counted the minutes between each event— gate open, cart in, gate closed, elevator up, cart full, elevator down, cart out. Adele muttered the schedule to herself until she had memorized it.

A key rasped in the big bronze lock in the door. Adele limped back to bed, breathing hard, but she was too late. The gargoyle of a nurse came in with a tray of food. Seeing Adele, she slammed the tray onto the bedside table. "I said not to walk."

"I was just trying a few steps." Adele stood by the bed, wobbling. The nurse clamped Adele's elbow in her cold, hard fingers, and they crossed the room. At the window, Adele flinched. The nurse stopped.

"Problem?"

"The shoes—I think I tied them wrong. Can you help?"

The nurse grunted and knelt by Adele's shoes, untying and retying them with brisk jerks that sent waves of pain up Adele's injured leg. Adele stared out the window.

She saw Kale.

His face was so covered with grime and he was so bowed down by the weight of the ice he was carrying that at first she did not recognize him. But as soon as he dumped his load into a cart, he took off his helmet and straightened, running a hand through his bright red hair. The gestures were so entirely Kale's that even without being able to see his face clearly, Adele knew this was he. She gasped so hard her chest hurt.

"Too tight?" said the nurse.

Adele nodded, pressing her lips together. The nurse ducked her head and adjusted the knots.

Adele glanced quickly out the window. The men were gone. Dust blew in the clearing.

The nurse guided her back to bed and yanked the orthopedic shoes off Adele's feet, making her wince. "Stay there till I get back," she said, putting the shoes under the bed.

"Yes, nurse."

As soon as the key turned behind the nurse, Adele struggled back to the window. By evening she had learned much. The razor wire surrounding the clearing would be impenetrable, that much was certain. The entrance to the camp was locked. A guard stood at the gate. Others patrolled the camp.

Adele sighed. This was not going to be easy.

The crowd filled the tavern with blood, sweat, and jeers. Bunny sat in the shadows, nursing a drink of fermented carrot juice with hops. On the stage, Till Eullenspiegel and his Merry Pranksters (for so the band was named) twanged a joyous tune. Till played guitar and lead vocals, his hair flopping over his owlish glasses. The group had no drummer, theirs having disappeared during one of Count Wilhelm Scream's Purges for Artistic Purity; and rather than find a new one, they had resolved to remain flagrantly drummerless until the Count himself departed, to leave visible the wound he had inflicted on them.

Seeing the boys, Bunny leaped up, the tools in her vest jangling. But her table was in a corner, and as Casper approached her on one side and Jasper on the other, she slumped to her seat. "Go away."

"We need some information," said Casper. They pulled up chairs and scooted in, their knees bumping hers.

"No you don't." She took a draft of her carrot juice and set down the half-empty tankard. She seemed very different from the shy, quiet Bunny they knew from the shop.

"What we want to know," said Jasper, "is why you turned that delicate shade of green when our lockets popped open."

"Not that we didn't all feel a bit queasy," said Casper. "What a shock."

"We didn't even know the darned things opened," said Jasper.

"Never mind that there were pictures inside."

"Or messages."

"Of hope, apparently," said Casper.

"And love," said Jasper. The boys looked at each other and sighed deeply.

"If only there were someone who could tell us more," said Casper.

"And finish the—what's it called?—train something."

"Train of thought?"

"No, that's not it."

"Maybe train's not the right word, then."

"Perhaps you're right."

"Something that sounds like train?"

"Like what?"

"Grain, brain, insoluble stain?"

"Chain of transmission," said Jasper. "That's it."

"I see what you mean," said Casper. "Someone who can finish the message."

"And reunite this sundered family."

Bunny played with a drop of water snaking down her condensation-beaded glass.

"Of course," said Jasper, "such a person would have to have nerves of steel."

"Bravery is the first of the virtues," said Casper, "for without it no others can exist."

"Casper," said Jasper severely, "have you been paying attention in class?"

Casper ducked his head. "Sorry. Won't happen again."

Bunny lifted her drink to her lips. Her fist clutched the handle. "Bravery," she muttered, and took a swallow. "Hah!"

"What about it?" said Jasper.

Bunny whacked her glass down on the table. The liquid sloshed. Her eyes, usually pink, had gone red and angry. "This isn't brave. Just stupid."

The Merry Pranksters struck up a tune about being unlucky in love. Bunny leaned across the table. The boys could smell the carrot juice on her breath. "You can't get in there," she said. "And you can't win against him and—*her.*"

"Who and who?" said Casper politely.

"I think you mean whom and whom," said Jasper.

"Now who's been paying attention in class?"

"Guilty as charged."

"Any idea what you're up against?" Bunny ploughed on. "What these people are like?"

"No," said Casper.

"But we're eager to learn," said Jasper.

"That's right," said Casper. "Depthless ignorance and boundless curiosity are the twin engines of our success."

"So where is it we can't get in?" said Jasper. "And whom can't we win against?"

Bunny grunted at her drink. A bubble in the foam popped saucily at her. Casper pulled out his locket, flicking it open with his thumbnail. "Bunny, are these our parents?"

Bunny looked away. "I don't know."

"Have you ever seen them?" pressed Casper.

A pause. As if in defeat, Bunny nodded.

Jasper opened his locket and held it in his palm. "Do you know where they are?"

"No," said Bunny.

"Do you know where they *might* be?" said Casper.

In Bunny's silence, Till Eullenspiegel sang, "Nothing's so whole as a broken heart, so baby you made me whole. I see the truth in your lies and the hurt in your eyes, shattering part of my soul."

"Maybe," said Bunny.

"And?"

"But." She shrugged.

"But what?" said Jasper.

"But it doesn't matter," Bunny snapped. "The Ice Mines are a fortified camp. The castle has trolls. Big ones, everywhere. And a *dragon.* Ever seen one? Didn't think so. The Food Mills are a fortress—everything's locked down. And that's even never mind the swamp—the forest—know who lives there? Who *hunts* there? You can't do it. You can't. No one gets out, no one gets in. So I'm not going to let you come. I mean go." She tipped her nearly empty glass into her mouth.

Casper and Jasper stared at her appraisingly. "Bunny," said Casper, "are you going somewhere?"

"Nobody goes there if they can help it," said Bunny. "Except maybe stupid kids pretending to be heroes."

"Stupid?" said Jasper. "Us?"

"I should say not," said Casper.

"We're bright underachievers."

"It's not the same thing at all."

"You shouldn't even be in here," said Bunny. "No place for kids."

The band belted the final chorus of the song, and the audience joined in. Bunny joined them, cutting off Casper's retort. "Shattering part of my soul," she sang. Her face crumpled.

Jasper touched her on the arm. "You've been there. Haven't you?"

Bunny set her glass down with a scowl. Jasper went on. "Wherever this place is, something terrible happened there."

"Oh, shut up."

"Did you see our parents?"

Bunny stared into a memory. Her pale skin and hair glowed in the shadows. "Go home to your uncle and aunt."

"Why?" said Jasper.

"You're an idiot."

"Again, why?" said Jasper. "I mean specifically."

"They're good people."

"We never denied it."

"Who care about you."

"And we them."

"Really?" she said. "Do they know where you are?"

"Ah," said Casper. "You see, sometimes *caring* and *sharing* aren't—"

"Go home," Bunny almost shouted. "Look at the time. They're probably worried sick."

"Only if they know we're gone," said Jasper, who was feeling practical.

Bunny shook her head. "No idea, do you? No idea how lucky you are." She took a pull on her nearly empty tankard. "Someone to worry about you."

"What about you?" said Casper. "Do you have anyone?"

Bunny shook her head.

"What happened to your family?" said Jasper.

"Never had any." And she began to weep.

24

The bartender's name was Brewski, and he was a stout fellow. Strictly speaking, he should not have sold fermented carrot juice to Casper; but when the boy presented a handful of coins (three stags and an eagle) and explained that the order was for a friend and that he personally never touched the stuff, the gentleman passed him a frosty one. Such relaxed standards were the foundation of the Tone-Deaf Troubadour's popularity.

Casper sat down and handed the juice to Bunny. Three empty tankards stood on the table; the bus wench had removed two more. "You were telling us about your family."

By now the boys had learned a great deal about Bunny. For starters, she was an orphan; and like most of her local ilk, she had grown up in Kinderdump. Unfortunately, just before she was old enough to leave, authorities discovered that the manager, Shifty Kenspeckle, was manipulating the price of gruel to pad his pockets. Shifty was summarily arrested, the orphanage was shut down, and the children were sent to labor for Count Wilhelm Scream. They were useful for crawling into jammed machinery in the Food Mills, or clefts in the frosty rocks of the Ice Mines.

The younger ones were soon returned to Middlemost, for Princess Abattoir despised children, especially orphans. But

Bunny, being older and stronger, was deemed useful and kept captive. She spent her days loading Rainbow Ice and bulky bags of flour and grain into carts destined for the surrounding towns, to be sold at prices no one dared dispute.

"That's how I saw them," said Bunny. "Your mom and dad." She lifted her glass and took a sip. "At least, it was the two in your lockets."

"Where?" said Casper.

After the first few drinks she had become blurry and slurry, to the point where the boys had trouble making out her words. But now some kind of carrot-juice stamina seemed to have kicked in, and although her eyes were glazed and she seemed sometimes to forget the boys were there, her speech was perfectly clear. She set her glass down. It clinked against the others. "The lady, your mom I guess, at the Food Mills. She had to help me load flour. I remember her especially."

"Why?" said Jasper.

"Because by rights she should have been dead," said Bunny. The boys flinched. "People don't last long under Wilhelm Scream. But she—she looked like she had a secret no one could steal. She looked...well, I wouldn't say happy, exactly. But like she could keep going." She tilted her glass and watched the orange liquid slip around. "Plus, she gave me a cookie. In all the time I was there, that was the only time that happened. How did she have anything to give? I couldn't understand it." She set the glass back down on the table and stared at it.

"And our father?" said Casper.

Bunny took another swallow. "Him I saw more. At the mines. He was nice—warned me away from places with Black

Ice. Oh, and kind to animals. I saw him giving Rainbow Ice to a fidelius bird once. They like sparkly things, you know."

"Aren't they swampland birds?" said Casper.

"Never mind," said Jasper hastily. "So, these mines—"

But it was too late. "Nest on cliffs, hunt in swamps and forests." Bunny sighed. "They're the most beautiful...big and bright. Green and gold feathers. Shines in the sun...you never saw anything like it...and when they sing...."

"Must be amazing," said Casper, hoping Bunny was not about to go down one of the side roads of her reminiscences. He wanted to get home before Aunt Becky and Uncle Zach noticed he and Jasper were missing.

"The song," said Bunny, settling in her chair. "It's...you just...."

"Most impressive," said Jasper. "And the man in this picture was with it?"

"Saved my life."

"He did?" said Jasper excitedly.

"*It* did."

"What did?" said Casper.

"The bird?" said Jasper.

"The song."

"Fascinating," said Casper, resigned.

"Most people have never heard a fidelius bird's song," said Bunny. "I'm unusual that way."

Casper and Jasper felt that Bunny was unusual any number of ways, but they held their tongues. After another gulp of carrot juice, she continued.

"It was a female. With two fledglings. In a tree just outside the mining camp. The princess was there. She hated them. Hah! They didn't care. Flew in together, lit on the branch, little ones on either side of the mother. Then the mom spread her wings wide—" Bunny thrust her arms out. The hand holding the tankard hit the wall, and carrot juice slapped on the floor. Bunny stared at it. "Oh, dear."

"Go on," said Casper, who was growing interested in spite of himself.

Bunny thunked the tankard back on the table. "The little ones went under her wings and she covered them. Like this." She hunched her shoulders, elbows out, in rough imitation of the bird's embrace. "Then she started to sing. Quiet at first. It sounds sort of like a flute, but more, I don't know, personal. Like no one else can sing that song. It got louder and louder, all this sound, it just filled the air and you felt like you were drinking it. And she lifted her wings, and the little ones touched her with the tips of their beaks. And her breast was gleaming like, like liquid gold, and her wings were green, green, green, like leaves full of sunlight. And then the little ones flew off! And she sang this high, pure note and flew away herself. And I knew then—I knew—" She stopped, voice cracking, as though the memory would shatter if she looked at it again.

"Knew what?" said Jasper gently.

Bunny drew a deep, shuddering sigh. "They didn't need her any more."

"She was singing because she was alone?" said Casper.

"No, idiot," said Bunny, this new Bunny who would never have spoken that way in the shop. "The only time they sing is—

for pure joy." She tried to drink out of her tankard, but most of the carrot juice was on the floor. She shoved it aside. Jasper caught it as it sailed off the table, and set it back with the others. "They were grown. Strong. That was her triumph. And that song, it saved me. Go on, ask me why."

"Why?" said Jasper.

"Because it showed me the world wasn't just me and my misery. There was a me, and there was a not me. And the part that wasn't me had room for light and color and music."

"And?" said Casper.

"And that's why I didn't die that day," said Bunny, "or the day after that."

"Because of a song?" said Jasper.

"Because every day I'd get up and I'd think, 'This exists, so I'm not going to die today.'"

Bunny seemed to feel the conversation was at an end. Her pink eyes unfocused and she hummed along with the band. The boys liked the song too, but now, they felt, was no time for humming.

"So," said Jasper, "it sounds like you're saying our father's in the mines and our mother's in the Food Mills."

"Nah," said Bunny. "Probably dead."

Jasper rolled his eyes. Casper scowled. "Why aren't you?"

"Why aren't I what?" said Bunny.

"Dead."

"I am," said Bunny.

Jasper sighed. "Bunny, please. What are you talking about?"

"My hair was dark then."

Jasper almost screamed. "So what?"

Casper poured the dregs of three glasses into a fourth and pushed it toward her. It slipped on the tabletop, which was patterned over with damp rings. "Go on, Bunny. Your hair was dark then. Bet it was lovely."

"It was," said Bunny. "Everyone said so. Then *she* showed up."

"Did she?" said Casper.

Bunny nodded. "She came often."

She, of course, was Princess Abattoir; and as Bunny explained, she visited the mills and the mines with a gleam in her eye and a poisonous smile on her lips, making sure the prisoners were properly wretched. She checked their food to be sure it was tasteless and gluey, and given in sufficient quantities that no one starved but no one ever really had enough. She made sure bags were heavy enough that they could be lifted, but not easily. She ordered the windows closed in summer and open in winter. And so-forth. Other people's misery was her chief happiness.

"So she *haaaaated* fidelius birds," said Bunny.

"Because she couldn't make it unhappy?" said Casper.

"Because it made us happy," said Bunny. "You didn't see them too often. But any day you might. Or hear it. That was my favorite thing. But *her* favorite thing...favorite...." And she stopped again, closing her eyes.

Casper and Jasper looked at each other in near despair. Jasper jostled Bunny's foot under the table. Her eyes opened. "She thought I was dead."

"What was her favorite thing?" said Casper.

"Death!" Bunny almost shouted. In a less noisy atmosphere, people would have turned and stared. "She lived for it. Whenever there's an accident at the mines—or the mills—she's there. Smiling like a crocodile. And of course—lots of accidents. She makes sure of that. Then she takes the—bodies—and dumps them. In the ocean, along with slag from the mine." She shuddered.

"So there was an accident," said Jasper quietly.

"On purpose."

"What was?"

"The accident," said Bunny. "They outsmarted her. Paid for it, of course."

"Go on," said Casper, with more patience than he had ever thought he possessed.

"She brought two new prisoners to the mines and tells 'em to bring up Black Ice," said Bunny. "She gives them gloves, I saw that—I was loading a cart at the entrance. And we all knew—she, she liked to do that. She'd give the miners gloves with pinpricks in them. Pinpricks. You couldn't see. But only one pair. So you didn't know which gloves were safe, which ones—weren't. It was a game, for her to see who would touch the Black Ice first.

"Those men. Their faces—they just stared straight ahead as the elevator went down. I kept loading. I didn't want to be there when it happened. But I was. It was summer, all hot and bright, and under our feet those men were playing her little game with their lives. One of them would die, and the other would never forgive himself. I don't know who I felt sorrier for.

"It was so quiet. And she sat there on the seat of her carriage and smiled. But you know what's funny? Under that smile I always thought she was afraid."

"Of what?" said Jasper.

"No idea. What did she have to be afraid of? We were scared to death of her."

"Then what happened?" said Casper.

"I heard a yell, then someone started laughing—not her. A really hard laugh. Like rocks breaking. One of the miners. He goes, 'They outsmarted her. Took off their gloves and grabbed the ice together. They're both gone.' So they had given her the corpses she wanted, you see, but robbed her of the game."

Casper and Jasper stared at each other, horrified.

"She was angry," went on Bunny. "Oh, you don't know. We were all terrified. She made the miners bring the bodies. They were still holding the Black Ice. It was dark but gave off light. Never seen anything like it. Say, you know Scream's throne is made of that stuff? I mean, that's what everyone says."

"The bodies," said Casper.

"Right, yes. She made the other miners take away the ice—she loved death, but not enough to check it out personally.

Then she made me put the bodies in her carriage. I got the first one on, but his hand was hanging off the side. She screamed at me to fix it, so I—touched his hand."

Onstage, instruments wailed. Till Eullenspiegel sang, "Our fearful trip is done. Your love for me is cold as frost, and takes away the sun."

"And?" prompted Jasper.

"And then I died," said Bunny brightly.

"No, you didn't," said Casper. "Dead people don't drink this much carrot juice."

"*She* thought I did." Bunny took a sip. "So did I."

"Why?" said Jasper. "What happened?"

"When I died?" said Bunny. "It was just the way I always thought it would be. I touched his hand, and suddenly I was cold, just pure cold all the way through. I fell over and I couldn't move or see anything. Someone said, 'She's dead.' And I couldn't talk. And *she* laughed and said, 'Marvelous. Load her on.' I couldn't see her but I knew exactly how she looked. You could hear it in her voice. Happy. No, not exactly. Relieved, I think. Yeah. Relieved and happy. Anyway, someone loads me on, and then the carriage started...and we must have driven to the sluice that dumps slag into the sea, because next thing I know I'm banging down the chute to the water, and I'm thinking, 'If I'm not dead already, this should do the trick.'"

"Then what?" said Casper in a low voice.

"It was high tide, or I would have landed on the rocks." Bunny's voice shook. "I hit the water, I sank—but it was so much warmer than the cold inside me—suddenly I could move, and my arms and legs started swimming even before I told them to. And my head broke through the surface and I could breathe...and I swam to shore."

She busied herself with her drink as Casper and Jasper imagined Bunny, her pink skin bristling with splinters from the sluice, sobbing on the sand with wavelets shushing around her legs and waterweeds tangled in her hair.

"Bunny," said Jasper. "How did you—"

"I started walking," said Bunny. "Don't know how long. Finally, I found a road. There was a sign, said 'This Way Inglenook,' 'That Way Middlemost.' I wasn't going back to Middlemost, so I came here instead. That's when I saw my reflection in a shop window. I figured I must have died, because I didn't look anything like myself. White hair, pink eyes...I still look dead, if you ask me."

"Why did you stay here?" asked Casper.

Bunny chuckled darkly. "To be close to *her.*"

"The princess?" said Jasper.

Bunny mumbled something under her breath.

"We can help," said Jasper.

"No you can't."

"We can," insisted Casper. "Give us a chance."

Bunny looked at him, a snarl in her eyes. "Forget it. You don't *have* a chance."

The Merry Pranksters finished their song with a flourish. Till Eullenspiegel stepped forward, mopping his sparkling brow. He took off his owlish glasses and rubbed them against his shirt while gesturing at his band. "How about it, folks?" he said. "Are they the best band you've heard all night or what? And how about our bass player? Needs no introduction—"

Feet stomped the wooden floor, and tankards thumped tables. Till put his glasses back on and beamed. "We've got one more set to close out the night. But while the band takes a quick break, I'm sending Flora around with a hat."

Tankards thumped even more enthusiastically, and boots drummed on the floorboards.

"And just remember," shouted Till, "the more you give, the more we have."

"You gonna play 'Archetypes in Action'?" shouted a patron.

"No!" yelled another. "'Gift of the Goddess'!"

"'Road of Trials'!"

"That one's a downer, man," shouted someone else. "Do 'Ultimate Boon'!"

"'Ultimate Boon'! 'Ultimate Boon'!" chanted a few more voices.

Till laughed. The musicians headed for the bar. The bass player stepped into the crowd, hat upturned. Jasper gasped and grabbed Casper's arm. "It's Flora," he cried.

"That's what he said."

"No, I mean—it's *Flora.*"

Casper's eyes widened. It was indeed Flora, the musician from the poster in their bedroom, the rebel whose songs they sang with Bunny in the shop. Her golden hair cascaded over her shoulders, and her white teeth flashed as she smiled at each drunkard or rabble-rouser as though they had been apart too long. Her hat sagged with coins.

"Flora is my favorite," said a thick, oatmeal-y voice.

They looked up. Guthrum Danegeld, aka Guthrum the Sinister, stood by their table with his shillelagh hanging awkwardly in the right-handed holster on his belt. Bunny raised her tankard. "Mr. Danegeld."

"What a lot of cups you have," said the troll, looking down at the table.

"Hello, Guthrum," said Casper. "Joining us?"

Guthrum shook his head. "My shift is over and I am leaving. Besides, I have no money now."

"No?"

"I gave my salary to Flora," he said happily.

"But Guthrum," said Casper, "don't you think you might need it?"

"She *smiled* at me." The troll's grin split his lumpy face, and his eyes were little sparkles of joy.

"Lucky you," said Jasper dreamily, watching the back of Flora's head as she traversed the room.

"Besides," the troll went on, "I will not be needing my salary now that I have magic." He patted his belt, where he had shoved the skein of yarn.

Casper felt a pang of conscience. "Yes—of course. But in the short term—"

Guthrum patted Casper's head. It felt like being whacked with a bag of flour. "Do not worry, little fellow. I am a troll of means."

"How so?"

Guthrum hitched up the belt. "I am off to my other job which I cannot tell you about because it is a secret."

"I'm sure you shine in that capacity," said Casper politely.

"Unh?"

"You're good at your job," said Jasper.

"You bet," said Guthrum. "I am on a secret patrol tonight that I also cannot tell you about."

"Discretion is the better part of valor," said Jasper, craning his neck around the troll's considerable girth to keep Flora in sight.

"Hah?"

"He means," said Casper, "that keeping a secret is a big part of being brave. Which we know you to be."

Guthrum drew himself up straight. "Of course I am brave."

"Exactly."

"That is why I have a secret mission tonight."

"I'm sure it was tailor-made for you," said Jasper.

"That is right," said Guthrum. "Tonight I am helping hunt fidelius birds."

Bunny started. "You're what?"

"It is very tricky and has never been done before and that is partly why it is a secret," said Guthrum.

"Why?" Bunny half-stood. "Why would you do this?"

"Princess Abattoir said to trap as many as we can while they are asleep because it is too hard while they are awake and it is a secret. Good night." And with these words the troll stumped away from the table.

"I'm going to give my money to Flora," said Jasper.

"What money?" said Casper.

"We must have some left." Jasper yanked his school backpack onto his lap and unzipped it.

"Do you really think she needs half a candy bar and a copy of 'An Uplifting Anthem to Count Wilhelm Scream'?" said Casper, peering into the backpack.

"What's in yours?"

Bunny stood up. "While you boys are giving everything you own to a woman you've never met, I have some personal business to attend to."

"What?" said Casper.

"Bathroom, you dope." Bunny took one last gulp from the closest tankard and, weaving slightly, walked away.

"Fine, fine," said Jasper as she brushed past him. "Casper, you can't give a lady raisins in that condition."

"I think they were grapes last week," said Casper. "Hold on—maybe a sandwich?"

"Maybe not," said Jasper, looking at it with distaste.

"I spent all my money on drink," said Casper, glancing at the forest of glasses on the table. "What a stinging lesson."

"And we didn't even have any."

"Bunny has an amazing capacity."

"Drinks like a parched desert."

"No wonder she has to run a wee errand."

Jasper looked up. "Where's the bathroom?"

Casper pointed. "I saw the sign when we came in."

"But—she went the other way." Jasper grabbed his backpack and jumped up so fast he knocked over his chair.

"She's given us the slip." Casper, who had been reaching into his pocket for his remaining change, leaped to his feet as well.

"No, wait—there." Jasper pointed. A door behind the bar opened, outlining a figure with ghostly white hair as it slipped out.

The boys whipped around the table, only to find their way blocked by Flora and her dazzling smile. She jingled the hat at them. "Spare change, boys?"

"Sorry," said Casper, edging around her.

"Not today," said Jasper, edging the other way.

Flora did not so much move as expand. Her smile became more brilliant, her eyes sparkled like fireworks on a hot summer night, and she tilted the hat toward Jasper. "Every little bit helps, sweetheart."

Casper and Jasper felt oddly as though they had never seen anything female before. It was suddenly very important that Flora like them, and that she know how much they liked her, and how very special she was.

"Hagah," said Jasper. He swayed slightly.

Casper dug in his pockets. Three coins and a ball of lint met his fingers. He poured all four into the hat.

"You are just the sweetest boys," said Flora. "Stick around for the last song, okay? It's special." She wove through the crowd, hat in her hands, wearing her smile like a summer dress.

"Flora," whispered Jasper.

"Bunny," said Casper. Jasper shook his head as if he had just stepped out of a swimming pool, and they dashed toward the bar.

Flora took up her bass as Till Eullenspiegel leaped to the stage. "Are you ready to dance?" he shouted. "One. Two. One, two, three!" The musicians sprang into their final song of the night, their chart-topping hit, "Belly of the Beast." A delighted roar filled the air as tosspots and troublemakers surged to the small dance floor in front of the stage, pulling Casper and Jasper with them.

"Excuse me," gasped Casper, trying to extricate himself from a tide of knees and elbows.

"Pardon us," wheezed Jasper, squishing his way through tightly packed chests and hips.

"Come on darlin'," wheezed a comely wench, grabbing Casper by the wrist. "Dance with me."

"No, thank you," said Casper.

"Are you dancing with my girl?" bellowed a troublemaker. He took a swing at Casper, who ducked. The comely wench caught hold of the troublemaker's fist, stopping it in midair.

"Oh, Chuckles," she cried, "you do care after all." She flung her arms around his neck and they staggered to the music.

Casper and Jasper struggled free of the crowd's cloying embrace, and raced behind the bar.

Straight into the belly of Brewski the barkeep.

"Garf," said Brewski, doubling over.

"'Scuse me," said Casper and Jasper.

Brewski straightened up, rubbing his gut. "Where do you think you're going?"

"Till sent us," said Casper.

"He said Flora needs another mead," said Jasper.

"With extra froth," said Casper.

The barkeep gazed at the stage. "Flora," he sighed dreamily. He turned a spigot in a barrel, filling a tall glass with amber liquid. "No need to take this over, boys. I'll do it myself."

"Great," said Jasper. As soon as the barkeep's back was turned, they darted to the door and nipped through it.

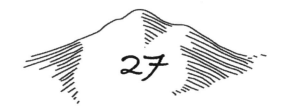

The boys tumbled down a flight of stairs and through a wooden door that stood ajar, as though the last person through had been in too much of a hurry to pull it shut. They found themselves in a storeroom. Music thumped through the low ceiling, shaking the lanterns that hung from it on chunky chains. Barrels stood along two walls. On the other two sides, huge sacks labeled FLOUR and PEANUTS and WALNUTS and LENTILS slumped next to bins of bread, barrels of apples, and crates of plates and tankards. Cured hams and whole turkeys hung from the ceiling. The floor was slick with flour, and gloom drenched the corners. In the center of the room a punching bag hung over a small pile of boxing gloves. Wooden swords and shields leaned against the wall behind it. In one corner stood a printing press next to a tidy stack of sheet music for Flora's more illegal songs. Casper recognized them from school.

"She's not here," said Jasper. He unhooked a ceiling lantern from its chain and gestured at the empty corners.

"Maybe she's in the bathroom," said Casper. He pointed to a door nestled between two stacks of barrels. It was labeled "Floozies or Cads."

"All that and she really did just skip to the loo," said Jasper in disappointment.

They knocked.

"Bunny," said Jasper. "Open up, please."

No answer.

"Not to be pushy or anything," said Casper.

"We value privacy as much as anyone," said Jasper.

"But we feel you were just getting to the good part," said Casper.

"For example," said Jasper, "where are these mines and mills exactly?"

"And what's the best way to get there?" said Casper.

Silence. Jasper shrugged and turned the knob.

The door swung open.

28

If the boys had been hoping for drama at this point, they were disappointed. The bathroom was cramped and entirely unexciting, with an ordinary toilet and an ordinary sink opposite an ordinary-looking cupboard. Fortunately perhaps for the more delicate sensibilities of the boys, Bunny was not perched on the toilet. Neither was she standing at the sink. Indeed, the defining feature of the room was, as far as the boys were concerned, its categorical absence of Bunny.

"She's not here," said Jasper, stating the obvious.

"Wait." Casper flung open the doors of the cupboard, which went from floor to ceiling. Its shelves held rolls of Count Wilhelm Scream's Excellent Toilet Paper (Medium Grain). The left corner of the cupboard was deeply scratched along its entire length. Tentatively, Casper reached out and pulled the shelf to the right.

It didn't move.

He pulled to the left.

It moved.

In fact, the entire back and left side of the cupboard shifted. Jasper put down his lantern and together the brothers dragged the shelves aside, revealing a dark tunnel plunging like a gullet to some unseen maw. They stared at each other, excitement leaping in their throats. Jasper picked up the lantern. The boys stepped inside and pulled the secret door behind them—leaving it ajar, for they knew how foolish it is to lock oneself into a tunnel.

Casper held up a silencing hand. They listened intently. An uneven tapping sound pattered into the distance. Within seconds it was gone, and all they could hear was their own breathing.

"She didn't get much of a head start," said Jasper quietly.

"Let's keep it that way," said Casper.

They set off. The tunnel went straight for some time, then dipped suddenly down so that the boys had not a moment to think about stopping before they found themselves running to keep from falling. Just as they were wondering how long this would go on, they collided with a wooden barrier.

Casper reached out to touch it. "Another door."

"Wooden and thick."

"With no visible lock or opening mechanism."

"We've missed our calling," said Jasper. "With our keen observation skills, we should have been detectives."

"In the meantime," said Casper, "how about getting this thing open?"

Jasper set the lamp down and ran his hands over the edges of the door. It sat snugly into the opening, with no crack at the earthen floor or the wooden walls or ceiling. Along with no lock and no knob, it was replete with no hinges. "How did she get out?"

"Dunno," said Casper. "I'd say she had a key, but there's no keyhole."

"It must open from the outside," said Jasper.

Casper surveyed the door. "Shall we knock?"

"It's that or go back."

Casper raised his fist to the door and knocked.

"Ow," said a splintery voice.

Casper jumped. Jasper froze. Their breath rasped in the cool, damp air of the tunnel.

"Did you say 'ow'?" breathed Casper.

Jasper shook his head. "Did you?"

"No."

"So who did?"

Jasper lifted the lantern. It made a yellow circle full of sliding shadows. No one appeared. "Knock again."

"Why?"

"Because *someone* said that and because what else are we going to do?"

Casper lifted his hand.

"Oh, no you don't," said the voice.

The boys looked around. "Who are you?" said Jasper.

"*Where* are you?" said Casper.

"In my day," said the voice, "people introduced themselves before asking personal questions."

Casper looked at Jasper. Jasper looked at Casper. They shrugged. "I'm Jasper and this is my brother Casper," said Jasper. "And whom do we have the pleasure of addressing on this lovely evening?"

"Dora."

The boys looked around again. They were still alone. Casper's eyebrows lifted. "You're—the door?"

"I am, young man, the portal, the gateway, the beginning of life's grand adventure. And I do *not* appreciate being treated as a mere obstacle."

"Of course not," said Casper.

"Our mistake," said Jasper.

"Nor do I enjoy being beaten like a tom-tom."

"I apologize," said Casper humbly.

"As well you might," said Dora. "I have feelings too, you know. If you prick me, do I not bleed? If you tickle me, do I not laugh?"

"I don't know," said Jasper. "Do you?"

"Indeed not. I have my dignity, young man."

"But you said—"

"No one has time for civility any more," Dora ploughed on. "The last person who came through barely said please or thank you. No, manners, no respect, no sense of—"

"Was it a woman?" said Casper.

Dora gave a sniff. "She was certainly no lady."

"Did she have white hair and pink eyes?"

"And a very poor attitude. When I was young, people paused for the niceties. How do you do, is your cousin still unhinged, aren't you looking well?"

"A more gracious time," said Jasper.

"Not like these days," said Casper.

"I blame a breakdown of traditional values," said Jasper.

"One knew one was appreciated," said Dora. "Things were pretty lively here in the old days, let me tell you, but people had manners. Common courtesy was still common. Not today!"

"It's a shame things have come to such a pass," said Casper.

Dora seemed lost in her reminiscences. "I met them all. Big bad wolves and merry men and jolly friars—I hear the friar is still at large, though of course no one's very jolly these days. Thank *you,* Count Wilhelm Scream! 'Adventure is the enemy of obedience,' he says. Pshaw! What's life without a little adventure?"

"Merest dross," agreed Jasper.

"We thrived on it back in the day. Everyone who came through here had *loads* of the stuff! Dreamers and schemers and unconquered heroes, all escaping from something or to something. Thieves and rogues and lovers meeting for trysts. A pretty steady stream of princesses dodging stepmothers—some of *them* had issues, let me assure you! But they all had time to ask politely for what they wanted. And—"

"And you let them all through," said Casper.

"That's my job, young man."

Jasper shifted his weight. "Um...why?"

"Why what?"

"Why did you let them through if you won't let us through?"

"Because, my lad, they used the magic word."

"So," said Casper, "if we use this magic word, you'll let us through?"

"Obviously," said Dora in a voice that meant "Duh."

"Hocus pocus," said Jasper. "Abracadabra. Open sesame."

Dora remained shut. If anything, she seemed to glower.

"Can you give us a hint?" said Casper.

Dora snorted. The boys had not known doors could snort. "If I did that, there wouldn't be much magic involved, now would there?"

Casper almost jumped up and down. "Dora, I don't wish to be rude, honestly I don't—"

"—and it's clear our generation lacks respect, breeding, and possibly hygiene—" said Jasper.

"—but our friend has given us the slip, and, well, we need to find her as soon as possible."

"If she's your friend, why did she give you the slip?" said Dora.

"Careless oversight, I'm sure," said Jasper.

"And she didn't tell you the magic word before hopping away like that?"

"Well, no," said Jasper.

"She doesn't sound like much of a friend," said Dora. "And it's hard to believe she wants to be found."

"Perhaps not," said Casper. "But either way, we have to find her."

"Goodness," said Dora in satisfaction. "This is so much more than the usual Thursday night doldrums."

"Alakazam," said Jasper. "Presto change-o. Klaatu barada nikto."

"What lovely elocution you have," said Dora.

"Dora, are you going to let us through?" cried Jasper.

"Not with that attitude."

Casper thought of Bunny leaping away from them. How far had she run already? How could they ever catch up with her? He wanted to jump up and down. "Dora," he cried, "open the door, for us, *please.*"

The door swung open.

Jasper goggled. "That was it?"

"All you had to do was ask nicely," said Dora as they walked through. "Just remember, always use the magic word."

Outside, Jasper hoisted the lantern. They were in a small clearing in a forest. To one side was a woodland pool, its surface gleaming darkly. Overhead, the fingers of a thousand dead trees scrabbled at the sky. The air was cold and smelled of something dank and rotten.

"Forward ho," said Jasper, hoping he sounded brave.

"Right," said Casper, hoping the same thing.

"Wrong!" shouted a voice. "Stop right there."

With a rustling sound, a dozen dark figures stepped from behind the trunks of the leafless trees. Every figure held a spear. And every spear was aimed at the boys.

That evening when the gargoyle of a nurse brought dinner, Adele's leg was so swollen it pressed against the gauze bandages. The burn marks were an angry red. The nurse set her tray down so hard that the bedside table gave a splintering noise. "How much did you walk?" she demanded.

Adele blushed. "Just a little."

"I told you to stay in bed."

"I'm sorry. I was just so eager to be on the mend and get back to my highly rewarding work for Count Wilhelm Scream, whom it is an honor to serve."

"Look at that leg. You'll be here at least an extra day."

"Oh." Adele groped for something to say. Her head was crowded with thoughts of Kale, of being able to hold him in her arms and look into his eyes. "Ah—gosh dang it."

The nurse narrowed her eyes and peered at Adele through her cardboard lashes. She was used to prisoners doing anything they could to stay in the infirmary. Some hit their heads on the walls, or tried to make themselves sick by eating the large and indigestible spiders that webbed the corners of the room. With quick motions that made Adele bite her lip, the nurse whipped off the bandages and rubbed fresh ointment onto the burns. She re-wrapped the leg and dropped it back into the sling, which hung over the bed from a metal pole. "Keep it in this way for the night."

"Yes, nurse."

"One other thing." The nurse leaned close to Adele. Her eyes were flinty, and her false eyelashes batted alarmingly. "If I find out that you are re-injuring yourself in order to stay here, I will report you to Princess Abattoir."

"Yes, nurse," said Adele, shrinking into her pillow.

"The princess is not as forgiving as I am."

"No, nurse."

The nurse straightened up and went to the doorway. She paused, her hand on the light switch. "You're smart enough to know that walking on that leg will make it swell up so you can't work. But I'm smart too. And if I catch you walking before I say you can, I will let the troll guards work you over before I even alert the princess to your insubordination."

"Yes. Yes, nurse."

"Do you understand?"

"Yes, nurse. Thank you, nurse."

The nurse flicked off the light and left the room.

In the silence, Adele reflected that the one thing she and Nurse Gargoyle agreed on was that no one was going to catch her walking. She breathed deeply and did her best to relax into the lumpy mattress.

Hours passed. Adele dozed, woke herself up with a start, and dozed again. Finally, when the infirmary was so quiet she could hear a troll sneeze three flights below, she got out of bed.

The floors were stone, which was cold but did not creak. Adele knew she could probably tap dance to the window and no one would hear. As quickly as she could, she put on the orthopedic shoes. She yanked the sheets from the bed and knotted them to the pillowcase, the mattress pad, and the sling. She tied one end to the middle of the sling's metal pole, and staggered over to the window with it.

The window did not, technically, open; but it was made of panes that stretched from waist height almost to the ceiling. Between the panes were metal bars, lest the prisoners should forget they were in prison. (To give the count credit, no one ever did.) Adele took a deep breath and, using the metal pole as a battering ram, shattered one of the panes.

In the silent room it sounded like an explosion. Adele waited, heart pounding. Distantly, she heard the trolls in the stairwell beyond her locked door.

"What was that?" said one.

"Nothing," replied the other. "Just outgassing."

"Ha ha. You said outgassing."

"That's not what it means, you oxymoron."

"Who you calling oxymoron?"

This exchange was followed by sounds of blows and troll curses. Adele breathed a sigh of relief. Wrapping her hand in the pillowcase section of her rope, she knocked out a few stray fangs of glass and set the pole across the window, bracing it against the iron bars. Gripping the makeshift rope tightly with both hands, she backed out of the newly smashed opening and walked down the side of the tower, gripping its stones with her orthopedic shoes. Every time she put pressure on her injured leg it blazed with pain. She clenched her teeth and concentrated on her steps. Her homemade rope reached almost to the ground; she barely had to drop. Thankful for the dark embrace of the night, she stumbled into the woods.

Jasper dropped the lantern. It went out. He looked to the right. Casper looked to the left. Dark figures closed in on them. They whirled toward the doorway.

"Don't even think of trying for that stupid tunnel," said the voice.

"Well, really," said Dora. "I don't need to keep myself open to insult." And with a soft *paf,* the door shut into the hillside.

"Hands up," said the voice. "On your knees."

"Well, which one is it?" said Jasper.

"Both," said the voice. *"Now."* The figures with the spears stepped closer.

It is not easy to get on your knees with your hands in the air when you are standing on uneven ground in the dark, but Casper and Jasper managed it. Two of the figures stepped forward. They ripped Casper and Jasper's backpacks off their shoulders. They yanked the boys' hands behind their backs. Tight, cold bands pinched their wrists. The boys heard the *klik* of handcuffs locking. The figures heaved the boys to their feet and gripped them firmly enough that Casper and Jasper knew they need waste no time on thoughts of escape.

"Spears up," said the voice. "Lights."

A dozen matches skritched. Lanterns flickered to life. And for the first time, Casper and Jasper were afraid.

A tall man stood before them, triumph glittering in his eyes. He wore thick-soled boots and a multicolored camouflage uniform. His chest twinkled with medals, and his armband bore the legend, *"CWS: Semper Tyrannis Ha Ha Ha"* above a picture of a muscular-looking crocodile. Although he did not recognize the boys and they certainly did not recognize him, it was none other than Wayne Dwop, now Captain of the Count's Special Police. Next to him, two patrolmen held a sagging figure between them. It was this that had given Casper and Jasper their jolt of fear.

Bunny's nose was bleeding, and her lower lip was swollen. Her vest was askew, and she curled over her stomach as if it hurt to stand up straight. She lifted her head to look at the boys. Her pink eyes said, *I told you so.*

Captain Dwop pointed at Casper and Jasper. "Who are these two?" he demanded, looking at Bunny.

Bunny rolled her head at him. "Never seen them in my life," she said, her words slurred by the bruises on her lips.

"Then why did they come out of the tunnel after you?"

"Maybe they're stupid," said Bunny.

Captain Dwop slapped her hard across the face. She gave a stifled cry and dropped her head. Her shoulders quaked. The captain turned to the boys, this time gesturing at Bunny. "Who are you?" he demanded. "Who is she, and how do you know her?"

Jasper cleared his throat. "Sorry."

"Can't help you there." Casper's hands felt cold, and they shook behind his back. "We've never seen her before."

"That is not true," said a familiar voice. The patrolmen parted as a bulky form with a bulging stomach stepped forward, his long hair swinging in the lamplight. His left hand held a wire cage containing what looked like a pile of damp feathers, and his bicep sported an armband like the captain's. "I watched them in the tavern tonight," went on Guthrum Danegeld. "They all sat together."

For this was the troll's second job: he was a proud member of the Special Police of Count Wilhelm Scream. His troop was often stationed in the forest of Gloamwoods, near Inglenook. The official reason for this was that Count Scream wished to protect his subjects from the dangers of the outside world. The unofficial reason was that the citizens of Inglenook did not seem nearly as fond of Count Scream as he was of them, and they had a habit of making a break for it on moonless nights.

"So," said Captain Dwop, breathing heavily, "these three do know each other."

"No," said Bunny.

"Certainly not," said Casper.

"Not us," said Jasper.

"Yes," said Danegeld.

"Aha!" said Captain Dwop. "They are spies, or criminals."

"Or both," said Danegeld.

"Either way," said Captain Dwop, "the count has ways of making such people talk." He lifted Bunny's chin with one hand. "Have you ever met Princess Abattoir?" he said softly. "I expect she'd be delighted to make your acquaintance."

Bunny's knees trembled, and one gave way. Captain Dwop laughed and dropped her head. "Start for the castle."

A patrolman stepped forward. "Sir, may I suggest we pitch camp instead?"

"Is the forest too frightening for you?" thundered Dwop. "Afraid of a few marshmallows and a pack of werewolves who haven't even unionized?"

"No, sir. But we haven't reached our hunting quota. The princess said—"

"Pitch camp immediately," the Captain bellowed. He gestured at Casper, Jasper, and Bunny. "Tie them to a tree. Set a guard. We march at dawn."

The patrol set their lanterns down or hung them from branches. They forced the prisoners to sit with their backs against a knurled tree trunk. As loops of rope went around their chests and pulled tight, Casper and Jasper looked at each other in consternation. But they were careful not to look at Bunny, and she did not look at them. They all understood the importance of pretending not to know each other, and no one wanted a telltale gleam of recognition to give them away.

Captain Dwop tested the knots, which were on the far side of the tree where none of the three could reach them, especially with their hands chained behind their backs. He made a goon place a ring of lanterns around the prisoners so they were bathed in light. "Make sure they don't talk to each other," he said as he stalked away.

The prisoners did not talk while the Special Police cleared brush and leaves from the ground. They remained silent as the patrol set up the captain's tent, a small shelter from the chill that suffused the night and crept up the prisoners' legs and backs. Their fingers, which rasped against the bark of the tree, were cold. The metal bands around their wrists were cold, too, and their feet were getting numb. And though they said nothing as the Special Police built a cooking fire, they did hope someone would feed them or at least offer them something to drink.

A kindly-looking goon glanced at the captives and stood up with a cup in his hand.

"No food or drink for the prisoners," barked Captain Dwop. The goon sat down again, looking away.

The Special Police cooked their dinner, and although it looked like cardboard and probably tasted a good deal like it, it was food. The boys' mouths watered. The Special Police drank their drinks and sang rude songs after dinner. The boys' throats felt parched, especially when smoke blew their way. And they could have suggested any number of additional lyrics for the songs, but no one asked them. They maintained their hush. So did Bunny.

After dinner Captain Dwop stood. He was not the sort of leader who would let pass an opportunity to bloviate, which means, "to speak pompously and get everyone really annoyed with you."

"Men," he began.

"And trolls," said Guthrum, who liked to help.

Captain Dwop scowled. "'Men' here refers to members of this patrol."

"So does 'trolls,'" said Guthrum.

"You're the only troll on patrol," snapped Dwop.

"Ha ha," said Guthrum. "You made a rhyme."

"Men," began Captain Dwop again.

"You are a poet and you do not even know—"

"Shut *up,*" said Captain Dwop.

"That is right," said Guthrum severely to the other Special Police. "You heard the captain." He put his shillelagh on his knee and looked at them reprovingly. The Special Police obligingly shushed. "You may continue, Captain."

"Very well. Now—"

"No one will dare interrupt you."

Captain Dwop gritted his teeth. "Now that I—have—your—attention," he said slowly and carefully, "let us examine our glorious missions. We have the prisoners—"

"Hooray," sang out Guthrum.

"Quiet, you moron," roared Captain Dwop.

Guthrum scowled. "That is hurtful."

The captain mopped his brow with the ribbon of one of his medals. "So. We have the prisoners, these wretches of scum and villainy. Next, we shall forge Princess Abattoir's triumph over the avian pestilence."

"I thought we were thumping birds," said Guthrum.

"'Avian pestilence' means 'birds.'"

"Then why not just say 'birds'?"

Dwop took a deep breath. "Our task is now doubly dangerous—"

"Goody!"

"Somebody shut up that troll," screamed Captain Dwop.

There was a silence.

"How?" said a bruiser.

Captain Dwop moaned silently and thought of his bed. He was not fond of nighttime patrols, but he had no wish to shorten his life expectancy by disappointing Princess Abattoir.

"Officer Danegeld," he said.

"Sir, yes sir!"

"I have a task for you."

"Sir, yes sir!"

"Guard these wicked prisoners while the rest of the patrol vanquishes the avian terrorists."

Guthrum frowned. "But I like thumping birds."

"Which is exactly why you aren't doing it any more," said Captain Dwop. "You know the princess wants them unharmed."

"It is not my fault," said Guthrum. "The right-handed shillelagh holster has a very quick release for a left-handed shillelagh. If I had a left-handed holster, it would not be a problem and the bird would still be alive." He looked apologetically at the cage full of damp feathers.

"But you don't and it is and it's not," said Captain Dwop, not entirely clearly. "Plus," and here he put his hand on the troll's hairy shoulder, "you have an advantage over the rest of us."

"Sir?"

"You, Danegeld, don't have to sleep. It makes you the perfect guard."

Guthrum scowled. "Is this because I am a troll?"

"It's because you don't have to sleep."

"Which is because I am a troll."

"Officer Danegeld—"

"I am the only troll on this patrol," sighed Guthrum. "It gets lonely." He brightened. "I made a rhyme."

"Yes—yes," said Captain Dwop. "Well done. Guard these scoundrels till dawn, and we'll discuss it then."

So as the rest of the patrol marched into the woods and Captain Dwop retired to his tent for what he felt was some well-earned rest, Guthrum Danegeld settled down on a massive rock next to the boys' backpacks. He put his shillelagh across his knees, thunking it into his cupped hand with a soft, pillowy sound, and glared at the three figures tied to the tree.

31

Captain Dwop's tent went dark. A few minutes later, the *hornk-hornk* of his snores filled the glade. Between each one the captain drew a whistling breath that sounded like someone ripping nails from old planks. The interval between snores varied widely. Sometimes Captain Dwop's tent said *hornk-hornk fneeee hornk-hornk fneeee* as if babbling frantically; other times the gaps were so long that the boys wondered if he had forgotten to breathe. But gradually the cavalcade of snores increased in duration and volume, interspersed with occasional hiccups and the sound of lip-smacking. When the din attained an exuberance that shook the canvas, Casper cleared his throat. "Hullo, Guthrum."

"So good to see you again," said Jasper.

"Be quiet," said Guthrum Danegeld.

"Why?"

"The captain said to make sure you did not talk to each other."

"We aren't," said Casper. "We're talking to you."

Guthrum thought about this. It was clearly a torturous undertaking, and he wrinkled his brow so hard his eyes disappeared in the folds. Casper and Jasper risked a look at each other. They nodded, and by the time Guthrum's small, glittering eyes reemerged, the boys were gazing at him with expressions of friendly concern.

"Guthrum, we are concerned," said Casper.

"In a friendly way," said Jasper.

"We think you're being taken advantage of," said Casper.

"How?" said the troll.

"This business of staying up all night," said Jasper.

"That is to guard you."

"Yes, of course," said Jasper. "But is it really healthy for a growing troll?"

"Sleep deprivation has felled many a warrior," said Casper.

"Hunh?"

"An army marches on its stomach," said Jasper. "But also on its mattress."

Guthrum frowned again. "Why would an army march on its stomach?" he said. "They would not make more than a mile or two a day."

"I think what my brother means," began Casper.

"Especially over rough terrain."

"It's more a figure of—"

"Rough terrain is difficult even when you are marching on your feet."

"Yes, of course. So—"

"On your stomach it would be very slow and painful." His eyes widened. "What if gravel got in your belly button?"

"Spoken like a true soldier," said Jasper.

"And why would they march on their mattresses? That would get them dirty."

"—is that nutrition and good sleep are essential—"

"Of course, I do not have a mattress anyway. Trolls do not need such things."

"Of course not," said Jasper. "But to be a good soldier, sleep—"

"I am a good soldier."

"We all know *that,*" said Casper. "Follow the captain's orders to a T, don't you?"

"By minding your Ps and Qs," said Jasper.

"It's clear why he selected you for this assignment," said Casper.

"Because I am a troll and I do not need to sleep," said Guthrum.

"Because you are stout of heart and swift of cudgel," said Casper. "Why, look in that cage."

"Why?"

"It's a fidelius bird, isn't it? I hear they're devilishly hard to catch."

"It is an ex-bird." Guthrum picked up the cage and poked a calloused finger through the bars. It was hard to tell in the flickering lamplight, but the boys thought the limp body shifted at his touch.

Bunny stiffened. The boys felt it because the ropes shuddered. They had supposed her to be asleep, as she had been silent and they could still smell carrot juice on her breath; but they did not greet her, for now was not the time to inquire how she was enjoying the evening.

"You say 'bird,' I say 'enemy of the state,'" said Casper.

"I bet you dispatched the miscreant with one blow," said Jasper.

Guthrum's lower lip quivered. "Now you are just making fun of me. You heard the captain say I thump too hard." His piggy eyes filled with tears, and he turned away with a sniff that sounded like a bed sheet being torn in half.

"But Guthrum, old man," said Jasper, "it's not your fault."

"It's the equipment," said Casper, trying to keep his voice low enough not to wake the captain.

Guthrum looked back over his shoulder, his eyes flaring with righteous indignation above his tearstained beard. "That is true."

"Of course," said Jasper. "Would Guthrum Danegeld, a troll who famously retrofitted his own truncheon, lack the skill to use it properly?"

"What nonsense," said Casper.

"The fault is not yours, sir," said Jasper.

"Now, assuming the bird is dead," began Casper.

"The bird is dead," said Guthrum.

"Then it, and you, Mr. Danegeld, are victims of what we call a Bastinado Blunder."

The troll blinked. "We are?"

Jasper wished he could lean forward for emphasis, but the rope across his chest prevented him. "Did you or did you not tell your captain that the right-handed shillelagh holster you are forced to use has a quick release for a left-handed shillelagh? That if you had a left-handed holster, the bird would still be alive?"

"Yes!" shouted Guthrum. The hornking in the captain's tent stopped. Casper and Jasper and Guthrum held their breaths. With a mutter that sounded like "Hezekiah's hairy fish nuts,"

Captain Dwop rustled as if rolling over, and the snoring began again.

"Guthrum," said Casper, "we are here to help you."

"No, you are not," said the troll. "You are here because you got caught."

"Details," said Jasper lightly. "The point is, we *can* help you."

"And you can help us," said Casper.

Guthrum frowned again. "How can you help me when you are tied to a tree?"

"By pointing out that you already have everything you need to secure that left-handed shillelagh holster," said Jasper.

"Where?" Guthrum glanced around.

"In—your—belt," said Casper with great emphasis.

Guthrum looked down at his belt. A craggy smile split his face as he pulled out the skein of yarn Jasper had given him at the Tone-Deaf Troubadour. He held it in his cement-rough palm.

"Remember what we told you?" said Jasper.

Guthrum nodded.

"We're now in a position to tell you more," said Casper.

"What?" said Guthrum.

"If we tell you—and mind, I'm not saying we will," said Jasper, "but *if* we do, do you promise to set us free?"

"Certainly," said Guthrum the Sinister. "I have already established that I can be bribed."

"Stout fellow," said Casper.

Jasper jerked his head to indicate that the troll should draw close. Guthrum squatted before them. His breath was hot and smelled like dead rabbits. "The magic in the yarn," Jasper whispered, "is most powerful if you plant the entire skein by starlight."

"No!" gasped Danegeld.

"And," said Casper, "you have to plant it fairly deep or the magic won't work."

"No skimping there," said Jasper.

"Rookie mistake," said Casper.

Guthrum Danegeld stood and shouldered his massive cosh. "Thank you," he said, and stumped away.

Casper and Jasper looked at each other, aghast. "Guthrum," hissed Casper, "aren't you forgetting something?"

Guthrum rubbed his chin. The animal skulls in his beard tinkled. "No."

"But you said you'd let us go!"

"I will," said Guthrum. "As soon as I make sure the magic is for real. Good night." He turned and disappeared into the woods.

"Guthrum!" cried Casper and Jasper as loudly as they dared.

Toads belched in the trees. Mist crept along the ground. Captain Dwop snored vigorously in his tent. But Guthrum did not return, and for once Casper and Jasper had nothing to say.

"Good job," said Bunny. "Are you boys OK?"

32

"Been better," said Casper. "How are you?"

"Busy," said Bunny, in a muffled voice. "Hang on."

The rope around the boys' chests moved. Presently it gave a twitch and fell to their laps. Bunny stood up, and in the light from the lanterns the boys could see something shiny hanging from her mouth.

"What's that?" said Jasper, keeping his voice low.

"Mini-saw," mumbled Bunny. Turning her head, she dropped it into one of the many pockets of her vest.

The boys lurched to their feet. "Does it work on handcuffs?" said Casper.

"No. But a lockpick does." She turned sideways. "It's in my right front pocket. I can't quite—ah, that's it. Thanks." Pulling her hands to one side of her body, she took the slim, curved blade awkwardly in her cold fingers. "Watch what I'm doing so you can do it," she told Jasper, and inserted the blade into Casper's handcuffs. She twisted the lockpick this way and that, then gave it a twitch. Casper's handcuffs fell to the forest floor. Bunny handed the instrument to him and turned her back. "Show him how to do it," she said to Jasper.

Of course, it is one thing to jimmy handcuffs if you have done it before. It is quite another if you have seen it only once, by flickering lamplight, when you are acutely aware of the fact that at any moment you may be set upon by Special Police who do not list your health and well-being among their chief concerns. But after several false starts and encouraging words such as, "A bit to the right, I think," and "I said right, you idiot," Bunny's handcuffs gave a satisfying click and released. From there it was the work of a moment to free Jasper.

All three huddled together, rubbing their pinched wrists and trying to get some warmth back into their stiff, dirty fingers.

"You have hidden depths," said Jasper in a low voice.

"And you're dumber than I thought," snapped Bunny. "Why did you follow me?"

"Why did you run away?" countered Casper.

Bunny rolled her eyes. "The troll said he was after fidelius birds. I know where they roost. Tried to cut him off, but he got there first. When I saw he was about to club one of them I gave a yell—OK, so I'm the blockhead here. He still killed it, and the patrol was on me like white on ice." She glared, not looking at the cage full of feathers that sat just inside the circle of lanterns. "What's your excuse? And don't give me that song and dance about wanting to rescue your parents."

"Can't oblige," said Jasper.

"It's all we have," said Casper.

"Plus, you did the same thing to save a bird," said Jasper.

"And almost got us all delivered to Princess Abattoir in a tidy package," said Bunny in disgust. "Get back in that tunnel and go home if you know what's good for you."

"'Good for us,'" mused Casper, turning the strange phrase over on his tongue.

"Not ringing a bell," agreed Jasper. "Is it your tunnel?"

"What do you mean, is it my tunnel?"

"Did you dig it?"

Bunny snorted. "Of course not. Innkeepers made them so farmers could deliver goods. After Scream took over, people started using them for escaping. So he filled them in—afraid of rebels—but if you bribe the right people they'll let you keep it open."

"Look," said Jasper in what he hoped was a reasonable voice, "why don't we do this together, Bunny? You know the forest, and we bring, ah—"

"Youthful energy and charisma," supplied Casper. "We can help each other. You save the birds, we find our parents."

Bunny put one hand on the back of each boy's neck and yanked them close. Her voice was low and fierce. "Now you listen to me. It's my fault that bird's dead, but there's others still out there. And maybe I'll get a crack at the princess later, or maybe I won't. But I'm leaving now, so don't even dream of following me again." She jerked her head at the door set in the hillside. "Go *home*."

With that, she bounded off into the woods.

"Have you noticed that she's a good deal tougher than we thought?" said Casper.

"Informative, too," said Jasper.

"What do you mean?"

"We now know there is a system of tunnels in and out of Inglenook."

"Good point," said Casper. "And did you notice that our good friend the Captain apprised us of a nearby swamp?"

"Where we doubtless need to watch our step."

"Let's follow Bunny."

"Good idea."

Tiptoeing, they retrieved their packs from the ground where Guthrum had been sitting, then headed into the woods. Just past the first tree, Casper touched Jasper's arm. "Stop. This thing's heavy."

The birdcage hung from his hand. Fidelius birds are large, which meant that although Guthrum found the cage a convenient size to carry, the same could not be said for a twelve-year-old boy.

Jasper frowned. "This is an inopportune time for larceny, Casper."

"I think I saw it move." Casper set the cage down and unlatched the door. He stroked the lump of feathers.

With an explosion of wings and a cry that sounded like a chain saw gunning, the bird shot past Casper's outstretched hands and into the tangled branches, knocking loose a shower of twigs and dead leaves. It flailed back into the clearing, upsetting two lanterns before gaining altitude, its frantic wing beats setting the canvas of the tent luffing as it plunged past.

"Hornk-whaa?" bawled Captain Dwop. The flap of his tent whipped up. His startled eyes took in the scene: the tree trunk, so lately replete with prisoners, now empty and surrounded by lanterns; loops of rope on the ground; three sets of handcuffs sparkling on the ground; and two pale, horrified faces peering at him from the undergrowth.

"Prisoner escape!" He grabbed a whistle and blew. Its shrieking blast tore the night.

At night, harsh lights illuminated the Ice Mines. This was to discourage escapes, but it also made the camp visible from far away. Adele limped toward it.

Now, if an able-bodied person thinks at all about walking, he or she probably thinks something like, "Step, step, step." Adele, however, had to think step-*OUCH*-step-*OUCH*-step-*oohCAREFULTHERE,* for every other footfall sent a hot jet of pain up her blistered leg. It slowed her walking. It made her fearful of capture. But she pushed on, for each torturous footfall brought her closer to Kale.

She hoped.

Before Count Scream's reign, Adele had often taken students to the edges of the woodlands to study plants and animals. She had always enjoyed these excursions. The depths of the forest, however, were a different story, full of ogres, manticores, talking plants, werewolves, and other creatures best confined to nightmares one can actually awaken from. But to find Kale, Adele could face these dangers and more.

She hoped.

The moon rose. Silver light bathed the trail, and liquid shadows drenched the woodlands. Adele reminded herself how important it was to stay on the path. Gloamwoods was especially treacherous at night. But if luck stayed with her, she would persevere.

She hoped. Oh, how she hoped.

Then an angry voice shouted, "Prisoner escape!" A whistle screamed. The forest exploded with yells and the sound of running. Getting louder. Closer. Boots hammered the hard earth of the pathway.

Adele bolted into the forest. Branches whipped her arms. Roots tripped her. Bushes stabbed her with thorns. She ripped free and ran. Each pounding footfall sent electric bolts of pain through her leg.

Finally she stopped, breathing hard. The sounds of pursuit were gone, swallowed by the forest. She leaned one hand on a tree trunk. Her legs were shaking, her arms were bloody, and every time she drew a breath her lungs felt as though she were scrubbing them with sandpaper.

The lights of the Ice Mines had vanished.

Adele was alone and lost in Gloamwoods.

At night.

She clenched her trembling hands and thought. She could use the stars for guidance. That would keep her going in a straight line, and eventually she would find something, perhaps a dwarf hostel or an abandoned gingerbread cottage where she could spend the night and regroup in morning. She just had to move quietly and not reveal her position, now that Count Wilhelm Scream's security forces were after her. She wondered how her escape had been discovered.

"Maybe trolls aren't as dumb as I thought," she said aloud.

"Certainly not," said a voice.

Adele jumped. A hulking shadow stepped from the trees. She saw its big, round stomach, and the mass of its shoulders. Her legs went weak. She clutched the tree trunk, staring up at a troll with a globular nose and a thick, full beard that rattled when he moved.

"Lovely evening," she breathed.

The troll crossed his arms. "It is not a lovely evening when I hear people saying trolls are dumb."

"No, of course not."

"I get enough of that at work, I can tell you."

"That must be very unpleasant."

"Yes, it is."

"I didn't mean it the way it sounded."

"Yes, you did."

Adele heard the *skrtch* of a match. A yellow light flared as the troll lit a lantern. He lifted it and examined her. She tried not to quake.

"Are you running away from Count Wilhelm Scream?" said the troll.

"Heavens, no."

"Sometimes people try to escape from him."

"How foolish of them," said Adele. "When he has been so kind to us all."

"It does not usually work," agreed the troll. "But it would explain why you are here. I should call the patrol, just in case." He lifted a pewter whistle to his lips and puffed out his cheeks like great, hairy balloons.

Adele clutched her burlap nightgown in both fists to show him. "I was sleepwalking."

The troll eyed her skeptically. "Why were you talking about trolls?"

"I had a dream," said Adele, improvising wildly. "About trolls. One was—a doctor. And one was a general, and one was a wizard."

"Hah," said the troll. "Trolls do not do such things."

"In my dream they did," said Adele. "And they led me here. Say, do you mind lowering that light a bit?"

"No problem," said the troll. He put it on the ground between them. "Go on."

"They led me here," repeated Adele, wondering where this was going. "They said—they said they would prove to me that trolls were smart. *Very* smart. They said as soon as I woke up I would meet, um, a genius troll."

The troll's eyes widened. "A genius troll?"

"Yes, exactly. And then I woke up and I said, 'Maybe trolls aren't as dumb as I thought.' And then you appeared."

The troll blinked.

"You appeared," repeated Adele. "The genius troll!"

"But I am not a genius," said the troll.

Suppressing a flinch, Adele patted his hairy arm. "Everyone has a special talent. What's yours?"

The troll rubbed his chin, setting the skulls in his beard tinkling like a dozen tiny wedding guests pinging their goblets with spoons. "Thumping."

"There you go, then."

"There is more skill involved than people think."

"Of course."

"Plus," went on the troll, "I am a financial hotshot."

"No! Really?"

The troll nodded. "I supplement my salary with bribes. One of them is going to make me rich tonight."

"Wonderful!"

"Want to know how?"

"Yes," said Adele, who didn't.

The troll lowered his head to Adele's ear. "Magic." He whispered so hard that her hair blew in the gust.

"What kind?" said Adele, hoping it was the kind that would get her to the Ice Mines and Kale.

The troll picked up the lantern and put a sausage-like finger to his lips. He gestured with his hand, and walked a few paces. Adele followed. The troll pointed proudly at a mound of dirt in the center of a small, moon-misted clearing.

"What is it?" breathed Adele.

"Magic," repeated the troll. "I just planted it."

"Oh." Adele tried not to sound disappointed. "Beans."

"Yarn."

"Yarn?"

"Yarn."

Adele thought about this. "I've never heard of magical yarn."

"The boys told me it was very powerful," said the troll. "Especially if I planted it by starlight."

They watched the mound. Nothing happened.

"Did these boys tell you what would happen when you planted it?" said Adele.

The troll scratched his head. "No."

"I think," said Adele delicately, "I think it is just possible that the boys were taking advantage of your well-earned reputation as a financial hotshot."

"Huh?"

"They lied," said Adele. "There's no such thing as magic yarn."

With a gargling cry, the troll leaped at the mound and plunged his arm in up to the elbow. He pulled it out, spraying dirt. In his palm, a skein of yarn dripped mud. He stared at it, his face contorted.

"I'm terribly sorry," whispered Adele.

The troll turned his craggy face to her. "There was no magic."

"No. There wasn't."

The troll lurched to his feet. "I am going back to those boys and make them pay."

"That's a fine idea," said Adele. "But before you go, I wonder if you could do me a favor?"

"Trolls do not do favors."

"But I just did you one," pointed out Adele.

"If you had not told me about the yarn, I would still be happy."

"If I hadn't told you about the yarn, you'd still be waiting for it to do something," said Adele. "As it is, you can find those rotten boys and give them the thumping they deserve."

"I am good at thumping," mused the troll.

"Exactly."

"Not everyone can do it."

"Quite right," said Adele. "At least not as well as you."

The troll turned his head as if blushing. "Now you are embarrassing me."

"Not a bit of it," said Adele. "And there's only one thing I ask of you."

"Oh, all right," sighed the troll. "What is it?"

"I need directions to the Ice Mines."

"Why?"

"The trolls in my dream told me I had to go there."

The troll's eyes widened. "The doctor and the general and the wizard?"

"Exactly. They said only the genius troll could give proper directions."

The troll puffed out his chest. He lifted the lantern and pointed. "Go straight that way until you come to the cliffs. Do not fall off the cliffs. Turn right. There is a swamp. Do not get lost in the swamp. Stay in the forest. If you do get lost, do not ask the grape vines for directions. They gossip. Do not go into any of the frozen clearings. You will freeze. Watch out for werewolves. Do not follow the friar with the lantern. He plays mean jokes. Go uphill, then downhill. You will see the Ice Mines after the boulders. It will take you until dawn. Good night."

He hoisted his lantern and stumped into the forest. Adele sighed and walked in the direction he had pointed, thinking about cliffs and clearings and talking vines and a cruel friar with a lantern.

It was going to be a long night.

34

Casper and Jasper ran. Every part of them hurt. Their feet ached from crashing against rocks and roots. Their legs screamed from stretching to dash faster. Their backpacks banged on their shoulders, and breath scraped in their throats.

Once they hid between two boulders leaning against each other. Once they climbed a tree but jumped out when something dark flapped past them. Twice they splashed across a stream, once going forward and once backward. The Special Police drew closer. They had lanterns. The boys did not. They knew the woods. The boys did not. The twins ducked behind what they thought was a rock but turned out to be a cauldron. Ordinarily this would have intrigued them. Now was not ordinary.

"This way, men," called Captain Dwop. "They can't get much farther."

Casper and Jasper looked about wildly. The forest was thinning. It would not hide them. The sky gleamed with moonshine, robbing them of darkness.

"This way," gasped Jasper. They plunged forward.

Their feet sloshed. They were ankle-deep in slick mud pocked with clumps of weeds. Cold water soaked their trousers.

"Swamp," groaned Casper. "He said there was a swamp."

Jasper tried to lift his foot. It stuck, and he lost his balance and fell. The noise wakened a flock of birds, and they flew away, gibbering.

"Sir, over there," shouted a bruiser.

"Keep going," said Jasper. The boys lurched forward, pulling their feet out of sucking mud with every step. Water spattered, and the mud said *scchhllop* every time they moved.

"Halt," bawled an all-too-familiar voice.

"No thanks," shouted Casper over his shoulder. He could see Captain Dwop and his band at the shoreline.

"Look out," yelled Jasper.

A blow knocked Casper to his knees. Something heavy oozed around his arms and chest. He yelped and kicked. It lifted him from the oily water.

He heard a cry and a splash. Looking desperately around in the silvery light, Casper saw his brother. Both boys hung a good ten or twelve feet above the swamp. Jasper was almost completely engulfed by a giant white ball atop a thick, green stalk. Only his head and one arm protruded. The more he struggled, the higher the glop rose around his body.

Casper, too, was mostly encased in a goopy, white blob. It pulsated with his movements. Somehow he knew that every time he struggled or shouted or breathed, it would suck him further in.

Captain Dwop hadn't been telling them to halt. He was speaking to his own men, keeping them out of the swamp.

Where Casper and Jasper were being eaten alive.

As per the troll's directions, Adele went straight until she came to the cliffs. Finding anything was no small feat for someone navigating Gloamwoods alone, and she was pleased with herself. Even better, a path meandered along the cliff side, illuminated by the moon. Adele turned right. Then she heard guttural voices.

"Stumpp, you promised," said one.

"Leave me alone," snarled a second, deeper one.

Adele ducked behind an outcropping as two enormous, doglike figures padded into view. Their eyes sparkled like green fire, and their mouths gleamed with teeth sharp and cruel.

Werewolves.

Adele shrank down, feeling sick and cold. Her injured leg burned.

The first voice rose in a keening whine. "The way you go running around, chomping and maiming—"

"For crying out loud, Lupita, you knew that when you married me!"

"Just once I think you could stay home. Heaven knows the den could use some tidying."

"Don't tell me you never head out with your girlfriends on a night like this."

"Well, at least I have the decency to shave my legs!"

Adele peeked around the outcropping. The beasts were standing nose to nose, hackles bristling. She backed away, hoping they would be too absorbed in their argument to notice her.

Unfortunately, it is almost impossible to move silently in a forest. Adele's feet crunched on fallen leaves and bracken. The werewolf called Stumpp lifted his head. "Quiet."

"Don't you tell me what to—"

"Listen." His ears perked up, and he swung his great muzzle around, sniffing. "Meat."

"Where?"

"Close." He sniffed again. "It's injured." His lips parted in a wicked grin.

Lupita inhaled deeply, shutting her eyes. She pointed her muzzle at the shadows where Adele hid. "This way," she hissed with a toothy smile. "Whoever bites first doesn't have to share."

Stumpp roared. His teeth gleamed like wet daggers in the moonlight. Lupita screamed with delight. They bounded toward Adele.

Adele did not think. She ran between the two monsters, so close she felt the hot puffs of Stumpp's breath on her cheek as she shot past. She skidded to a halt at the edge of the cliff. A full moon hung in the sky, but the base of the cliff was lost in shadows.

The werewolves leaped. They landed all fours on either side of her. She could not outrun them. She could not out-climb them. The cliff plunged away behind her.

Lupita crouched. Stumpp reared up on his hind legs. Adele jumped.

36

Captain Dwop leaned on the cauldron the boys had hidden behind, and watched them struggle. "Carnivorous Marshmallows," he announced.

"Yes, sir," said a tough.

"Well, that makes our job easier."

"Yes, sir."

"Now we've only got that other one to capture."

"Don't you mean re-capture, sir?"

"Shut up."

"Yes, sir."

"A dangerous criminal or spy, a suspected confederate of those two," he gestured at Casper and Jasper, "is at loose in Gloamwoods. Find her."

"Yes, sir."

The police melted back into the woods. Captain Dwop rocked on his heels and whistled a cheery melody.

"Sir?" The tough poked his head through the bushes. "Do we find the confederate, or eliminate the avian pestilence?"

Dwop rubbed his chin. "First confederate, then pestilence."

"The princess said—"

"Pestilence first." Dwop turned back into the forest to join his men, looking back at the boys with a sigh of regret.

Casper looked at Jasper. Jasper looked at Casper.

"We could call for help," said Jasper.

"Why?" The marshmallow moved a little higher up Casper's chest.

"They...might not come," agreed Jasper with difficulty.

"Even if they did," said Casper, "what's the advantage?"

"True." The marshmallow flowed up Jasper's arm to the elbow. "I like these things better when they're boiled down into candy."

"They—might say the same about us."

A swamp slug slithered past in the water. Unseen insects hissed. The marshmallows burbled with gentle but relentless undulations.

"My feet are getting hot," said Casper.

"Mine too." Jasper wriggled. The marshmallow pulsed up to his shoulders, constricting his chest. "What...do you think it means?"

"It means you are being digested," said a familiar voice.

They peered down. "Guthrum!" exclaimed Casper.

"Are we ever happy to see you." Jasper wished he could wave in a chummy fashion, but one of his arms was deep inside the marshmallow, and he didn't want to move the other one if he could help it.

The troll stepped forward, lantern in hand. He scowled. "I am not happy to see you."

"Why not?" said Casper.

"Because you are a couple of stinking liars."

"Why, Sinister, old sport, whatever do you mean?" gasped Jasper. His feet were uncomfortably warm. The heat was creeping up his legs, and in places where his trousers were thin it was beginning to burn.

"I buried the yarn. It did not grow."

"Well—not in a forest, of course," wheezed Casper. The marshmallow was squeezing his chest, and he was having difficulty breathing. "It needs—direct sunlight—"

"Last time you said starlight," said Danegeld.

"A mix—of the two," explained Jasper. "For optimal growth and—ouch, this is really hot—the—ah—accelerated photosynthesis associated with—"

"All I got was muddy yarn," said Danegeld.

"So—urk—sorry," said Casper with what little of his breath he could summon. "Get us down—we'll try again."

"We'll—give you—a hand," agreed Jasper, though his voice was pinched.

Danegeld shook his head. "I am going to sit here and watch you get digested," he said. "Because you are rotten stinking liars." He swept aside a pile of firewood by the cauldron and sat down cross-legged, his shillelagh on his lap. A smile split his ugly face.

Jasper gave up all pretense. "Guthrum," he cried. "Help us. Please."

The troll smiled more broadly. "Danegeld the Sinister," he said.

"Danegeld the Sinister," choked out Casper. "Please. We're dying."

"I know," said Danegeld. "People die here often. See?" He pointed. A work boot sat in a puddle next to a downed mallow stalk, its laces trailing in the water. Mud partly covered a design of interlaced hearts on one side. "The marshmallows do not like shoes and belt buckles and such," he went on. "They spit them out when they are done with the rest."

Jasper waved his free arm. "Danegeld the Sinister," he said, "we're sorry we tricked you. Please, help us and we'll never do it again."

"No." Danegeld leaned against a hummock and put his arms behind his head.

"What do you want?" cried Casper.

"To watch you die," said Danegeld reasonably. "You were mean to me. And I still do not have enough money for a left-handed shillelagh holster."

Casper clawed at his chest. His fingers found his locket, and he pulled it free, letting it swing in the air. It glinted in the moonlight. "Here," he gasped.

Danegeld stood up. He peered at the locket, then sat down. "Too small. I could not buy a holster with that."

"I have one too," said Jasper. He held his so Danegeld could see it, even as his elbow was being sucked into the marshmallow.

Danegeld considered this. "Two might be enough."

"Of course it is," said Casper. "You could buy—the best holster—in the Count's—Special—Police."

Danegeld nodded. "All right. I will wait till the plant is done eating you. It will spit out the gold after."

Casper gagged as the marshmallow pulled him in up to his chin.

"It's well known that marshmallows—eat gold," said Jasper.

"It is?" said Danegeld.

"An essential nutrient for the mallow—family," gargled Casper. "There'd be—none—left." And with a choking cry he disappeared into the sticky white ball.

"Well in that case," sighed Danegeld, "I guess I have to rescue you."

He splashed through the water. Lifting his shillelagh over his shoulders, he struck the stalk of Casper's marshmallow with all his might.

The first blow dented the stem. The second sent cracks through it. The third shattered it. The heavy top of the plant crackled through the branches of dead trees and splashed into the slough, sending up a wave of muddy water full of twigs and beetles.

Danegeld reached into the marshmallow ball up to his elbow, then to his shoulder. Mumbling deep in his throat, he probed the sticky mass. Finally his face brightened, and he pulled Casper out by his ankles and dropped him.

Casper sat up to his waist in cold water. He coughed, and marshmallow phlegm shot out of his mouth and nose. He drew a ragged breath and wiped sticky tendrils from his face and neck.

"Thank you," he said, his voice cloudy.

"Pay me." Guthrum Danegeld held out his enormous palm.

Casper stood, shaking his head. "Not till you get my brother."

"That was not part of the deal."

Casper looked up at Jasper disappearing into the marshmallow. "It is now."

Danegeld sighed. "Sometimes I think you do not play fair. But I will do it."

So he felled the marshmallow holding Jasper and fished him out. But he kept a firm grip on the boy's arm.

"Ow," said Jasper. Then he vomited marshmallow mucus onto Danegeld's muddy boots.

Danegeld was unswayed, and if you are familiar with trolls' personal habits, this will not surprise you. Plus, like trolls in general, Guthrum Danegeld had a singularity of purpose that made him an outstanding bouncer and reliable Special Police officer. "Gold."

Casper pointed at Jasper, who was examining the vomit with great interest. "Let go of my brother."

"Pay me first."

Casper reached into his shirt and drew out his locket, the locket with the letter C that had always been with him, night and day, as long as he could remember. He dropped it into Danegeld's outstretched palm with a sigh.

Danegeld set Jasper on a tuft of soggy grass. "Now you."

Jasper handed over his locket, wishing he had just one more moment to memorize the faces of the nice-looking mother and father he had never known.

"Have a nice night," said Danegeld. "I am going to buy my holster now." He sloshed back to shore and disappeared into the moonlit forest, stumping along rutted tracks leading away from the cauldron.

Adele shot through the air. Wind screamed in her ears. She screwed her eyes shut, waiting for the bone-smashing impact she hoped would kill her instantly.

WHOMP.

Adele gasped and opened her eyes. The moon and stars swung crazily. Overhead, two shaggy heads peered at her from the cliff's edge. Their eyes glowed, and their teeth gleamed in the moonlight. But they were too far away to reach her.

"Lycanthropy," rasped an educated voice. "A little-understood social ill."

Adele tried to sit up. A blaze of pain shot through her leg. Waxy leaves fluttered with her every movement, and rough ropes of bark supported her.

"There are those," said a similar voice, "who feel it is sometimes mistakenly attributed to the disease known as porphyria. The discolored teeth, extreme sensitivity to light, and antisocial attitudes might come under such a heading."

"Nonsense," said a third voice. "It describes some of the symptoms, certainly, but how do you account for the fact that when in human form the sufferer has no attributes such as might be accounted for by the disease?"

Adele heard a bristling noise. "Are you impugning my thesis, Cornelius?" said the second voice.

"Not happily, Eli," said the third. "But I do think that hypertrichosis is arguably a more valid place to start. The excessive hair growth—"

"I see what you mean," mused the second voice. "But the behavioral aspect is more salient, don't you think? Perhaps a cross-contamination with rabies might describe the condition more fully."

"No matter the origin, it's a full-blown epidemic," said the first voice. "How do we respond? Blaming the victim has been a catastrophic failure. Would rehabilitation work? And if so, how do we fund it?"

"Hey," hollered the werewolf named Stumpp. "You done with that?"

The leaves and vines rustled. "Why, no," said a voice. "We can dissertate everlastingly once we get started."

"I meant our dinner," said the werewolf.

"Your dinner?"

Stumpp gestured at Adele with a hairy paw. "That."

"This?" Tendrils waved over Adele's head. She shrank against the leaves and bark.

"Yeah, that," said Stumpp with some irritation. Even from her distance, Adele could see his hackles rising.

"I mean, if you're not going to eat it, mind giving it back?" said Lupita.

A tremendous rustling ensued. Vines thrashed; voices muttered and hissed. The strange web that held Adele surged, and as she clung tight to the bark-rough vines, she could only marvel that from now on the phrase "the leaves whispered" would mean something entirely different to her.

"We've reached a consensus," said the first voice.

"Good," said Stumpp. "Toss it up, willya?"

"Ah. No, I'm afraid we can't do that."

"We saw her first," cried Lupita. "She's ours."

"Possession is nine-tenths of the law," said the voice called Eli.

"Oh, not that old saw," said the first voice. "What about the issue of consent? Miss," it said gently, "do you wish to be these animals' dinner?"

With a start, Adele realized the voice was talking to her. "No," she said. "Not at all."

"Then I'm afraid it's not your night, Mr. Stumpp, Ms. Lupita," said the voice. "Some other time, perhaps."

"Oh, great," snarled Stump. "We do the hard work—"

"—chase her right to you—" chimed in Lupita.

"And now you're just going to eat her in front of us?"

Adele choked. She tried to leap to her feet, but the vines underfoot swayed with her every movement. Her leg cramped and gave way. She collapsed, heart pounding.

"Certainly not," said another voice. "But we do have standards to maintain."

"High ones," agreed yet another.

"Perhaps," said one of the voices gently, "if you'd prefer to take some time off and re-apply in the future—"

With a snarl, Stumpp turned and dashed away. Lupita followed him.

"Drat," said the voice called Cornelius. "I was hoping to interview him for my paper."

"That would be quite a feather in your cap," said the Eli voice admiringly.

Adele shoved herself to a sitting position. It set everything bouncing, and leaves tickled her neck. "Excuse me," she said. "Where am I? And, if I may ask, who are you?"

"For heaven's sake, where are our manners?" said the first voice. "Miss, I beg your pardon. We are a group of eight like-minded vines who have been growing together here in Gloamwoods for some time. I'm the eldest. My name is Veritas. Would you like to get down to the ground?"

"Yes," said Adele. "Very much."

In a process that felt like a cross between square dancing and going over a waterfall in a fishnet (a popular sport in Larkspur), Adele found herself passed from one vine to the next. It involved dropping a few sickening feet, being introduced to the vine that caught her, and being dropped again. The bouncing hurt her injured leg, and she clenched her teeth to keep from crying out. The last vine, Cornelius, set her on the forest floor at the base of the cliff, solicitously inquired after her health, and brushed a few twigs out of her hair. Looking up, Adele could see that the entire cliff face was covered with a dense growth of ivy. The dark, waxy leaves rustled when the vines spoke, and tendrils waved excitedly whenever anyone wanted to make a point.

"Thank you so much," she said. "You saved my life."

"Think nothing of it," said Veritas. "It's part of our social obligation."

"Well, I'm very grateful." She shook her nightgown; a few leaves fluttered to the ground. "Can you tell me how to get to the Ice Mines?"

"Now, that's a good question," said a vine named Penn. "Are you speaking literally or metaphorically?"

"Literally, of course," said Adele.

"Oh." Adele thought Penn sounded disappointed. "Are you sure?"

"Quite sure."

"There's some doubt as to their location," said a vine named Leo. "If indeed they exist at all."

"We suspect it may be a local legend," said Veritas. "Of course, all legends have a germ of truth, so the trick is to analyze the evidence and see where it leads you."

Adele shook her head. "No, it's not a legend. I've seen them. I was going there but I got lost, and then the werewolves—"

"Among competing hypotheses, the one with the fewest assumptions tends to be the most valid," went on Veritas, who seemed rather fond of his own voice.

"An essential guideline, especially when one considers that a hypothesis is merely a proposed explanation for a phenomenon," said a vine named Big Greene.

"Exactly," said Penn. "And one must beware the temptation to combine conjecture and data beyond necessity." He chuckled. "I don't suppose any of us need to be reminded of *that*."

The vines all guffawed in agreement, setting the leaves shivering as though in a downpour.

Adele gritted her teeth. "Yes yes yes," she said. "But do you know where the mines are?"

The laughter stopped. "Not really," admitted Veritas. "We don't get out much."

A chortle sounded from near Adele's knees. "Yah, no kiddin'."

She jumped. The ground was crowded with blue figures in high, broad-brimmed red hats. In the moonlight she could see that some carried bindles on sticks, and many had pickaxes tucked into leather belts around their waists. Others wore capes, and a few had tidy red jackets. Two who were slightly taller than the others stood at her side, grinning cheerfully.

"Kobolds," groaned a vine named Burnbright. "Now, there's something I wish were just a legend."

"Ach, you remember us," said one of the creatures in delight.

"The Ivy League has a long memory, my friend," said Eli. "Even of things we might prefer to forget."

"Now, Eli," scolded Veritas. "Remember, this community was among the first to be victimized by the count. Let us not fall prey to his propaganda."

"They were a pain in the neck long before he came aboard," grumbled Eli.

The kobolds beamed, and several fist-bumped one another. "Tanks," called one.

"Yah, we bin away fer some time," said the tall kobold.

"Do tell," sighed Big Greene.

"We wintered at Skunk Haven de first few years, but de service, it was not so good. It was not like *das Frözenshaften.*"

"And de cruise, it was too long," said the figure by his side. "De beds were too soft. Not like our beds in *das Frözenshaften.*"

"Yah, and de ice, it was chust terrible."

"No color."

"No flavor."

"It was like water," lamented the slightly shorter kobold. "Not like de ice in *das Frözenshaften.*"

"So, yah, we done a lot of travelin', you know, looking for a place dat was chust right," said the first kobold. "Did some hauntin' and herdin' here and dere. But nowhere is like *das Frözenshaften.* Now Herschel say dere is five columns at de mines wid lots of danger, so—we komen back." He grinned again.

"Any chance you might head out again?" said Leo hopefully.

"*Vaksen zolstu vi a Tsibele, met dem Kop in Dred!*" shrilled the second of the tall kobolds.

"Well, really," huffed Leo. "There's no need to be offensive."

"Dat's what you tink," said the kobold smugly.

"Excuse me," said Adele, who had been trying to follow the conversation. "Did you say you were from the mines?"

The first kobold looked her up and down. "Yer no Ivy Leaguer."

"My name is Adele. And you are—?"

The kobold swept off his hat and bowed, indicating the figure at his side. "Starski and Hütchen, pleased to meetcha. And we are from *das Frözenshaften*, yah."

"It is de best place for us," said the kobold named Starski who had offended Eli. "De service is good, and de beds are not too soft."

"The Ice Mines?" pressed Adele. "The mines of Count Wilhelm Scream?"

As if she had pressed a button, every kobold turned his or her head and spat. Hütchen scowled and jammed his hat on his head. "Dat *Schweinporker*. His mines? Hah! He stole dem from us."

"He is *das Jerkweasel*," called someone from the back of the crowd.

"But you're headed there now?" said Adele with rising excitement.

Starski twisted her hat in her hands. Several other kobolds looked at the sky and puffed their cheeks out as they whistled off-key. One or two became very interested in their capes.

"It is taking longer dan we thought," admitted Hütchen.

Starski pulled on Adele's nightgown. "Hütchen will not ask for directions," she hissed in a stage whisper. "Herschel Wulfgrim, he go ahead to *das Frözenshaften* for to tell de column of five dat we is coming. But it is many years we are away and now we is walking and walking in Gloamwoods for much time." She dropped the nightgown and glared at Hütchen. "Instead of *das Frözenshaften*."

Deep in this glorious swirl of words Adele glimpsed two facts: the kobolds were returning to the Ice Mines, and they were lost. "But I have directions," she exclaimed.

All faces turned to her, eyes wide with hope. "Yah?" said Hütchen.

"Well, sort of." Adele repeated the troll's words. "He said not to fall off the cliffs, so I guess we have to climb back up."

She glanced at the vine-covered cliff, and thought of Stumpp and Lupita. Her leg throbbed painfully.

"Well, why didn't you just say so?" exclaimed Veritas. "Good heavens, miss, there's no need to go scaling cliffs willy-nilly. What haphazard methodology."

"There isn't?" said Adele.

"Not a bit of it. Just walk along the base of the cliff until you get to Contrition Cleft. There's a staircase carved into the rock. It will take you all the way to the summit, and hey presto you're back in the game."

"Plus, it puts you past the worst of werewolf territory," said Big Greene.

"Werewolves?" said Starski hopefully, and suddenly every kobold was gripping a dagger and glancing about excitedly. Adele began to feel quite optimistic.

"The stairs are uneven," said Penn. "Medieval in vintage. Dreadfully weathered, you know."

"They were carved by Friar Spooklight as part of his penance," said Leo. "He was caught leading travelers into the slough with his lantern. Kept telling them there was faerie gold hidden there. Of course it was just his idea of a practical joke."

"Rotten trick," huffed Cornelius.

"That's what Friar Uptight thought too. Took away the lantern till Spooklight had carved the stairs. Of course as soon as he got it back he was up to his old tricks, so I'm not sure what good it did in the long run."

"You guys talk a lot," said Hütchen. "Hey lady, you komen wid us or what?"

"Certainly," said Adele. "And you Ivies—thank you so much for all your help. You've been lovely, really."

Starski gestured with her dagger. "C'mon, lady," she shouted. "We need your directions."

"Best of luck with your endeavors," called Big Greene.

"Indeed! May the weight of your task never bear you down, but carry you aloft to the height of your dreams," said Penn.

"Godspeed," agreed Eli heartily. "Never give in and never give up."

"Why Eli, you old ruffian, you've ended a sentence with a preposition," said Veritas. "That is something up with which I will not put. Ha! Ha!"

Adele waved goodbye to the chortling vines. Surrounded by a sea of kobolds with hats bobbing and capes flapping, she limped along the base of the cliffs, hoping that each painful step was bringing her closer to Kale.

"When does he sleep?" said Casper as the troll disappeared into the forest.

"I guess he doesn't have to," said Jasper.

"Well, I do," yawned Casper. He and Jasper had spent several hours tied to a tree anticipating being delivered to the local despot for torture and interrogation; undertaken a mad flight through woodlands and wetlands; and nearly been devoured by marshmallows. If that has ever happened to you, you will understand that it is not conducive to a pleasant evening's rest. (If it has not happened to you, you will just have to use your imagination.)

Jasper pulled on his brother's arm. "Come on."

"Where?"

"This way." He gestured at the swamp.

"Are you barking bonkers? Let's take the road." Casper pointed at the rutted tracks the troll had taken.

"I'm sure that would be very useful if we wanted to rejoin Guthrum and his charming friends."

"Point taken." Casper yawned again, and his eyelids drooped.

"We can't nod off here," chided Jasper.

"Maybe you can't," muttered Casper, but he stood up all the same, sloshing to a tuft of grass to stand on.

As soon as he put his weight on it, half the tuft broke loose. Casper slid into the water again, soaking any part of himself that had been dry before. It was the latest in a series of dousings in cold, muddy water, and did nothing to improve his mood.

"Your vocabulary has positively burgeoned," said Jasper admiringly when Casper was done explaining his feelings about the swamp. He shifted his feet on the tussock where he stood. "And I can't say I disagree. Getting out of here is going to be a challenge."

Casper wiped a weary hand across his cheek. "Walk carefully," he said. "Assume the water hides treachery."

"Absolutely," said Jasper. He stepped off his tussock and plunged into muck up to his chest.

"Give me your hand," said Casper, and began to pull.

But the harder Casper pulled on Jasper, the deeper he pushed himself into the gunk at his own feet. "Let go," panted Jasper finally. He reached out a muddy hand and grasped the gnarled roots of a swamp tree. They held, and the boys clambered free of the cloying embrace of the mire.

"Right," said Casper, clinging to a trunk. "Off we go."

"How?" said Jasper, clinging to another.

Casper pointed at a weed-free channel curving through the water. "Looks like a swamp slug canal. If it is, the mud is compacted at the bottom. Maybe we can walk it."

"Can't get any wetter, that's for sure," said Jasper. He stepped in, keeping one hand on his tree. The base held, and Casper joined him. The boys sloshed along. It was not a pleasant walk. The water was cold, and brimmed with insect shells and rotting leaves from autumns past which pricked against their skin. A bird flew over them, as if mocking their mudbound plight. Several times the boys had to move aside to let swamp slugs ooze past, filling the channel with their grey girth. Twice they splashed to safety as Venom Clutch reached out with vicious tendrils. Once they startled something that thrashed away from them on wings that might have been green. Finally, exhausted, they stopped to sit on a fallen log with a skirt of weeds at the waterline. Casper gave a yelp. "Look!"

Jasper looked. Gleaming in the moonlight were a cauldron and three downed marshmallows. One was twitching slightly.

"Right back where we started." Jasper felt like crying.

"I can't do it." Casper's head drooped. "Not if every step is like this."

"We can't stop here. They'll find us."

Casper closed his eyes. "They think we're dead."

"If we don't move, they'll be right. Remember the boot?"

Casper's chin fell to his chest. "We can't go on."

"Yes, we can."

"No, we can't."

"Yes, we can."

"Stop talking banana oil."

"Stop being a moaning fleshlump."

"Stop being a goon-faced trogglewhopper."

Ordinarily such fightin' words would have roused either twin to a joyous fistfight, but now Jasper merely sighed. "You're just saying that because you want to sleep and you're afraid."

"Yes," said Casper. "I do. And I am." He drew his knees up to his chest and burrowed his forehead into the crook of his elbow.

Jasper poked his brother in the arm. "Come on. At least we can find dry land."

"No, we can't." Casper's voice was muffled. "Dry land is where the police and the troll are. We can only walk in the channel, and it goes in a circle. Face it, Jasper. We're sunk."

Hütchen was the first to notice Adele's injury. "Hey, lady, what's up wid dat leg?" he demanded as they made their way along the base of the cliffs. "You is all walkin' steppy-limp, steppy-limp. We got no time fer such nonsense."

"Sorry," said Adele. "I'll go faster."

"Dat's no answer," said Hütchen sternly. He threw up a hand and everyone halted, many bumping into each other. "How kin we fix it if you wone tell us what's wrong, eh?"

Adele sighed. "I got mauled by a marshmallow." She lifted the hem of her burlap nightgown to show the burns.

"Oooh," said the kobolds admiringly.

"Is dat all?" said Hütchen. "We can fix dat no schwett, yah." He put two fingers in his mouth and whistled. "Hashtag! *Cuttenzee ein Kripplesticken, yah? Und makeit schnappy!*"

A sprightly kobold leaped into a nearby tree and hacked off a stout branch. In short order she had stripped it of its leaves and bark, leaving a fork exactly the right height to slip under Adele's arm. A short branch, neatly trimmed, made a handle for her to grasp. Adele took two steps, marveling.

"Thank you," she said. "This is much easier."

They continued, Adele keeping up better now. Presently Starski trotted up alongside her. "Have some munchies, yah?"

she said. "We kobolds brings our own food when we travel. It is so hard to get de best wurst away from home. It is not like *das Frözenshaften.*" She pressed something spicy-smelling into Adele's hand. Suddenly realizing how hungry she was, Adele bit it. It turned out to be a hearty sausage, full of meat and onions. The flavor shocked her almost to tears, reminding her of her old life when such things were common.

"This is heavenly," she gasped when she had swallowed.

"Try it with *Loafen* and sometink to drink, den," said Starski with a grin. "Hey, everybody, time fer *Snacken!*"

The kobolds cheered. Those carrying bindles dropped them, assuring each other there was nothing like a midnight snack, yah? Others pointed out it was well past midnight, and got smacked for their trouble; but most were intent on pulling out the contents of their bags and setting them out on clean cloths their companions had spread on the ground.

Of all the magical things Adele had seen that night, nothing seemed more enchanted than the loaves of dark, chewy bread, the spiced wine, the hearty beer, and mountains of sausage links and cooked cabbage that came out of those bags. Soon she was talking and laughing with the kobolds as they expounded on their favorite soccer teams and how much better everything was in *das Frözenshaften.* With each mouthful she felt braver and stronger; and with so many daggers out to cut bread and spread butter, she almost wished Stumpp and Lupita would appear again.

Please understand that the kind of hunger Adele had endured for years was in no way the kind of energetic appetite that comes from, say, playing outside on a winter day. That sort of hunger, especially when followed by a good meal, is no more like Adele's experience than a cranky housekeeper is like a giant, especially if your name is Jack and you have invaded his personal space with your dang beanstalk. No, Adele's hunger had stabbed in her gut, making her feel fragile and helpless. She had kept those feelings hidden: from Spudd, who hated her so, and from the other mill workers, who looked to her for strength. But now she could eat her fill, enjoying something other than prison rations or what she managed to scrounge from the slough. Furthermore, for the first time since that dreadful day in Middlemost, Adele was surrounded not by fellow prisoners but by allies. Even her injured leg seemed better.

She felt a surge of confidence. *We're going to win this thing, she thought. Das Frözenshaften, here we come!*

Jasper snorted. "Sunk? Pshaw!"

"Tell me one thing we could do that we haven't already done."

Jasper opened his mouth to refute Casper's logic, and shut it when he realized he couldn't.

Whomp.

"Yarg," yelled Jasper.

"Hey," shouted Casper, flailing his arms.

A green and gold form flapped on the log between the brothers. Gaining its balance, it folded its wings and twitched its head first at Casper, then at Jasper. The sky was lightening, and they could see it clearly.

Casper recognized her first. "So it's you, is it?"

Jasper glared at the creature. "Troublemaker. Come back to gloat over a job well done?"

For it was none other than the fidelius bird the brothers had liberated from the Special Police. She fluffed her feathers and smoothed them with her beak. She hopped off the log and looked over her shoulder at the boys.

"Go take a flying leap," said Casper.

"You heard him," said Jasper.

The bird spread her enormous wings and sailed to a cluster of dry grass a few feet away. She skipped and danced, staring at Casper and Jasper.

"Go *away*," said Jasper. But she didn't.

"You know," said Casper finally, "I think she's trying to tell us something."

"Like what?"

"Like maybe that that spot is safe to step on."

Jasper looked at the bird, now bouncing on the hillock and seeming more impatient with every passing moment. "You're nutters."

"It hasn't broken under her weight."

"That's because she doesn't have any."

"We set her free. She must know she owes us."

Jasper gritted his teeth. "No, she doesn't."

"How do you know?"

"Because she's a *bird*."

"Fine," said Casper. "You cash in your chips. You stay here on this mucky log, feeling sorry for yourself. Forget our family history. Forget the whole thing. You can be the one who drops the thread just when we had a chance to darn the hole in the tapestry of our lineage."

"Now, that's unfair," said Jasper, "especially considering who was moaning to cash in *his* chips mere moments ago."

"The appearance of our plumed guide has revived me," said Casper. "Come on, but let's step carefully."

"Or we might get wet," said Jasper.

"Here goes," said Casper.

"In one swell foop," said Jasper grudgingly. They stepped into the water, making a beeline—or fish line—toward the tiny island where the bird waited. The water was shallow, and they reached it easily. Casper stepped onto the spot of dry land. Jasper followed.

It held.

"Great!" said Casper.

"Coincidence?" said Jasper.

The bird flew ahead. It landed on a second hillock and looked at Casper and Jasper. Its eyes glittered even in the dank atmosphere of the swamp.

This time the island was close enough to jump. They made it, with Casper slipping just a little and muddying the heel of one shoe.

The bird flew off again. Tuft by tuft, clump by clump, the boys followed her. Sometimes they landed on miniature islands a few strides long. Sometimes they straddled moss-slicked logs and pulled themselves forward in a process that left them looking as though a goblin with a head cold had blown its nose on them. Once the fidelius bird seemed to land on water. It turned out that she was using submerged rocks as steppingstones. The boys raced after her, moving too fast to slip. As Jasper pointed out, half of luck was speed; and as Casper added, the laws of physics were easier to break if you didn't slow down to think about them.

Finally they stopped on an island larger than the rest, a jumble of trees whose roots plunged into the water, gripping the swampland muck. Silt and leaves had collected in them, and grass had sprouted in the mat of debris, making a ruff of land around the trunks. The boys leaned against the trees. Although they were dirty and tired they were no longer soaking wet, for hard work and not falling into the water every time they took a step had mostly dried them out. They were also fairly warm, though they knew that would wear off if they held still too long.

The bird strutted back and forth along the edge of the island, staring at them with her head turned to one side. She fluttered to a nearby cluster of twigs and hopped up and down, flapping her wings.

"She thinks we're slackers," said Jasper.

"She's right," said Casper.

Jasper spread his hands and looked at the bird. "Not all of us can fly, you know."

The bird squawked and flew back to the island, landing on a knobby root. She folded her wings with an attitude that said, "Humph!"

"Seriously, we need a rest," said Casper.

"And we have a list of demands," said Jasper.

"Fifteen-minute breaks every hour."

"And a dental plan."

"Don't say we didn't warn you."

The bird flapped away.

"Hope she comes back," said Jasper.

"Me too."

"After our breather."

"Right," said Casper. "We couldn't stay here if we wanted to."

"Too lumpy."

"Too wet."

"This glop has got to end somewhere."

"Exactly."

"I just wish I knew we were going in the right direction."

Casper shrugged. "I'm going to assume our feathered friend is easing her conscience by leading us to safety."

Jasper stretched out his legs and rolled his shoulders. Casper shifted his spine, trying to work out a kink.

"I wish we had something to eat," said Jasper.

"And drink," said Casper. Even without their camping experiences with the League of the Crocodile, they would have known better than to drink the fetid liquid at their feet.

Jasper sighed. "The next time we set out to rescue our parents, let's take provisions."

"And boots." Casper wiggled a toe through a brand-new hole in his shoe.

"And a map."

"And a road."

"You see," said Jasper, "that was our big mistake right there."

They chuckled, and lapsed into silence.

"Seriously, though," said Jasper, "I'm hungry."

"I'll be in charge of thirsty," said Casper.

Jasper looked at the black leaves and dim sky overhead, and the vine-choked trees that stabbed the water on all sides. "There must be something here we can eat." Croc League outings had not focused on swampland excursions, an omission Jasper now found downright offensive.

"Ideally that doesn't try to eat us first." Casper stood up. "Let's go see."

Stepping carefully, the boys explored their tiny island. "Not much to look at, is it?" said Jasper. Once you had seen the trunks and the roots and the mat of rotting leaves spiked with grass, you had pretty much done the tour.

"Fnark," said something over their heads.

They looked up. Casper beamed. "Hullo. Good to have you back."

The bird bounced atop a spiny bush. Her feathers seemed to cast colored light instead of shadows. With a twitch of her head, she plucked something from the bush and tossed it at their feet.

Jasper picked it up. "I never noticed these." He held a cluster of berries. Even in the milky, predawn light, the fruits were bright red.

The boys looked at each other. They looked at the bird. She looked back with an expression that seemed to say, "Go on, you twit."

Now, birds don't really have facial expressions. Seriously, they don't. Try looking at a chicken sometime and saying, "Extra crispy!" It will of course be terrified, but nothing will show on its face. The fidelius bird is exactly the same in this regard. What was really happening was that Casper and Jasper were doing something called "projecting," which means they were imagining their emotions onto someone else—in this case, a creature with no facial muscles. They did this because they were dreadfully hungry and thirsty, and being presented with strange berries that might sustain them or, alternatively, might poison them. If you have never faced such a dilemma yourself, be grateful for your uneventful existence.

"You or me?" said Casper finally.

"I was in charge of hungry." Jasper plucked one of the fruits and bit it. Juice squirted onto his shirt in a fan pattern, and he coughed.

Casper's eyes widened. "Are you all right?"

Jasper nodded, chewing, and swallowed. "Just wasn't expecting so much juice. It's like biting a water balloon." He popped a second one into his mouth. "These are d'lish's," he said with his mouth full. "If they don't kill me, we'll have a feast."

He swallowed. Casper waited.

"Any stiffening of the limbs?" said Casper when he judged enough time had passed.

"No."

"Erratic heartbeat?"

"No."

"Cold sweats?"

"No."

"Hot sweats?"

"No."

"Blurred vision?" Casper waved his hand in front of his brother's eyes. "Impulsive decision-making?"

"No more than usual." Jasper swatted Casper's hand away.

"Then let's eat." Casper plucked a berry from the clump and bit it. If he chewed carefully, he found he was eating and drinking at the same time. The boys ate slowly, making the fruit last.

The bird dropped a new bunch at their feet.

"Thanks," said Jasper. He started to pluck one, but the bird gave a *skwak* and hopped in place.

"She's right," said Casper. "We should save them." So Jasper dropped them into his backpack and stood up.

"Ready when you are," he said to the bird.

The fidelius bird plunged her head between the trees' ropy roots. She came up in a spray of water, something dark clenched in her beak. It was perhaps half the size of a ping-pong ball. She slammed it onto a stone. The object splintered, revealing a black, thumb-sized worm that wiggled from side to side. She snatched it from the stone and swallowed it. Stepping to one side, she glanced down. The boys looked. Between two roots was a shallow pool, its sides encrusted with round, dark objects like the one she had just smashed. The boys thought she looked rather smug.

"Surely you jest," said Jasper.

As if in irritation, the bird reached into the water and pulled out another round object. The boys had just enough time to see it was a snail before she crushed its thin shell. She stepped away and looked from it to them, all but tapping her feet at their stupidity.

Casper watched the naked snail writhe. "Ewg."

"The thing is," said Jasper, "there's a difference between, um, you know, food for birds and, yes, well, the rest of us."

The bird nudged the snail at them. Casper and Jasper looked at each other.

"Some people eat snails as a delicacy," said Casper.

"Some people are whackos."

Casper sighed. "You tried the fruit. I guess this one's mine." He picked up the snail and, trying hard not to think about it, swallowed.

"So?" said Jasper anxiously.

Casper burped. "Slimy. But not bad."

The bird brought up two more snails and cracked them. Then she flapped to a low-hanging branch and waited

"While we wait to see if you drop dead, I'll bring up a few more," said Jasper. He lay on his stomach and pulled snails loose, piling them on dry land. When a few minutes had passed and Casper had obliged them by not dying, they set to work unpacking their lunch. And really, once they got used to the idea of eating something so completely foreign, the snails were not bad at all. As even Jasper admitted on his tenth one, with a little butter and garlic they would be quite tasty.

What Casper and Jasper had discovered was this: wetlands, though perhaps not the best places for a long walk, are rich in plant and animal life, much of which is useful to humans. In this realization they were far ahead of the Special Police, who never ventured past the Pernicious Perimeter of the Slough of Despond. They feared what they did not know, and chose not to learn more. Such lack of imagination is common among Special Police the world over.

"Thank you," said Casper to the bird when they had eaten their fill. "I can honestly say that was one of the best—"

"—and weirdest—"

"—meals of my life."

"When this whole thing is over, perhaps we'll come back and open up a little bistro," said Jasper

"'Swampy's,'" suggested Casper. "People will flock to us."

"Or wade," said Jasper.

"And speaking of wading," Casper turned to the bird again. "Ready?"

She flew to a knot of roots, then a stump. The boys followed. Presently they realized that the footholds she found for them were getting closer together, and that their steps no longer raised squirts of muck. The land shifted upwards. Casper sighed with joy, and Jasper smiled a tired smile. They were out of the swamp.

"What a relief," said Casper.

"This isn't much better," said Jasper. A forest stood before them, dense and dark and tangled. Shadows stood under its branches like sentinels of midnight that defied the breaking dawn, and insects hissed in the gloaming.

"Fortunately, we have a guide," said Casper cheerfully. He glanced around for the fidelius bird. So did Jasper.

It was gone.

41

"Where did she go?" said Casper.

"Think she'll come back?" said Jasper.

They waited.

"No," said Casper.

"Well," said Jasper, looking around, "we're out of the swamp, anyway." And they headed into the dark, mesmeric woods.

Please remember that Casper and Jasper had no map, few supplies, and only the wispiest idea of their location. Happily, however, they knew better than to panic. When people panic in the wilderness they can endanger themselves by crashing through the landscape, walking into trees, or running blindly through underbrush until they collapse, often far from any place rescuers might find them. Drawing on their long experience with the League of the Crocodile, however, the boys used the sun to reckon a straight line and hiked uphill, forcing their way through brambles and over boulders draped with roots. Trunks crushed in from all sides, and vines tumbled thick as ship-ropes from their dark branches. Every third or fourth tree leaned on a neighbor as though about to fall. The air was heavy. The boys panted but dared not speak, for any trunk or twig might hide an enemy eager to betray them. Or eat them, depending on its principles and the condition of its larder.

Casper and Jasper knew that what they needed most was shelter. Perhaps you might think water more important, or food; but any healthy person can survive for days without food, and almost any place has water, even if it is only dew that one collects at dawn. No, the crucial need in a wilderness situation is protection from heat or cold. Shelter also provides peace of mind, which cuts down on the impulse to panic. So they kept an eye out, and eventually found a patch of flat ground uphill from a stream. They shucked off their backpacks and let the breeze cool the splotches of sweat on their backs. Then they set about pitching camp.

They checked the ground for sharp rocks and root tangles, which are unpleasant to sleep on. Then they searched until they found two long, straight branches. They propped each against a tree, with one end about waist high and the other end jammed into the dirt. (These were of course live trees: the boys knew enough to avoid dead ones, which sometimes fall, creating dead campers.) Casper's branch slid until he steadied it with a couple of rocks. Then they placed smaller branches against the long ones like ribs along a spine. They piled great armfuls of dry leaves onto these frameworks, leaving gaps at the trunks just big enough to creep in. They topped off the debris with a layer of light sticks to hold everything down in case of wind. Then they filled the insides with the softest, driest leaves they could find. They crawled inside to compress them, then stuffed the insides again. Their bodies ached, their muscles were soggy, and their heads spun with exhaustion. Still they worked, gathering and stuffing, for they knew that each handful of leaves would keep them warm once they snuggled inside.

"Best hotel in Gloamwoods." Casper looked at the bare earth they had cleared in their leaf-quest. "Think we can risk a fire?"

"No."

"Me neither." He sighed. "I hate wet socks."

"Oh, Casper," said Jasper reproachfully. "We all hate wet socks. That doesn't make you special."

"Curses," said Casper. "I pinned my whole identity on that one."

They took off their socks and draped them across the ridgepoles of their leafy huts. Then they sat together and ate some of the berries from the swamp, wiggling their pink, shriveled toes in the dust of the forest floor.

"I'd like a fire too," said Jasper in a low voice.

"No need to apologize. I know it would telegraph our position."

"Just like that idiot over there is telegraphing his."

Casper looked where Jasper pointed. Sure enough, a light glistened in the shadows. "Let's not jump to conclusions," he said softly. "The idiot could be a girl."

"I don't think we need to be quiet," said Jasper. "It's pretty far away."

Casper stood up. "You don't suppose it's the castle, do you?"

Jasper stood too. "Or those Ice Mines Bunny was talking about?"

"Or that Food Mill."

The boys grinned through their fatigue.

"Still," said Casper. "Sleep first."

"If we don't, I'll keel over," said Jasper.

They marked the direction of the light by drawing an arrow in the earth by Jasper's tree. And just in case forest creatures walked all over it and changed it from nor'nor'east to sou'sou'west, they scratched a second arrow in the bark of the tree. Then they retrieved their still-damp socks and wriggled into their lean-tos feet first so their heads remained at the doorways.

"Seems strange to go to bed first thing in the morning," yawned Casper.

"Would be stranger not to," yawned Jasper. "I'm beat."

They pulled in their backpacks for pillows, and shoved their socks into their underarms to warm them up. This is a very disagreeable sensation, but it works. They plugged the doorways with debris and curled up inside, feeling warm and relatively comfortable. Soon they were asleep. From the outside, the leafy mounds blended with the forest. Creatures made of knuckles and spit scuttled past, peering at them with rheumy eyes as birds grunted overhead.

Adele hobbled through the night. The troll's directions, together with the vines' additional details and the swarm of kobolds eddying about her knees, led her steadily on: up the uneven stone steps of Contrition Cleft, around the swamp, uphill, downhill, and to a spill of boulders mere yards from the razor wire coils encircling the Ice Mines of Count Wilhelm Scream.

Somewhere in there, so close she could see him if she knew where to look, was Kale.

Adele's hands and face were scratched. Her eyes were gritty from lack of sleep, and she was covered with bug bites. Her feet were blistered. Her arm was sore from the crutch. Her leg hurt like blazes.

She hadn't been so happy in years.

Adele turned to Hütchen. "I memorized the guards' schedules, and the workers'," she whispered. "There's only one gate. It's locked most of the time and there's always someone watching it."

"I don't tink dat will be a problem," whispered back Hütchen.

"Great," whispered Adele. "What's the plan?"

The kobold gestured. "I tink Starski has one."

Adele looked. A diminutive figure in a natty hat and cape trotted across the bare lawn toward the guard at the gate. "You *think* she has a plan?"

"Den again, maybe not," admitted Hütchen. "Dat Starski, she *shooten from das Hip.*"

Adele groaned. It was too late to call the little creature back without revealing their location. All she could do was watch and listen.

Starski planted herself in front of the guard, arms akimbo. In the still air, her words carried crisply. "Hey, *Schweinface!*"

The guard looked up. He looked around. He scratched his head. Starski kicked him in the shins. He yelped and bent to clutch his leg. Starski whipped her dagger out of its sheath and held its tip to his nose. "'Scuse me," she said sweetly. "I tink you are on my property."

The guard stared at the small but very sharp dagger pricking the end of his nose, and the small but very angry kobold holding it. His next words proved that whatever else he was, the guard was no fool.

"What do you want?"

Starski's eyes glinted. "Dat's some honker you got dere. Mind if I call you *Lumpenschnoz?*"

"I'd rather you didn't."

"Okey-dokey, *Fungusface,*" said Starski cheerfully. "Here's what I want, den. I want you to step aside an' let me and my family back into *das Frözenshaften.* Tink you can do dat?"

"No," said the guard. "Count Wilhelm Scream and Princess Abattoir would kill me."

"Dat," said Starski, "was de wrong answer." She slashed his belt with her dagger. The guard's pants dropped around his ankles. He grabbed them. Starski shoved him. He fell. She jumped onto his chest.

The guard flailed. "I'll never open that gate."

"Hokay," said Starski.

The hasp from the gate clunked to the ground in pieces. Herschel Wulfgrim pushed the doors open, spitting shards of metal. "You guys take de scenic route or what?"

"Nice work, Herschel." Starski threw back her head and shouted, *"Gai kakhen af en Yam!"*

"Gai kakhen af en Yam!" roared the kobolds. A blue and red horde poured from the forest. Some carried swords, others pickaxes. Many clenched daggers in their teeth. They swarmed through the open gate.

"My Starski, she is a bit of a potty mouth," said Hütchen proudly to Adele. "Whatcha waitin' fer?" And he joined the throng.

Adele bounded through the gateway with her crutch. The camp was engulfed. The cheerful sprites of the evening before bore no resemblance to this whirlwind of terrifying creatures with glittering eyes and sharp teeth. Guards collapsed under the onslaught. Kobolds whizzed onto rooftops and down chimneys into the prisoners' barracks. A group of men in miners' uniforms tumbled out. Some swatted at the blue mites on their shoulders. One, a tall redhead, tried to pull his boot away from a kobold who wanted to keep it as a souvenir.

"Kale!" screamed Adele.

She ran into his arms.

43

No one seeing Princess Abattoir would have recognized in her the young girl kneeling before Count Wilhelm Scream all those years before. Whereas Prissy Anders had been uncultured and awkward, Princess Abattoir was elegant and refined. Prissy had torn, ill-fitting clothes. Princess Abattoir wore gowns of flowing silk. Prissy had been spontaneous; Princess Abattoir was cunning. The only thing they shared was an ever-present anger, but even this had refined over the years as Prissy's impulsive rage had transformed into Princess Abattoir's icy cruelty.

Guthrum Danegeld knew none of this. The princess had summoned him to her office to report on his mission, as she often did. The troll was perhaps not the most brilliant intellectual light in the Inglenook firmament, but he could speak words of more than three syllables, if given time and perhaps a little coaching; and his memory was good. Thus he was valuable to the princess, for his reports were accurate, and unadorned by suppositions.

The princess sat at her desk. "Did you catch the fidelius bird that's been stealing my sparkleberries?"

"Yes, your Highness," said the troll.

"Bring it to me."

"No, your Highness."

The princess was not used to being denied. Her eyes snapped. "And why not?"

"It escaped."

"How?"

"I do not know, your Highness," said Guthrum Danegeld. "When I asked Captain Dwop, he told me to shut my pie hole."

Princess Abattoir tapped her fingers on her desktop. "Why would he say that?"

"He was angry because the prisoners escaped."

Princess Abattoir jerked upright. "Prisoners?"

"Yes, your Highness."

"How many? Where are they now?"

"Three, and I do not know."

The princess shut her eyes briefly. "Are you telling me that Captain Dwop caught the fidelius bird and three prisoners?"

"Yes, your Highness."

"And let everyone escape?"

"That is what the patrol told me after Captain Dwop was done shouting and breaking things."

"Would you recognize these prisoners if you saw them again?"

"Yes," said Guthrum. "They are the boys from the Tone-Deaf Troubadour and their friend."

"The what?"

"The tavern where I moonlight because I am a young troll and I do not have to sleep much."

Princess Abattoir looked Guthrum over from head to toe. "What is that object hanging from your belt?"

Guthrum beamed. "That is my brand-new left-handed shillelagh holster. I got it this morning at the Holster Emporium."

"Give it to me."

Guthrum unhooked the holster from his belt and handed it to the princess together with the shillelagh. She ran a pale, manicured finger over the careful stitching and the finely oiled leather. "This is an expensive holster."

"Yes, your Highness," said Guthrum proudly.

The princess put it down on her desk. A suspicion had begun to form in her mind.

Now, it is a strange fact of human nature that people tend to judge others by their own moral standards. Honest people tend to assume others are honest, but dishonest people are generally on the lookout for anyone who would wrong them. Princess Abattoir was Machiavellian, which means she ruled by power and deceit. She was also avaricious, which means greedy. Guthrum Danegeld was not, though he was venal, which means he was willing to be bribed. But in her narrow-mindedness the princess forgot all this and assumed that the troll was just as evil and clever as she was.

"So you met the prisoners at a tavern where you work."

"No, your Highness."

"Do not lie to me."

"No, your Highness."

"Did you meet the prisoners early in the evening?"

"No."

"But you said you did."

"They were not prisoners then."

The princess clenched one lovely fist under the desk. "But you met them?"

"Yes, your Highness."

"Did you speak to them?"

"Yes, your Highness."

"Did you take them to Gloamwoods?"

"No, your Highness. They went by themselves. But I helped capture them because I am a good Special Policeman." He puffed out his chest.

"I see," said the princess. "So you met them in Inglenook and again later the same night in Gloamwoods."

"Yes, your Highness."

"Then they escaped from the Count's Special Police."

"Yes, your Highness."

"And now you have a brand new, very expensive holster."

Guthrum smiled again. "That is right, your Highness."

The princess glared. The troll's smile looked to her like a smirk. She rang a bell on her desk. The door opened and half a dozen goons tromped into the room.

"Guthrum Danegeld, you are under arrest," she said. "Guards, take him to the dungeons. Then bring Captain Dwop to me."

"Adele!" gasped Kale. He crushed his wife in a hug, thrust her at arms' length so he could be sure he had the right woman, and crushed her again.

"Kale!" she cried, hugging and crushing back.

She looked up at him. His red hair was threaded with grey at the temples. She thought it made him look distinguished.

He looked down at her. The corners of her eyes were laced with fine lines. He wished he could have been there as each one appeared.

Wordlessly, they kissed.

"Kale!" cried Bob. "This is it—our break!"

"Now or never!" yelled Jerry.

Kale pulled himself free. "It's fight time," he said to Adele. "Care to join in?"

"More than anything."

As you will probably recall, the men had not been idle during their captivity. When the expert on farming taught his class, they planted secret gardens and grew nourishing food. When the constellations enthusiast taught his class, they memorized the sky so they would be able to walk in a straight line through the woods at night without lanterns. When Kale taught his class on history and rebellion, they made weapons and stashed them under mounds of rock and ice deep in the mines. Now Kale ran to retrieve the armory.

He needn't have bothered. The kobolds had shot down the shaft in great numbers, and were now enthusiastically throwing out everything they didn't like, which was pretty much anything that hadn't been there when they had last seen the place. A geyser of billy clubs, boomerangs, darts, spikes, and other hand-crafted weapons shot from the opening, accompanied by muffled exclamations of, "Wouldja believe what dey done to *das Frözenshaften?*" and "What kind of *Schmendrick* mixes up de ice dis way?"

Kale grabbed a pike. "That was easier than I thought. Charge!"

Adele fought alongside Kale, whacking guards with her crutch. It felt good to do something together as a couple.

Plotz barreled out of his quarters, smacking at his head while a grinning kobold yanked his ears. Plotz grabbed him by the ankles and smashed him against the wall with a sickening clunk. The little body flopped to the ground.

An elderly kobold in a flowered muumuu ran to his side, crying, "Balkan!" Plotz caught hold of her and whirled her over his head like a lasso. She screamed.

Herschel Wulfgrim shot through the crowd in a blur and sank his teeth into Plotz's knee. The bone crunched. Plotz howled and dropped the kobold. She staggered dizzily. Herschel gripped Plotz's leg with both arms and both legs, jaws clamped on the knee, worrying his head and growling like a terrier. Plotz raised his truncheon to smash the little man's skull.

"Don't."

The overseer froze. Bob had thrust a pickaxe into the soft underside of Plotz's jaw. His eyes flashed like broken glass. "Unless you want to make me very, very happy."

Plotz was a man of few virtues. One of them was an instinct for self-preservation. "Drop your weapons, boys," he gasped.

Herschel put his arm around the elderly kobold still weaving in circles. "You hokay, Bubbe?"

"*Ach,* sure." She put her hands on his shoulders to steady herself. "How's Balkan?"

Herschel glanced at the limp form. "Sleepin'."

"Too bad. Balkan love a good fight." She hugged Herschel close. "Nice work, *Boychik.*"

"Tanks." Herschel buried his head in the old lady's shoulder.

Hütchen held the door to the prisoners' barracks while the miners shoved the guards inside.

"The princess will never let you get away with this," sneered Plotz.

"We've managed so far," said Kale.

"Your luck is about to run out."

"What's that mean?"

Plotz only sniggered. Kale locked the door and tossed the key down the mineshaft. "Herschel," he called.

The kobold trotted up to him. "Yah?"

Kale squatted. "I think Plotz is up to something. Can you keep an eye on him?"

"Sure ting."

"Don't let him see you."

"No? 'Cos I was gonna play cards wid him an' have some tea, but if you don' wan' him to *see* me—"

"Please?"

"Chust kiddin'." Almost before Kale could blink, Herschel had swarmed up the side of the building and zipped down the chimney.

Adele shaded her eyes to watch him. "Friend of yours?"

"One of the best."

Kale asked two kobolds to watch the barracks so no one escaped. They were happy to oblige, especially once he explained that it was the guards who were responsible for some of the more appalling decorating choices in the depths of *das Frözenshaften.*

"No worries about dem," said a bright blue kobold named Mandrake. "We only letten dem out if we want some target practice, yah?"

"Or fer playin soccer wid der heads," suggested another named Walther.

"Just keep them inside, please," said Kale.

"But kobolds is wicked fond of soccer," groused Walther.

"Tell you what," said Kale. "If these men are safe and sound when I get back, I'll bring you the best soccer ball I can find."

Mandrake rubbed his chin. "Dat is schweeten de deal," he admitted.

"And some wurst," said Adele.

"And wurst," agreed Kale. "Deal?"

The kobolds cheered and threw their hats in the air. Adele would have given at least even odds that the guards would survive the day.

Kale and Adele walked past the mineshaft, which was still spewing intermittent bursts of weaponry and mining equipment. They held hands, one calloused palm against another. Kale smiled at her and asked his first question.

"How?"

Adele explained about the marshmallow attack and her sojourn in the infirmary, her flight through the woods and the help from the kobolds. "I could see the mines," she said. "I even saw you yesterday. I thought I would shatter into a million broken pieces, you were so close."

"Oh, my darling." Kale hugged her again. When they emerged, he asked his second question. "Now what?"

"We have two options. Fight or flight."

"Flight," said Kale. "We've memorized the woods, and I bet we could get to Inglenook from here. I've heard there are secret passageways under the walls."

"Fight," said Adele. "If the count or the princess catches us, we're doomed. We only have a chance if we attack them before they know we're free."

"She's right," said Jerry, tucking a guard's truncheon into his belt.

"The princess would rip your guts out and tie up her hair with them," said Bob, his rusty pickaxe on one shoulder.

"Not a metaphor," said Jerry.

"This is the time to strike," said Bob. "They'll discover your escape pretty soon, if they haven't already. They'll look here. We can't afford to stay."

Adele blinked. "We?"

"We're pretty sick of this place," said Jerry. "Confidentially."

"What he means," said Bob, "is that we're coming too." He gestured at the crowd around them. Each miner had a glint in his eye and a set to his jaw; each gripped a weapon; and Adele saw that what she had taken for a group of exhausted, defeated prisoners was in fact a well-armed militia thirsting for its next victory.

"Goodness," she said.

Kale beamed. "Do I have the best co-conspirators or what?"

"I guess you do."

"All righty." Kale rubbed his hands together. Adele saw that after so many years in the mines they were scarred, and webbed with cracks and dirt. "Ready to storm the castle?"

"With you, I'd storm a thousand castles," she said. "And as soon as this is over, we're going to get off this stupid mountain, go home—"

"—and find the boys," said Kale. "I know. I can't wait."

45

Wayne Dwop, Captain of the Special Police of Count Wilhelm Scream, staggered into his girlfriend's kitchen and half-collapsed into a chair at the table. He buried his head in his hands and moaned.

"What's the problem, ducky?" said his girlfriend. "Rough night on patrol?"

Dwop lowered his hands. His expression was ragged. "I—was just interrogated by Princess Abattoir."

The girlfriend smirked. "Why?"

"She wanted to know about some prisoners we captured. Get me some coffee."

"Get it yourself."

"Get it for me or I won't tell you how I escaped her wrath."

"Like I need to know," huffed the girlfriend. But she went to the stovetop and handed Dwop a steaming mug. He took a sip and screwed up his face.

"This is even worse than usual."

"If you can't chew it, I didn't brew it," said the girlfriend. She sat down across the rustic wooden table from him, and not for the first time Wayne Dwop mused at her astonishing resemblance to a gargoyle. "So tell me about it. How mad was she?"

Dwop lifted the mug to his lips, remembered the first sip, and put it down. "Terrifying. Somehow she found out about a couple of kids and their friend we caught near the slough. Said it's my fault they escaped. Said one of my men signed a confession saying I was guilty."

The gargoyle took a sip of her coffee. "What were they, poachers?"

"Dunno. But my life wouldn't be worth a stuffed swamp slug if she thought I was to blame for their escape."

The gargoyle burst out laughing. "You are so dramatic," she chortled. "Look at you, all shaking like an undercooked egg."

Dwop scowled. It was at times like these he wished he had a few more options, girlfriend-wise. But since his job kept him close to the castle or tromping through Gloamwoods most of the time, his pickings were necessarily slim. "I fooled Princess Abattoir," he said. "How many people can say that?"

"Are you sure?"

"Of course I'm sure."

"Of course you are." She smiled into her coffee.

Dwop frowned. He tapped the table. He tilted his mug to watch the coffee ooze to one side. "She's had it in for me from the start."

"So you've mentioned."

"If she thought I'd done something—but she'll never know."

"She knows," said the gargoyle.

"No, she doesn't."

"Yes, she does." The gargoyle took another sip. "Unlike you, she's no fool."

Dwop forgot to be angry. His hands felt cold, and he was sick inside. "What do you mean?"

"This officer of yours signed a statement?"

"Yes. She said."

"Which one?"

"Guthrum Danegeld."

The gargoyle threw back her head and laughed. "You are such an idiot."

Dwop slammed his hand down on the table. "I won't be talked to that way."

"Yes, you will." She paused, carefully wiping tears of laughter from her cardboard eyelashes. "Danegeld is a troll. Trolls don't write. He never signed a confession. She lied to you to get you to talk." She laughed again. "Oldest trick in the book. Still works on some people."

"It didn't work on me," shouted Dwop. "I said he was lying."

"Did he, ducks? Did the troll lie?"

"I don't know."

"But you did. You lied about him to protect yourself."

"I had to."

"Of course you did," she said. "What happened to him when you lied?"

"I don't know."

"Don't you?"

Dwop scowled. "She had him put away."

"So where is he while you're here enjoying your coffee?"

"I'm not enjoying it." Dwop felt this point was worth clarifying. "He's probably in the dungeon."

"How brave of you."

"It was him or me."

"And what's a captain for, after all, if not to look after his officers?"

"My loyalty lies with Count Wilhelm Scream."

"Naturally," she simpered. "What else did you lie about?"

"For your information," snapped Dwop, "I lied about the entire situation. I said there never were any prisoners."

"Tidy."

"It was better than saying they got away from me, you stupid—"

The gargoyle put a hand on his sleeve. "Now, ducks, let's not get too excited. I'm sure you did your best. Would you like a muffin?"

Dwop sighed and settled back in his chair. He didn't have much experience with people being kind to him, but it did seem to him that his girlfriend could have been a bit more consistent. He could never tell whether she loved him but was sometimes nasty, or was nasty but occasionally fed him. "Sure."

The gargoyle put a muffin on a plate and set it on the table. "Nothing like a muffin after a nasty scare like that." Her voice still held a hint of snigger.

Dwop looked up, his mouth full of muffin that was so dry it had exploded to powder as soon as he bit it. Even the raisins were dusty. "If I'm lucky she'll keep believing me and execute the toll." He swallowed with great effort. "I'll just have to keep my nose clean from now on."

"Of course."

"Work extra hard."

"That's my man."

"Prove myself to her in every way."

"So she believes you the next time you lie."

"Exactly."

The gargoyle took a sip of her coffee. "Did you ever think, my poor handsome fool, that it's really not that complicated?"

"What do you mean?"

"I mean skip the lying. Why tell her anything at all?"

"I didn't. She asked me." He shuddered. "Over and over again."

The gargoyle smiled a self-satisfied one. "That's the difference between you and me, ducks."

"What is? Other than the fact that I know the difference between coffee and tar."

The gargoyle giggled girlishly. "I don't get caught."

Dwop frowned. "What do you mean?"

"Just that." She took another sip. "Unlike some people, I don't get caught."

"I didn't get caught."

"You, ducky, got interrogated by Princess Abattoir. That's caught if you ask me."

"She believed me. She arrested the troll."

"This time."

"Fine," snapped Dwop. "What makes you so—so special and uncatchable?"

"Nothing," smiled his gargoyle. "Ever."

"What's that supposed to mean?"

"It means there's nothing to report and nothing to get caught for."

"Great." Dwop cradled the mug of coffee in his hands. It was safer than drinking it. "Nothing ever happens to you, so you don't get in trouble. Very nice, I'm sure. But when you're in my position—"

"I am in your position, you idiot. I had a prisoner just last night."

Dwop set his mug down. "What do you mean, you *had* a prisoner?"

"Just what I said. A mill worker came in with an injury. Last night she was in her room and this morning she wasn't."

"She escaped?"

"I certainly didn't tell her she could leave, ducks."

Dwop gaped at her. "You had an escape and didn't report it?"

"What's to report?" She shrugged. "I had the guards transferred to other stations. I doubt any of them will remember her anyway. You know trolls. And when her overseer comes for her I'll say she was sent back ages ago. That overseer looks like a potato and thinks like one too. But she won't dare admit she's wrong. As soon as I'm done with my coffee I'll clean up the mess my little escapee left by the window, and we're all set." Her teeth flashed briefly in a grin of satisfaction before she took another sip of coffee.

Dwop walked to the sink. His coffee made belching noises as he poured it down the drain. He set the empty mug on the counter and turned to face his girlfriend, his arms folded across his chest.

"So," he said, and his voice was thick with emotion, "you had a prisoner escape from the rightful custody of Count Wilhelm

Scream and her Magnificence, Princess Abattoir, and you didn't tell anyone."

"My goodness, ducky, you sound like a propaganda leaflet all of a sudden."

Dwop took a step forward. "Do you know how valuable this information is?"

"Of course. That's why I didn't tell anyone."

Dwop grabbed her by the elbows, lifting her to her feet. Her chair screeched backwards. Her mug fell to the tabletop and spun in a circle, spilling lumps of coffee. The gargoyle screamed, but Captain Dwop of the Special Police only held her tighter. He grinned into her ugly, terrified face.

"Princess Abattoir will reward me handsomely for this, you traitor."

Count Wilhelm Scream watched as Princess Abattoir dropped a deep curtsey. "Your Grace," she said.

The count prized two things in life: Princess Abattoir, and the throne where he now sat. The throne enabled his rule within Castle Mirkstone; the princess gave him power without. It was, he felt, a good system. "What have you for me today, Princess?"

The Princess presented a long, flat, leather object. The count took it in his gloved hands, turning it over for inspection.

"It's a left-handed shillelagh holster," said Princess Abattoir.

"I can see that," snapped the count, who in fact had not. He did not know a shillelagh from a shellacking, and they both knew it.

"I took it from one of your Special Police, a troll named Guthrum Danegeld. I sensed you would find its presence as disturbing as I do."

"Continue."

"Your Beneficence is of course far too wise and thrifty to overpay the Special Police," said Princess Abattoir. "The troll could not afford such an extravagance on his salary. I was immediately suspicious and asked him how he procured it. He said he extorted gold from two hapless travelers."

"Well done."

"Yes, your Beneficence. However, the travelers may not have been as hapless as reported."

"No?"

"Danegeld is moonlighting as a bouncer in a tavern in Inglenook. It was there he first encountered these supposed travelers, along with a confederate. The next time he saw them, they had breached the walls of the town and were deep in Gloamwoods. By this time the troll had assumed his station with your Beneficence's Special Police, and he assisted in their capture and interrogation, as well as that of their companion from the tavern. Last night the ruffians somehow effected an escape."

"And in the process the troll acquired enough gold to afford a custom-made holster."

"Exactly, your Beneficence."

"Did you corroborate his story with his commanding officer?"

"Captain Dwop assures me he has never had a prisoner escape from him, much less three, and that his men were out hunting fidelius birds as per my orders, not looking for trespassers."

Count Wilhelm Scream ran a finger down the fine-grained leather of the left-handed shillelagh holster. "It appears Mr. Danegeld is being less than honest."

"Yes, your Grace."

"He certainly came into extra money by some means."

"Yes, your Tactfulness."

The count frowned. "Perhaps he encountered a group of subversives who let him know they wished safe passage through Gloamwoods, and agreed to help them for a price."

"It is far more believable than his version of events, your Beneficence."

"As soon as he had their gold, he abandoned them to their fate."

"Yes, your Cleverness."

"Where is the troll now?"

"In a cell beneath your throne."

"How far below?"

"Several stories."

"Have him shot."

"Yes, your Beneficence." The princess's beautiful face was like a mask, but her dark eyes gleamed as black as the ice of the count's throne. "But I fear there may be more to the story."

"The travelers?"

"Yes, your Grace. We don't know what happened to them."

"Devoured by swamp plants or werewolves, most likely."

"One hopes, your Charmingness. But I fear they may be the vanguard of an invading force."

"Why?"

"Your Beneficence may be aware that among your Beneficence's prisoners are some who harbor resentment against your person."

"Prisoners can get awfully cranky," admitted the count.

"Exactly. So the missing travelers may be spies or scouts intending to connect with co-conspirators."

"What co-conspirators?"

"I suspect the group called the Ascendant Defenders. They have had the longest to plan a rebellion."

The count rubbed his chin and thought about the years the rebels had been in his prisons—longer than anyone else, with no hope of release.

The princess continued. "Just yesterday I received word from Overseer Plotz that we have enough ice for our purposes. Perhaps spies intercepted the message."

The count straightened. "The project is top secret."

"Of course. But every time that dragon lays an egg she makes those horrid noises, and colored smoke bursts out the tower windows."

"How many eggs has she laid?"

"Half a dozen, your Benefaction."

"Half a dozen times she announced her presence," mused the count.

"Exactly."

"Princess, you may once again have uncovered a threat to our order and stability."

"Thank you, sire. But yes—we could be set upon by foes within and without. The danger rises like a foul tide. It is best to eliminate your enemies immediately."

"How would you proceed?"

The door at the end of the chamber burst open. Captain Dwop of the Special Police stormed in, dragging a gargoyle of a nurse. She was crying and shaking all over, and her false eyelashes clung damply to her cheeks.

"Tell them," roared Captain Dwop. "Perhaps the count will be merciful."

He shoved her. She fell to her knees, wailing and wringing her hands. The princess grabbed the nurse's hair, yanking it back so the wretched woman had to look up. "Speak," she snarled. "What have you done?"

"It's not my fault," howled the nurse. "She was up in the tower—the room was guarded—how could I know she would escape?"

"Who?" The princess shook the nurse's head.

"A prisoner from the Food Mills, your Majesty," said Captain Dwop, for the nurse was gargling incoherently. "She broke a window and slid down her sheets."

The princess dropped the nurse's hair. The woman fell on her face. "Please," she moaned. "Have mercy."

"Have her shot too," said the count, who had a short list of solutions to his problems. Captain Dwop barked a command. Two Special Police tramped in. They hooked the gargoyle under her arms and trotted briskly out the door as she yowled and kicked.

"More of the spies' plot?" said Count Scream as the door slammed shut.

"I fear so, your Beneficence," said Princess Abattoir. "May I suggest a course of action?"

The count tented his fingers. Captain Dwop leaned in eagerly.

"The captain and I will take a platoon to the infirmary," said Princess Abattoir. "Perhaps some of her friends are still there. If so, we will deal with them. From there we proceed to the Ice Mines and have the prisoners load the Black Ice for transport. Any who survive we bring here to put the ice in the dragon's tower. In the meantime, your Efficiency should, if I may be so bold, summon the rest of the rebels so we can execute the lot of them."

The count sighed deeply, for the prospect of so much bloodshed pained him. Still, he could always get new prisoners. "Very well. And arrest more people as a show of power."

"It will be my pleasure." The princess smiled. Not for the first time, the count thought that if he were to kiss those perfect, red lips, he would die of poison.

It is astonishing how restorative even a few hours of sleep can be. When the boys emerged from their debris huts, everything seemed bright and merry.

"You have leaves in your hair," chortled Casper as he put on his nearly dry socks, which were warm from their stay in his underarms.

"You have dirt on your face," grinned Jasper as he tied his shoelaces.

"Are you disguising yourself as a tree to slip past the castle guards?"

"Maybe your mud mask will do the trick instead."

They broke down their huts and scattered the debris. For breakfast they devoured the last of the swamp berries, and drank water from the stream.

"When we get back to the shop," said Casper, "I plan to plunge headfirst into the pastry display and chew my way from one end to the other."

"Not if I get there ahead of you," said Jasper.

Casper frowned. "Jasper. We are brothers. Oughtn't we to do this thing together?"

"Oh, very well. We'll both dive in, and I'll meet you in the middle." Jasper shrugged his backpack onto his shoulders. "Ready?"

"Set."

"Go."

When they had got their bearings from the arrow in the dirt, Casper scuffed it out with his foot. Jasper ground dust into the scratches they had made in the tree. "After you," said Casper politely; and with Jasper leading the way, they trudged into the forest, hoping they were headed for something, anything that could lead them to their parents. They walked as briskly as they could while trying to be noiseless, which, as we have already established, is impossible in the woods. Even mice and squirrels can't manage it, and this stuff about stepping on the blade of your foot and rolling it so as not to rustle the leaves is nonsense. Casper and Jasper knew this, but they also knew better than to talk; so their silence, while imperfect, was as good as they could make it.

Presently they came to a place where trees stopped as though they had been cut down in a wide swath, which is in fact what had happened. The edge of the woodland was thick with tryllions, a woody shrub with thousands of blooms amid pea-green leaves. Casper and Jasper crouched behind one. Before them stood a stone tower encircled by a greensward. Casper grabbed Jasper's arm and pointed. Jasper looked. His eyes widened.

Standing in the doorway of the tower was a troll, sword at his side and crossbow in hand. His armband bore the insignia of Count Wilhelm Scream. He was looking the other way.

The boys slipped around to the far side of the tower. It was sheer rock, broken occasionally by barred windows, but there were no doorways and no guards. Casper put his mouth close to Jasper's ear. "That was close."

"Too close." Jasper squinted up the tower. Keeping his voice low, he said, "What's that?"

Casper looked. A high window was broken, and from its bars hung what looked like a long kite's tail made up of lengths of cloth tied together. It reached almost to the ground.

"Shall we?" said Jasper.

"Why?" said Casper.

"Better view than any tree. We might be able to see the castle or the mines or the mills or, oh, I don't know, our parents, if they're still alive and we can recognize them from a distance. We're getting nowhere down here."

"Will it hold us?"

"There's no flattened corpse below it," said Jasper. "If it held whoever made it, it should hold us."

"Your logic is impregnable," said Casper. "Let's hope the same can't be said of yonder tower."

"I wonder if it's a dolorous tower," said Jasper as they walked forward.

"I hope there's no one needing a rescue," said Casper. "We're in a bit of a rush."

"That's what you think," said a cold voice.

Casper and Jasper whirled around. For the second time in two days, they were at the center of a circle of toughs with leveled weapons. A beautiful woman with dark hair and angry eyes stepped forward.

The boys did not need to be told who she was. They had seen her likeness every day of their lives: on commemorative coins bearing her exquisite profile; in life-sized portraits lining the walls of their school; and on monuments in every town and city they had ever known. They had never wished to meet her in person, and could not help thinking that now was a particularly inopportune time to do so.

"I arrest you in the name of Count Wilhelm Scream," said Princess Abattoir. "You will tell me everything you know about the rebellion."

"Bind them," ordered the princess. Two eager Special Police stepped toward Casper and Jasper, who were standing with their hands above their heads.

It was at that moment that each noticed something. Casper noticed a glimpse of white in the woods.

Now, many things in the woods are white. Deer tails are white, and deer flash them when they run because if anyone is chasing them, the bouncing flag of a tail confuses the predator. It is hard to follow visually. Rabbits' tails are white for the same reason. Certain birds, such as flickers, flash white parts of their bodies when they fly, and of course there are all sorts of white or pale flowers and plants in your average forest. But what Casper saw was not a plant or an optically confusing part of a middle-of-the-food-chain prey species. It was a shock of white hair so fine that it floated with every breeze, and it was located directly over a pair of pink eyes peering out at him from a tryllion shrub.

Casper wished he could create a diversion.

"Why, Captain Dwop," said Jasper in delight. "How lovely to see you again."

For this is what Jasper had noticed: the captain, who was not one of the eager Special Police to have stepped forward, was hanging in the background, rocking on his heels and studying the sky while whistling a nonchalant tune. Princess Abattoir looked at him in momentary confusion.

"Don't tell me that's you," said Casper as an officer pulled off his backpack and chained his hands. "Good heavens, you don't look a day older than when we last met."

"Though he is, when you think about it," said Jasper as another did the same to him.

"I count half a day."

"I suppose it was just last night, when you get right down to it."

"We're none of us as young as we used to be," said Casper. "Remember third grade?"

"Those were the days."

Princess Abattoir's bewilderment turned to rage. Most of her moods turned to rage fairly quickly. "Captain Dwop. Who are these two?"

"No idea," said Dwop.

"Captain," said Casper reproachfully. "After all we've meant to each other."

The princess glared. "Are these the prisoners you say you did not capture yesterday?"

"Ah." Captain Dwop drew a pattern in the dirt with the tip of his hobnailed boot. "About that."

"Did they escape from you?"

"Of course not," said Dwop, shocked.

"We most certainly did," shouted Casper. He decided to risk her wrath, because as she stepped closer to Captain Dwop she was also stepping closer to the tryllion shrub. The Special Police officer holding Casper whomped him in the gut with his truncheon. Casper fell, the wind knocked out of him. The pink eyes in the shrub disappeared.

Princess Abattoir swept down on Casper like a hawk. She gripped his chin, forcing his head up so he had to look her in the face. "Did this man arrest you?"

"Yes," said Casper in a strangled voice, because having your head held by the chin after being sucker punched makes it surprisingly difficult to speak.

"Did you escape?"

"Obviously."

The princess kicked Casper in the chest. He fell, his body curled up with his face on his knees. She whipped on Jasper. "How did you escape?"

"Captain Dwop fell asleep." Jasper stole a sideways glance at his brother. Casper lay on the ground, his mouth opening and shutting.

The princess whirled back to Captain Dwop, who had developed an acute interest in his shoelaces. When she spoke, her voice sang like a blade in battle.

"You allowed enemies of the state to escape."

Dwop's shoulders quaked. "Yes, your Highness."

"You lied to me, Princess Abattoir."

"Yes, your Highness," bleated Captain Dwop.

Princess Abattoir gazed at him with disgust. "Bind him as well." She pointed to a thug. "You there."

The thug stepped forward, trying not to look terrified. "Yes, your Highness."

"What is your name?"

"Officer Jacques Boute, your Highness."

"You are now Captain Boute. Take half the unit to the Ice Mines. Have the prisoners load the ice. Bring it and any survivors to Castle Mirkstone."

"Yes, your Highness."

Princess Abattoir stepped close to him, something wild and barely restrained in her eyes. "That ice must arrive today, Captain. *Today.*"

"Yes, your Highness."

"The count does not accept failure. Neither do I."

Jacques Boute, who had woken up that day not knowing that before noon he would be a captain, gulped. "I am your obedient servant."

"Then shut up and get to the mines." She turned to the patrol. "Forward to the castle. The count has ways to deal with traitors and villains."

Captain Boute did not hesitate. "All odd-numbered officers, follow me!" He and half the patrol tromped into the woods.

A Special Policeman chained Captain Dwop's hands behind his back. Another heaved Casper to his feet. The boy looked pale and sick. Jasper tried to smile encouragingly at him, but found he could not.

The princess and the remaining Special Police marched the prisoners toward the castle, past a tryllion shrub that trembled at their heavy steps.

Kale flung open the doors to the prison garage, revealing a rugged little military vehicle emblazoned with the insignia of Count Wilhelm Scream. It blinked at him and hiccupped.

"Not that thing," moaned Jerry. "It gets lost even when it's not drunk."

"You've seen it not drunk?" said Bob.

"It's what we have," said Kale. He wiped his eyes, which were watering from the vehicle's boozy fumes. "Hey, are you sober?"

"How dare you, sirrah?" roared the vehicle. "Such vile aspersions will not go unanswered."

"I think that means no," said Bob.

"Quite," agreed the vehicle. "Now shove off. The fewer men, the greater share of sherry."

Bob tugged Kale's sleeve. "Call him Colonel. Tell him there's a secret mission."

"Bob, be serious."

"I am. Plotz does it." Bob saluted crisply and addressed the vehicle. "Sir, his Excellency the Count needs you for a covert assignment."

The car perked up. "Does he, old bean?"

"We are at war, Colonel. Didn't you hear the battle just now?"

"I was resting," said the Colonel with dignity.

"Resting?" cried Bob. "Heard you not the clash of arms calling you to honor and glory? Heard you not the valiant cry, 'We shall fight in the mines, we shall fight in Gloamwoods, we shall fight in the hills, we shall never surrender'?"

The Colonel shook with excitement. "V for victory!" it shouted. "Stiffen the sinews to the sticking place and let sound your barbaric yawp, what? What? Motor vehicles never, never, never shall be slaves!"

"That's the spirit," yelled Bob. "For Scream and Abattoir! For Cypher Mendatius!"

The Colonel, who had just begun to explain that loose lips sink ships, snapped to attention. "At your service. Huzzah!"

"Thanks," muttered Kale. Quickly he selected four erstwhile prisoners to head to Middlemost to find sympathizers. They rifled the guards' quarters and pulled on uniforms. They didn't fit very well, and the men were covered with grime from years of mining. Everyone hoped the resemblance was passable.

"Bit of a sticky wicket, what?" bellowed the Colonel as they climbed in.

"Just stay on the road," begged Norbert from Nether Wallop. He was in the driver's seat and had just discovered that the steering wheel seemed to be entirely for show, since it certainly didn't have any effect on where the Colonel went.

"Absolutely, by Jove." The Colonel let out an enormous backfire and sped out of the camp in a spew of dust. "Some talk of Alexander, and some of Hercules—"

"Left," called the driver.

"Of Hector and Lysander, what? And such great names as these—"

"Left!"

The voices were growing fainter.

"But of all the world's great heroes—"

"*Leeeeeeeeeeeeeefffffft!*"

Kale and his friends looked at each other as the vehicle disappeared into Gloamwoods.

"They'll be fine," said Kale firmly. "Really. Just fine."

"What next?" said Jerry.

"We'll stick to the woods," said Kale, glancing at Adele's burlap nightgown and the miners' prison uniforms. "When we get near Mirkstone we'll lay low till reinforcements come. Meantime, we'll analyze the castle's weaknesses. Every place has them."

It was a good plan, and they picked their way through the trees with care. So it was just unfortunate that they were headed downhill at the exact moment that Princess Abattoir and her Special Police were headed uphill. At first, both groups thought it was an ambush.

"Rebels!" shouted Princess Abattoir. "Seize them!"

"Police!" shouted Kale. "Run!"

It wasn't much of a contest. The miners were hopelessly outnumbered, and it was their second battle of the day. By contrast, the Special Police were fresh and perky. They were also scared stiff of Princess Abattoir, who did not suffer defeats philosophically. They spread out. They beat the bushes. In short order the prisoners were kneeling in the dirt before the Princess, stripped of their weapons, hands on their heads.

Princess Abattoir stood over Casper and Jasper, who had watched the proceedings in helpless horror. Her eyes gleamed. "I was right. You *were* part of an advance guard. You *were* going to meet your confederates and rebel against the just and lawful rule of Count Scream."

"That's what I thought too," called Captain Dwop from the back of the crowd.

"Oh, shut him up, someone," said Princess Abattoir. A troll obligingly cuffed Captain Dwop on the side of the head. He fell to the ground with his feet twitching. Princess Abattoir pointed at the kneeling prisoners. "How did you contact them? Speak."

Casper swallowed. "I'm afraid you've got it all wrong."

"We've never seen these people before in our lives," said Jasper.

"Do you expect me to believe that?"

"'Expect' is perhaps too strong a term," said Casper.

"'Hope' is more like it," said Jasper.

"We've been marvelously lucky so far."

"That we have."

"Quiet," snarled the princess. She stood uncomfortably close, so they could see the icy perfection of her skin and the bleak mirrors of her eyes. Her breath smelled like sleet. "You have conspired with this sleeper cell."

"No, honestly, we haven't," said Casper.

"We're not that organized," said Jasper. "Just ask our teachers."

"We don't even know what a sleeper cell is," said Casper. "At least I don't. Do you?"

"No," said Jasper. "Could you explain it to us?"

The princess gnashed her pearly teeth. "A sleeper cell," she snarled, "is a group pretending to be innocent people, sometimes for years at a time, until they receive a signal to strike."

Casper brightened. "And you think we're the signal."

"I *know* you are."

"Seems unlikely," said Jasper. He gestured with his elbow, since his hands were chained behind his back. "Aren't they in prison uniforms? So they don't look terribly innocent to me."

"This one is not," called a troll. He poked one of the kneeling figures with his truncheon.

"Stand him up," ordered Princess Abattoir, striding over for a closer look.

The troll officer yanked the figure upright. Casper and Jasper stifled gasps.

White hair wafting around her head, eyes glaring red, Bunny stood nose to nose with Princess Abattoir.

50

Jacques Boute expected to see guards patrolling the Ice Mines and prisoners attending fearfully to their tasks amid the hum and hiss of machinery. He did not expect to see the camp empty and silent with the masticated remains of a lock littering the ground by a wide-open gate.

The place was, of course, teeming with kobolds; but most of them were in the mineshaft figuring out color schemes so their new curtains would complement the carpets but not be too matchy-matchy, yah? As for Mandrake and Walther, they had spotted a mostly intact set of manticore ribs half-buried behind the camp that worked so perfectly as a goal net that they had abandoned their post and were engaged in a celebratory game of soccer. Boute mistook their cheers for the trills of woodland birds.

Like everyone else his age and younger in the Lands of Yonder, the captain had been trained in the League of the Crocodile. His specialty was tracking. He examined the ground. Footprints patterned the dust. The majority were from boots. Many were oddly small. Most converged on the prisoners' barracks.

Boute signaled silence. He and his patrol drew their weapons and arranged themselves on either side of the barracks door. At a nod from Boute, a troll punched it in and they tumbled through the splintery opening.

"Aiiiiii," screamed Plotz from the floor where he had been resting his mangled knee.

Boute heaved Plotz to his feet. "Where are the prisoners?"

"Beats me," gasped Plotz. "They headed out and left the little blue guys at the door singing drinking songs."

"What?"

"In two-part harmony," babbled Plotz. "For *hours.*"

Swiftly, Boute latched on to the single fact that mattered. "They're *gone?*"

"We were attacked. They have teeth."

Terror churned in Captain Boute's gut. He knew how Princess Abattoir felt about escaped prisoners. How would she feel about an entire escaped prison camp?

"Patrol, divide into three groups," he barked. "Two search the woods for escapees. Report back in an hour. Last group, stay here." As two-thirds of his men thudded out, he pulled Plotz closer. "Load the Black Ice into the carts, all of you. You're going to Castle Mirkstone to report to Princess Abattoir and Count Scream."

Plotz's face went slack with terror. "Please, no. They'll kill me."

"Probably," said Boute. "Now load that ice."

Numbly, Plotz and his men pulled on gloves and unlocked the door to the storehouse. A wave of burning cold rolled out. They groaned and bent to the terrifying task they had so often forced upon their prisoners.

High above the barracks, Herschel Wulfgrim popped out of the chimney and onto the ridgepole. From there he and Bubbe had a clear view of Mandrake and Walther's soccer game.

"De game is tied," said Bubbe contentedly. "Who you rootin' for?"

"*Ach,* nobody. I gots to warn de guys."

"Not stayin', den?"

"Kale is my friend."

"He seem like a nice boy," admitted Bubbe. "Chust be back for supper, yah? I is gonna make borscht wid Rainbow Ice garnish."

"Nuttin' better dan Bubbe's borscht." Herschel whisked down the drainpipe and over to the warehouse.

The guards loading the carts shook with cold. Their breath rasped, and jagged pains shot up their arms whenever their gloved hands touched the Black Ice. So they never noticed a little blue figure slip into the lead cart and cover himself with the frosty, black lumps.

I bet you are wondering how Bunny got captured.

Having released Casper and Jasper from the tree they were tied to, and having told them in unambiguous terms to go home and pursue her no further, Bunny took off. However, like anyone who had known the twins for more than about five minutes, she suspected they might not follow instructions. Her worries proved well-founded when, moments later, she heard Captain Dwop sound the alarm. The woods exploded with troops thundering through the underbrush. Bunny ran, clutching her vest to keep the tools from clanging.

Later that night, having found shelter in a hole under a tree, she considered her options. With the Special Police hunting escaped prisoners, the fidelius birds were safe for the moment, but Bunny could not say the same for herself. No one could live in Gloamwoods for long, with its panoply of monsters, swamplands, and deadly frozen clearings. Plus, the Special Police would eventually remember her. Ultimately, there was no protection for her, or the birds, or Casper and Jasper—unless someone stopped Princess Abattoir and Count Wilhelm Scream.

With a deep breath, Bunny faced the truth. She would have to do the very thing she had told the boys was impossible: go to Castle Mirkstone and confound the two villains.

Bunny was tired of waiting for the right moment. Instead, she would make the moment right.

She did not know if she was the right person for the job. But no one else seemed willing to take it on; so as the moon spilled its silver light across the opening of the hole, Bunny curled into a ball and slept, determined to find the castle in the morning.

She awoke at dawn. As she made her way around the swamp and through the woods and up the mountain and ever closer to Mirkstone, she kept an eye out for the boys. Eventually she found herself at the infirmary. It was part of Count Scream's mountain compound, though it was some distance from the castle. This was by design: the count felt that infirmaries were for sick people, and sick people often turned into dead people, in which case he wanted them downwind.

Like Casper and Jasper, Bunny saw the makeshift rope hanging from the tower window, and it occurred to her that if she climbed it she might be able to see any approaching Special Police. She had just decided to do so when the boys walked out of the woods; and so, cursing volubly but inwardly, she hid in the tryllion bush. She hoped Casper and Jasper would not see her. She hoped that if one of them climbed the rope and reported on what he had seen, she might be able to hear. And she hoped most fervently that none of the forces at the command of Count Wilhelm Scream would choose that morning to do a sweep of the infirmary or its environs.

Bunny was not lucky that day.

When the boys were captured, Bunny cursed a bit more. She thought about the Inglenook Sweet Shoppe. She thought about singing forbidden songs with the boys, and smiling at their jokes. She decided to follow them. Besides, the Special Police were going to Mirkstone. Perhaps she could remain unseen and enter with them. So she kept herself at what she hoped was a safe distance, her heart pounding every time she spotted Princess Abattoir's perfectly coiffed, gleaming hair or a flick of her manicured hand.

When the Special Police and the runaway miners encountered each other, Bunny was naturally among those captured. The troll who caught her was named Herkimer Grunt, and he had only entered the count's employ because his aunt pressured him into it, but that is not important to the story. What is important is that Bunny now faced the person she hated most in the world.

"Who are you?" said Princess Abattoir.

"No one you'd care about," snapped Bunny. All the fear seemed to have burned out of her.

"Bring Dwop over here," ordered Princess Abattoir.

The troll who had smacked the captain dragged him through the leaves by his collar and propped him up before the princess. It is very difficult to look dignified when your hands are chained behind you and your jacket is pulled up to your ears and your bottom is covered with leaves and twigs. Dwop did not succeed even remotely.

The princess gestured at Bunny. Her fingers were white, and her nails were blood red. "Do you know this creature?"

"No," said the Captain.

"Hah!" said Bunny. "Ask him again."

Princess Abattoir nodded to the troll. He punched the Captain on the side of his head. Captain Dwop toppled to the ground like a felled tree. Princess Abattoir pointed to Bunny. "Think carefully, Captain. Have you ever seen this...person before?"

"Maybe," gasped Captain Dwop.

"Right before I escaped from him and his unit last night," said Bunny. "But don't blame yourself, Princess. Good help is hard to find."

Princess Abattoir crooked her finger. The Special Police shoved Casper and Jasper forward. "And these?"

"So—difficult to say," gurgled the Captain.

"Because it was dark," chortled Bunny, who seemed to be having the time of her life. "Nope, they got away too. You're losing your edge, Captain."

Princess Abattoir struck Bunny full across the face. Her white hair whipped to one side, and when she straightened up her lip was bleeding. She grinned. "A little to the left," she said. "You missed a spot."

It is very unladylike to stamp your feet and hiss like a basilisk having a temper tantrum, but that is what Princess Abattoir did. "To the castle," she snarled. "We have means for uncovering the truth."

During the march up the mountain, Princess Abattoir had the Special Police keep Bunny close by so she could slap her occasionally. Each time this happened, Bunny smiled. This did nothing to improve the Princess's temper.

Her foul mood infected the troops. The trolls wanted to sing a song of triumph, but the men in the unit complained about being forced to do the high harmonies when the real fun was in the melody, which the trolls always hogged for themselves. Princess Abattoir settled the controversy by announcing that the next person to so much as hum would be executed on the spot. An unhappy silence reigned.

Captain Dwop brought up the rear, escorted by a troll with a truncheon and a gleam in his eye. The captain concentrated on marching.

Near the front, Casper and Jasper stumbled along rocky, root-strewn paths. Their hands were still chained behind their backs, which made balancing difficult. Because the princess still believed that they were part of a conspiracy, the boys were kept separate from everyone else.

The miners had to walk with their hands on their heads, fingers laced together, which is very uncomfortable after a few minutes.

Adele was allowed to keep her crutch because otherwise she would have slowed everyone down. She and Kale managed to stay together. Despite the Special Police's order to look straight ahead, they dared to glance at each other occasionally as they shuffled along the path. The glances said, "Can it be?"

Kale and Adele were astute observers, meaning they noticed things most people did not. This was part of what had helped them survive so many years of captivity. So when Princess Abattoir had brought Casper and Jasper forward for questioning, Kale and Adele had paid attention.

They noticed right away that the boys had red hair.

Kale had red hair. So did Adele.

They noticed that the boys had green eyes.

Kale's eyes were hazel, and Adele's were like emeralds.

Adele noticed that the shape of the boys' chins was exactly like her mother's.

Kale noticed that the boys' noses were exactly like his eccentric uncle Dafydd's.

They both noticed that the boys looked about twelve.

So now, even as they were being led to an audience with Count Wilhelm Scream that was almost certain to end in their deaths, Adele and Kale glowed with a luminous elation that blazed in their hearts and sparked in their eyes. Who cared if they were captured? So what if the count had it in for them? If their boys were alive, miracles could happen.

They chanced another round of secret glances. These said, "If there's an opening, we move." Each nodded in a way that was so slight as to be barely perceptible. Indeed, the Special Police officer who was closest to them missed it entirely, and

one who was a little further away thought they were quaking
with dread.

53

Castle Mirkstone was everything Bunny had said. It was big. It was scary. Its archways bristled with trolls. They lifted the portcullis for Princess Abattoir. She sailed past them with barely an imperious glance, followed by her patrol and the captives.

The prisoners found themselves in Mirkstone's grey, stone courtyard. Overhead hung banners depicting Count Scream's victories over his enemies. Even these were black and grey and earth tones. Smoke reeked from the highest tower, and shadows hung in the corners like bad dreams.

The portcullis slammed down behind them.

At the far end of the enclosure, encircled by Special Police, a crowd of women knelt in chaff-covered overalls. Their heads were bowed, and the air shook with their fear.

The princess pointed to Bunny and Captain Dwop with her salt-white hand. "Take these two inside. Keep the others here." She smiled. "It's a lovely day for an execution."

Captain Dwop paled. "No," he begged. "I have given—years of loyal service to the count. I revealed the escape from the infirmary this morning. I did that! Have mercy, please."

"Oh, shut up, you big baby," said Bunny. "This will be fun."

Princess Abattoir's teeth gleamed. "Yes," she said, drawing the word out as though it tasted sweet in her mouth. "I'm sure His Beneficence will enjoy it tremendously." She laughed with a sound like breaking glass, and the Special Police herded Bunny and Captain Dwop away. "On your knees, captives of the count."

The prisoners knelt. They kept their hands on their heads. Kale and Adele tried to get the boys' attention by moving only their eyes, but the boys were in front of them and did not see. Minutes crawled past like wounded animals.

A fanfare sounded. At the far end of the courtyard, two oaken doors bound with iron bands scraped open. The police stomped in a special rhythm that sounded like an avalanche. Princess Abattoir commanded, "All hail his Beneficence, Count Wilhelm Scream."

The prisoners looked.

The count sat tall and straight on his throne of Black Ice. He was dressed entirely in black, including black velvet gloves that glittered with diamonds and bracelets of fresh Rainbow Ice. He smiled a withering smile.

The throne grated against the stones as it moved forward, giving off waves of bitter cold. The women were closest to it. They flinched. The ice was not like any other black they had ever seen, but a cold, hungry bleakness that looked as if it had frozen all other colors to death.

Bunny and Captain Dwop were shackled to the ice. Special Police Officers prodded them forward with spears.

They were pushing the throne.

Bunny's vest was gone, and with it any tools that she might have used to escape. Her hands, and Captain Dwop's, were wrapped in strips of cloth to keep them from touching the deadly throne. Even so, they quaked with every step. Captain Dwop's legs went into spasm and he collapsed. Bunny held her head high, but her arms shook and finally she, too, fell to the ground.

Rage filled the courtyard.

The count curled his finger. Two Special Police Officers dragged Bunny and Captain Dwop before him. Their chains clattered on the flagstones. Languidly, the count stretched out his booted feet and rested them on his fallen enemies. Dwop's leg still jerked, but Bunny lay still.

"Look on the doom of those who oppose the count," ordered Princess Abattoir.

The prisoners looked. They had to. The count smiled, enjoying their helplessness.

But what he did not see was this. Because he was between the two bands of prisoners, anyone looking at him also saw the other group. A gasp filled the courtyard. The count thought it was terror, or defeat. It was not. Instead, a flush brightened many a dust-clouded or flour-encrusted cheek. For of course, the prisoners who had been brought to the courtyard ahead of the mineworkers were the laborers from the Food Mills.

For the first time in a dozen years, the Ascendant Defenders were united.

It was easier for the women to recognize the men. Under the dirt their faces had not changed much, and as they were all required to be clean-shaven, beards were not an issue.

It was harder for the men to spot their wives, who had to wear kerchiefs over their hair to keep it from getting caught in the mill gears. This was not so much out of concern for their safety as it was for the upkeep of the machinery. The result, however, was that they all looked much the same from a distance. Stella, who happened to be kneeling in the front row, could see a man she was pretty sure was her husband. She pulled off her kerchief and let her hair flow onto her shoulders. It was a rich chestnut, and even despite her long captivity it gleamed in the dull light. "Jerry," she breathed.

Jerry heard. He saw her hair, how it framed her face and made her eyes stand out. A huge grin broke out on his face, and in a moment of rocket-fueled exuberance, the first she had felt in many a long year, Stella threw her kerchief in the air.

"Who did that?" roared a Special Police Officer. He raised his truncheon.

Ingrid whipped off her kerchief and threw it aloft. Her hair was short and blond and spiky. "I did it!"

Suddenly the air was full of flying kerchiefs and cries of, "I did it!" and, "No, me," and, "Over here, kelp-face!" As the women shouted they rose, hitting and punching.

The Special Police crashed down on them, clubs raised, laughing the laugh of bullies who know their victims cannot escape.

They forgot about the men.

The miners had just had their first glimpse of their wives in years, and they did not intend it to be their last. Roaring, they surged forth in a dark and dusty wave.

There are times when training and organization win the day. Such times are called "most days."

Other times, the rage and desperation of people who have nothing to lose makes a tide that nothing can withstand, and justice pours down like a mighty stream. That is what happened this day.

Kale grabbed two goons by their collars and bonked their heads together till they went limp. Ingrid and Bob jumped up and down on a hoodlum's stomach. Jerry and Stella hung from the beard of a moss-colored troll, dragging him to the ground. Everywhere the enemy collapsed. Victory seemed certain.

"Stop!" cried a horrible voice.

No one did.

"Or I will kill these boys," said Count Wilhelm Scream.

Everyone froze. Princess Abattoir, her face alight with cold fire, pulled Casper and Jasper before the throne. A troll with a black eye yanked Bunny and Captain Dwop aside. The boys thrashed and kicked, but could not break free. The princess's talons seemed to dig through their flesh and scrape their bones.

"Your Beneficence," purred the princess, "these traitors are my gift. Dispatch them as you will."

From the back of the courtyard, Adele cried out. At her side, Kale choked and was silent. A truncheon seized from a Special Police Officer dropped from his suddenly numb fingers, ringing against the flagstones.

The count looked at Kale and Adele. He looked at the boys. And he knew.

He snapped his fingers. Several battered toughs picked themselves off the ground. They dragged Adele and Kale to the count.

"I won't make you kneel," said the count softly. "I want you to have a perfect view of this."

"We weren't planning on kneeling anyway," said Casper, who thought the count was talking to him and Jasper. The boys did not see Adele and Kale being pulled up behind them. Everyone else was frozen in horror.

The count looked down his beaked nose. "You are disobedient, low-born ragamuffins."

"Absolutely," said Jasper.

"So good of you to notice," said Casper.

The count peeled off one of his black gloves and dropped it. The diamonds clinked on the flagstones. The glove lay like an inky pool. He stretched out his hand. Cold came off his fingers. Casper felt the skin of his face tighten till it stung. Jasper flinched and turned away.

The count laughed a long, slow chuckle. "Does it hurt?" he said softly. "Oh, yes, it does. And it will hurt much more."

"No," said a voice.

The count did not turn to look. He dropped his second glove. It swirled to the ground. Casper and Jasper yanked away again, but Princess Abattoir's claws held them as tightly as the chains around their wrists. Behind them, Adele screamed the terrible cry of someone who is again about to lose what she loves most in the world.

"*I said no,*" shouted the voice. And this time the count looked.

Bunny staggered to her feet. Grasping the chains that bound her to the throne, she pounded it with all her might.

Princess Abattoir threw back her head and laughed. She gripped the boys tighter. Her nails pierced their skin, raising droplets of blood.

The throne cracked. Bunny gasped. The count leaped to his feet. The bandages on Bunny's hands smoked. She hit the throne again. The count lunged at her, chalky fingers outstretched. She dodged, striking the chair with both fists. Her chains flew through the air. Her bandages turned black and fell away like soot. The count clung to his throne as if he could hold it together. Bunny raised her hands over her head and crashed them down. Her face contorted. She shuddered. Chips of Black Ice clattered to the flagstones. The count screamed. He leaped at her. She smashed her chain-wrapped fists down on his head.

He fell.

"Stop her," snarled the princess. But the Special Police backed away from the Black Ice, eyes wide.

A shard fell from the throne. Bunny gripped it with both hands. She stumbled forward on tottering legs.

The Special Police holding Kale and Adele let go and ran. Princess Abattoir shoved Casper and Jasper before her like a shield. Bunny lurched. Her weakened legs would not obey her, would not stop. Her pink eyes grew round, horrified. The princess gleamed with vicious delight.

Adele punched Princess Abattoir. She loosened her grip on the boys. Kale grabbed Casper. Adele grabbed Jasper. They threw them to the ground as Bunny fell forward.

She drove the blade of ice into Princess Abattoir's heart.

The princess screamed. She clawed Bunny's face. Bunny's lips pulled back in a grimace. She leaned in closer. Her arms shook. A groan dripped from her throat. The princess fell back against the fractured throne.

It shattered with a white and silver sound. Light filled the courtyard. Locked doors sprang open, and the manacles on Casper and Jasper's wrists vanished like smoke. The banners overhead turned to mist and drifted away.

Princess Abattoir slid to the cold, stone floor. Bunny still clutched the icy dagger. The princess stared at her. A dark, bubbling sound came from her lips. Her wide eyes focused, and she took a slow, gargling breath.

"You," she said. "Now I remember...you."

She gave a final sigh. Her limbs loosened, and her eyes glazed over.

Bunny knelt over the body of Princess Abattoir. Swaying, she dropped her icy blade.

Casper pulled himself to his feet. "Bunny! You did it!"

Bunny drooped. Casper and Jasper caught her and eased her to the floor.

"Hang in there, Bunny," said Jasper.

"We'll get a sorceress. Or an apothecary," said Casper.

As though it were a terrible effort, Bunny shook her head. "I touched the ice," she whispered. She held up her hand. It was as white as flour, and even as the boys watched, the deathly pallor spread up her arm. Black cracks appeared, encasing her skin in a dusky web.

"No," said Casper desperately. "No, no, no."

"Stay with us," cried Jasper.

"It's okay, boys," said Bunny softly. "I did what I set out to do." She drew a deep breath and relaxed. "Oh, my," she said. "It's so late...I really must be going."

Her head lolled to one side. Her hand dropped to the ground, lifeless.

"They killed the princess," gasped a bruiser.

"Kill them back," yelled a strong-arm.

"This way!" shouted Adele. As the Special Police advanced, the rebels bolted to the archway that had admitted the count and his throne. They pulled the doors shut behind them and dropped a huge oaken beam into brackets, locking them. The planks shook as the enemy pounded outside.

"We need reinforcements," said Adele.

"Let's find the dungeons," said Kale.

"Which way?" said Jerry.

"Upstairs is the dragon," said Bob. "I saw the smoke."

"Downstairs it is," said Kale.

"We're coming too," said Casper and Jasper.

"Fine," said Kale. "Everyone else, watch the windows. Keep low."

They dashed through dank and dewy corridors and tumbled down slippery staircases until they found a doorway with a sign over it that said, "Abandon All Hope Ye Who Enter Here."

"Derivative," sniffed Bob, who had studied poetry in school.

"It's an homage," snapped Jerry, who had a background in copyright law.

"It's the dungeons," said Casper.

"It's locked," said Kale.

"It's not," said Jasper. He pointed.

When the Throne of Black Ice shattered, every lock in the castle had opened. So although a padlock the size of a ham hock still hung from its iron hasp, it was sprung. Kale flung it to one side and threw the door open.

Prisoners cascaded forth. Some leaped with joy. Others walked. A few crept with uneasy steps, leaning against each other for support. A small number needed to be carried. The strongest ones scooped them up like rag dolls, or made seats of their hands.

"Can I leave now?" said a deep, oatmeal-thick voice. Guthrum Danegeld, sometimes known as Danegeld the Sinister, surged to the front of the crowd with his enormous troll strides.

"You sure can," said Casper.

"Where is Princess Abattoir?" Guthrum asked. "She still has my left-handed shillelagh holster."

"She's dead," said Jasper.

"Oh, good," said Danegeld. "Then she will not mind if I go get it."

"Do you know where it is?" said Kale.

"It is in the Weapon Room."

Kale wondered if he could possibly be this lucky. "Do you know where that is?"

"Certainly." Danegeld lifted his shaggy arm to show his *Semper Tyrannis* armband. "I am employed by the Special Police. I know where the weapons are stored."

"Can you take us to it? Now?"

"I was going there anyway."

Danegeld led them around corners and up a staircase and into a room they would never have found by themselves. The walls bristled with weapons: swords, bows and arrows, daggers, spears, and, sitting on a table in one corner, a particularly fine left-handed shillelagh holster encasing a custom-modified shillelagh. Danegeld strapped it on, a craggy grin splitting his face. "Now I am ready for some action."

"Just to be clear," said Kale, "whose side are you on?"

"The Special Police put me in the dungeon," said Guthrum. "You let me out. So now I will break a few of their heads."

"Much obliged." Kale grabbed weapons. "Let's go."

And so it happened that about a minute and a half later, the rebels waiting at the double oak doors found that they were no longer unarmed. "Have a dagger," yelled Casper, tossing it (still sheathed, of course) to Adele. "Have a spear. Have a truncheon."

"Don't worry," yelled Jasper, running through the doorway with his arms full. "We brought enough for everyone."

Guthrum lifted the oaken beam. Stella and Ingrid pushed open the doors. The Ascendant Defenders crashed down upon the Special Police. Guthrum waded through the throng, thumping pates with his left-handed shillelagh. A tattered stream of the healthier prisoners followed in his wake, lashing out at their former captors. Those who were too weak simply lay down and hoped someone would trip over them.

Casper and Jasper were in their element. Their eyes flashed like sword blades, and their muscles thrummed like bowstrings. This was like every schoolyard battle they had ever fought, only bigger and better: more enemies, more shouts and cries, more at stake in every way. Once again, victory seemed certain.

"Open the gate!" shouted a guard on the ramparts.

The portcullis rose. Framed in its stone arch stood Jacques Boute and his patrol. Behind them, carts of Black Ice glistered in the bleak light.

56

Jacques Boute knew an uprising when he saw one. "Forward! Pile the ice in the center of the courtyard. We execute the traitors immediately. Trials next week."

Guards with ashen faces pushed the carts inside. A cold miasma filled the air.

Encouraged by the appearance of reinforcements, the count's forces stomped and grabbed. Everyone else fought and ran.

Herschel Wulfgrim sprang from the lead cart with a warrior's howl. It died on his lips when he saw smoke boiling from the highest tower above the courtyard.

He leaped onto the only troll not rounding up prisoners and pulled himself up to its shoulder, gripping its wiry hair.

"Ow," said Guthrum Danegeld, swatting.

Herschel bobbed away from the great hand. "Hey, you. Tink you can trow me up to dat tower window?"

Guthrum squinted at it. "Yes."

"Do it."

"Why?"

This was no time for exposition. Herschel grabbed one of the troll's vast, drooping ears. "Because if you don', I bite dis off right now."

"You are a hostile little fellow." Guthrum was pained. But he cupped his hand anyway. Herschel jumped in. With a mighty, left-handed heave, Guthrum hurled the kobold heavenwards. And though his heart may not have been pure, his aim was true, for Herschel landed, flailing, on the stone windowsill of the Dragon Tower of Mirkstone.

A woeful sight met his eyes. The dragon, a great, scaly creature, was shackled to the floor by an iron collar. The chains were so short she could barely lift her knobby head. Her wings lay slack about her serpentine body, like collapsed tents. Behind her lay a clutch of pearly white eggs the size of bed pillows. She glared at him with one red-and-gold eye.

"Hey," said Herschel. "Wanna get back at the *Schnitzelhunden* who done dis to you?"

The dragon heaved against the shackles. Her wings thrashed, and acrid smoke snorted from her nostrils.

"*Oy,* I'm hopin' dat means yes." Herschel bit the fetters in half. The dragon lifted her bulbous head and roared, shooting white sparks and flame. Herschel jumped onto her back, just in front of the wings. The dragon rocketed out of the window with a gut-sucking leap, Herschel clinging to her collar as if his life depended on it—which, of course, it did.

Now, to understand how extraordinarily brave this was, you must remember that Herschel was chthonic, a jaw-cracker of a word meaning that unlike you or me, he ordinarily dwelt underground. Nothing in his nature was meant for soaring through high windows into wide-open spaces. And now imagine wings powerful enough to hoist a full-grown dragon into the air, and the pounding sound that filled Herschel's ears with every enormous flap. Wind burned his eyes; tears whipped his cheeks. His legs struggled to keep him astride the dragon as her shoulder muscles roiled under him. No, this was not how Herschel Wulfgrim would have chosen to spend his day.

Wishing he didn't have to, Herschel looked down. In the center of the courtyard stood a mound of Black Ice big enough to sled on. The carts were empty. The exhausted mine guards had fallen, some to their knees, others on their faces. The Special Police and castle guards had penned the rebels and dungeon escapees in a corner.

"Kill the cripples first!" ordered Jacques Boute. Two thugs grabbed Adele and shoved her toward the ice pile. Kale lunged forward. A troll sat on him.

Herschel pulled down on the collar. The dragon swooped. "Now!" cried Herschel. *"Blitzen-zee das Nacht-Iss! For das Frözenshaften! Hot Ziggety!"*

Flame blasted from the dragon's mouth. Ice exploded in a glittering, black cloud, obscuring Herschel's view until the furious wing beats dispersed it. Gritting his teeth, he chanced another glance down into the courtyard.

The ice was gone, leaving only a charcoal-colored smudge on the flagstones. All eyes turned upward, and every mouth was agape.

"Herschel!" cried Kale. "What are you doing? Come down!"

But though Herschel tugged desperately on the iron collar, the dragon wheeled up and away, vanishing into the bright afternoon sky as his despairing cry faded with her.

"We won," cried Stella.

"Never!" bellowed Boute. A military vehicle emblazoned with the insignia of Count Wilhelm Scream barreled under the raised portcullis. Guards leaped out, weapons at the ready. "Anyone wearing a uniform—hands up," shouted the driver.

Groaning, the rebels raised their hands for what seemed the hundredth time that day. Captain Boute whooped.

"Ah. I can see I wasn't clear enough," barked the driver. "Not prison uniforms. Police uniforms. That's right—in the air, *now.*"

Only then did everyone notice that the guards' uniforms didn't fit, and that their faces were covered with dust.

Uncertainly, the Mirkstone guards and Special Police raised their hands. Kale, who had gotten away from the troll sitting on him when it fled from the ice cloud, helped Adele to her feet. She pointed. "Look!"

To say that the hillside beyond the archway was black with advancing forces would be misleading. For one thing, many wore bright colors. But as they emerged from what seemed to be every tree and rock and dip in the ground, they certainly appeared to cover the land.

"Those aren't reinforcements," said Boute.

"Oh, yes, they are," said the driver.

At this point, Captain Jacques Boute realized two things.

First, the crowd seething toward Mirkstone was not with Count Wilhelm Scream, but against him—exactly like the gaggle within the courtyard. This meant he was sandwiched between two groups of people who were distinctly unhappy with him.

Second, all that remained of his deadliest weapon was a smudge.

"RUN," he roared. And just so everyone would understand what he meant, he turned and ran. (This is called "leading by example.")

As Boute careened toward the archway, the driver stuck out his foot, sending him sprawling on the flagstones. The driver stepped on Boute's back, pinning him. He waved to Kale. "We got halfway to Inglenook before we ran into a patrol," he called, for of course he was none other than Norbert from Nether Wallop. "Stopped us and demanded to see our papers. I have to say, this guy was a prince—we'd never have made it without him." He patted the vehicle affectionately.

"All in the line of duty," said the Colonel modestly.

"Told us to pretend to be drunk while he pretended to be sober. Then he said he was the designated driver for a group of hard-working public servants on furlough, so where's the nearest pub, officer? We ended up at the Tone-Deaf Troubadour. Met up with some real helpful folks there. And then *he* put out the word."

A stout fellow stepped from the vehicle. He saluted Kale. "Commander Brewski, at your service. We've opened the tunnels." He gestured at the hordes on the hills.

"How did you do all this?" marveled Adele.

"I heard from Sergeant Eullenspiegel and Lieutenant Flora as soon as they made contact with your advance guard. We've been training in secret in the storerooms under the pubs in Inglenook. You know, just waiting for the right moment."

"Us too," said Kale.

Flat on the stone floor, Captain Boute wheezed. "We surrender."

"Yes," said Kale. "Yes, you do."

With the aid of their new comrades, the rebels rounded up Special Police, many of whom babbled that it wasn't their fault and they were victims of an unjust society. Soon they were grumpily relinquishing their weapons to the Army of the Recently Liberated, or ARL, as they now called themselves.

"Put them in the dungeons," said Commander Brewski. "Are they troll-proof?"

"Yes," said Guthrum Danegeld in his thick voice. "Very."

Brewski scowled at the troll, who still wore the badge of the Special Police on his hairy arm. "Agent of the count, eh? You can just go straight to lockup with everyone else."

"By no means," said Adele.

"He's one of the heroes of the Battle of Mirkstone," said Kale.

"He tossed the kobold," said Adele, who had seen it happen.

"Kobold?" said Commander Brewski.

"Herschel," said Kale.

"Who's Herschel?" said Adele.

"The dragon rider," said Kale.

"What dragon?" said Commander Brewski.

"Oh, wait," said Adele. "That was before you got here."

"The troll threw the kobold," said Kale.

Commander Brewski arranged features into a patient expression that said this would all make sense eventually.

"This troll and the kobold—Herschel?—and the dragon saved the day," said Adele. "To be brief."

"Oh, well, then, that's different," said Brewski. "What's your name?"

Guthrum drew himself to his considerable height. "I am called Danegeld the Sinister, Slayer of Enemies, Wielder of the Left-Handed Shillelagh."

"Very well, Danegeld the Sinister," said Commander Brewski, smiling. "Any chance you could herd these hooligans into the dungeons for safekeeping?"

"It will be my pleasure," said Guthrum. "This one was not very nice to me." He nudged Captain Dwop with his shaggy foot.

"Say," said Commander Brewski, "what's wrong with him?"

Captain Dwop's manacles had evaporated from his wrists when the throne broke apart, but he had not tried to escape. He lay where he had fallen on the flagstones, barely moving. His breath was shallow, his eyes were glassy, and his back was festooned with footprints.

"Ice poisoning," said Kale. "Doesn't look too bad. Give him some hot broth and keep him away from frozen desserts for a while."

"Okey-dokey." Danegeld tucked Captain Dwop under one arm. He and the ARL herded the count's guards and Special Police into the dungeons. Adele hung the broken lock in the staple on the door, where it functioned just as well as if it had been whole.

"We'll get out," shouted Jacques Boute, his voice muffled by the door. "And when we do, you'll be sorry. We will crush you. We will *destroy* you. We will—"

"Guthrum the Sinister," said Adele, "would you mind guarding this door?"

"My pleasure," said the troll, and he settled himself on the floor with his back to the thick planks of the door, tapping his shillelagh in his open palm and humming a chipper ditty.

Back in the courtyard, Adele drew a deep breath. "Where are those two boys?"

Kale pointed. His face was tired, and deeply lined.

Casper and Jasper knelt by the shattered remnants of the throne. It had turned white when it broke apart, and it sparkled so brightly it almost hurt to look at it. Somehow the boys knew they could touch the powdered ice with no danger, but neither one tried. As gently as they could, they lifted Bunny and carried her away from the pale and dreadful corpse of Princess Abattoir.

They laid Bunny out on the flagstones in a patch of sunlight. They brushed her fine, white hair from her face, and wiped the blood from her lips and a small cut under one eye. Bruises were forming on her fair skin, but she would never feel them. They straightened her limbs and pulled her clothes so they were neat and unwrinkled. And with the tips of their fingers, they closed her pink eyes for the last time.

Kale and Adele waited till they were done. Finally, Adele stepped forward. "Who was she?"

Casper wiped his eyes but could not speak. Jasper looked at the still form. "A friend," was all he could say.

"I'm sorry," said Adele. "She was so brave."

Casper nodded. Jasper stared at his hands.

Kale moved to stand beside Adele. "Where did she live?"

"Inglenook," said Casper. "Where we're from."

Kale and Adele exchanged a look. "Not Middlemost?" said Kale.

Jasper looked up at them. "Why Middlemost?"

Kale cleared his throat. "We used to live there."

"A long time ago," said Adele. She and Kale were watching the boys very closely.

Jasper stood. Now that battle no longer raged, he had time to notice things, such as Kale and Adele's red hair and the color of their eyes. He saw that Kale slouched on one side when he wasn't thinking about it, just like Casper, and that Adele was fidgeting with her thumb just as he himself did. "How long ago?"

"Twelve years," said Adele. She placed her words carefully, as if each were so fragile it might break.

Casper rose to his feet. "We were born in Middlemost," he said. "Apparently."

"Apparently?" said Kale.

"We didn't know till a few days ago," said Casper.

The four stared at each other. All around them activity swirled. The Army of the Recently Liberated thumped through the castle and its environs. Commander Brewski barked orders. The army barked replies. Every few seconds someone yelled with excitement over some new discovery. But to the four people in the center of the hubbub, it all seemed very far away.

They were in a bubble of silence, a small world that contained only them.

Adele couldn't stand it any more. "Are you—Charles and James?"

"No," said Casper.

Adele gave a soft cry. Kale jerked his head back.

"Yes," said Jasper.

"I mean, sort of," said Casper.

"We don't have the necklaces," said Jasper.

"Right," said Casper. "The necklaces. That would have been proof, yes?"

"Necklaces?" said Kale.

"The medallions," said Casper. "Our parents, I mean our aunt and uncle—"

"They're not our aunt and uncle exactly," said Jasper. "But we always called them that, so—"

"Were they on your wrists?" said Adele.

"What, the medallions?" said Casper.

"Lockets," said Jasper. "Yes, on our wrists."

"Till we got older. Then we wore them on our necks."

"Where are they?" said Kale.

"Lost them," said Jasper.

"Well, not lost in the strictest sense of the term."

"We're not that careless."

"We had to pay a troll," said Casper.

"One had a C and one had a J," said Jasper.

"We didn't know they opened till a few days ago," said Casper. "Then we saw—oh."

Casper looked hard at the two people in front of him. He remembered the pictures from the locket. Those faces were young and unlined. That happy mother and father had not spent years toiling in captivity. But these were the same faces, of this he was sure. "And so," he said, "you are...I mean, you must be...."

Adele burst out crying. She covered her face with one hand and reached for her sons with the other. Kale's shoulders shook and his face collapsed as he, too, embraced the boys. And suddenly Casper and Jasper, who had not realized they were holding back tears, found themselves sobbing as they clutched two total strangers who had saved their lives years ago.

Far overhead, from a ledge on the castle wall overlooking the courtyard, a fidelius bird began to sing.

"Commander Brewski reporting to Commander Brandiwygn," said a voice.

"And they moved to Inglenook with us so no one would know," said Casper.

"Good thinking," said Kale.

"Commander Brandiwygn, I am ready to make an interim report," said Commander Brewski.

"Bully for you," said Adele. "Go on, boys. What happened next?"

"Well, it's kind of a long story," said Jasper.

"I need to report to Commander Brandiwygn," said Commander Brewski.

Kale barely glanced at him. "Who's Commander Brandiwygn?"

"Your men tell me you are, sir."

"Yes, yes, lovely," said Adele. "Charles, how did you get that scar on your chin? I bet there's a story there."

Kale turned his back on Commander Brewski. "Go ahead, then."

"Quick status report," said Commander Brewski. "The prisoners are liberated, the princess is dead—"

"Great," said Kale.

"Tell us a little more about that couple who raised you," said Adele. "What were their names again?"

"However, we still face challenges," said Commander Brewski loudly.

"We all face challenges," said Kale. "James, I mean Jasper, I used to love fishing when I was your age. Is that something you're interested in?"

"Count Wilhelm Scream is missing," said Commander Brewski.

"What?" said Adele.

"What?" said Kale.

"Also, the lands around the castle are rife with his minions," said Brewski. "I'm afraid, sir, that despite our victory the danger is still great."

Kale rubbed his chin. Adele sighed. Casper turned to Jasper. "Just when I thought things were getting easier," he said.

Indeed, in a number of ways the real work was just beginning; for now everyone engaged upon the great task of ridding the land of the shadow of Count Wilhelm Scream.

Casper and Jasper dug a grave for Bunny just outside of Mirkstone and laid their friend to rest. With Guthrum's help they erected a stone spire over it. Since no one knew her real name, the letters carved into the stone read, "Here Lies Bunny, the Hero of Our Liberty." They cleared the underbrush around it so they could plant her favorite vegetables in the spring.

"We'll call it Bunny's Bounty," said Casper. "Everyone should know about her."

"It's a long way to come for a carrot," said Jasper. "But I suppose that's not the point."

Adele decided to turn the Food Mills into a museum about Scream's reign. It would be good for field trips. She and her friends set to work collecting memorabilia and dismantling the horrid machinery, as well as clearing dead vines and other detritus from the windowsills in order to create nesting habitat for fidelius birds.

Commander Brewski dispatched runners to cry aloud the glorious news. Throughout the Lands of Yonder, joyous bells pealed. In Larksong and Inglenook and Nether Wallop, eager crowds toppled statues of the count and the princess. Secret libraries in Widdershins and Deasil threw open their doors and wheeled out books of poetry and adventure, of cabbages and kings. In Middlemost, lanterns were hung on every street and byway, and people danced all night to music that had been forbidden mere hours before.

When word reached Inglenook that a pair of exuberant redheads had been in the thick of the battle that had quite literally dethroned the count, Becky and Zach nearly collapsed with relief. They loved the boys dearly and had been frantic at their disappearance. They considered galloping to the castle to retrieve them, but Gloamwoods was seething like a broken wasp nest as former lackeys of the count tried to escape and former prisoners of the count tried to make sure they didn't. Skirmishes between these two groups were common, and the Zuckermans had no wish to become what military people call "collateral damage" and everyone else calls "dead." So instead they wrote a hasty letter to the boys, rolling it into a little tube that they sealed with honey-scented wax, as was the custom.

They handed it to the runner from Mirkstone, who eyed it suspiciously. "Is it cheerful?"

"Cheerful?" said Becky.

"Who cares?" said Zach.

The runner drew himself up. "My job description is quite clear: I 'cry aloud the glorious news.' So if this news isn't glorious, it's not my responsibility."

"It's *mostly* cheerful," said Becky. "It says we love you and we miss you and yes, we're a little miffed because did you even *think* about how we would worry and we've been absolutely *frantic* but the main thing is we understand how strongly you felt about going but if only you'd checked in with us first we would really have preferred that but we forgive you and we'll talk more about this later but things just haven't been the same without you and have you been eating properly and—"

"Got it," said the runner hastily. He sprinted out of Inglenook's gate and up the mountain.

When Casper and Jasper read the letter, they did not know how to respond. They were still adjusting to their new status as war heroes, which was overwhelming in itself; and they had just been reunited with long-lost parents whom they had until recently believed to be dead. Staying with Kale and Adele seemed best in some ways. On the other hand, they did not wish to hurt the Zuckermans with their absence any longer than was necessary.

"Then that's what you should tell them," said Adele when they told her and Kale their problem. She spoke lightly, but she, too, was torn. She did not want to say goodbye to the boys, but she knew only too well how the Zuckermans must feel. So

Casper and Jasper penned a quick note, assuring Becky and Zach that they were well, and promising to return when they could.

In the midst of all this activity, the wiggle-dragons hatched. They had wings and four legs, like their mother, and in most respects appeared to be perfectly normal dragons such as one might see curled around any perfectly normal pile of treasure in any given cave. Thanks to Herschel Wulfgrim, the eggs had not been poisoned with Black Ice, so the little creatures did not spew the deadly frost intended by Princess Abattoir and Count Wilhelm Scream. Indeed, the only indication of their wyvern paternity was a slight Scandinavian accent when they roared.

"What on earth are we going to do with them?" said Kale.

"When they get a bit older they'll be very helpful," said Adele. Her leg was healing nicely and she no longer needed a crutch. Instead she leaned on a cane Guthrum had kindly made for her by splicing together billy clubs from the Weapon Room. "For now, just get them hot toddies and a few dead rats."

Thanks to the assiduous efforts of the ARL, Gloamwoods was soon minion-free. The judge in Middlemost, who had not had a great deal to do for the past dozen years, set to work scheduling trials and scouring the hinterlands for unbiased jurors.

Late in the summer, Adele and Stella and Ingrid laid trails of rancid goat meat to coax the wiggle-dragons to the frozen patches in Gloamwoods where nothing had grown since the count took power. They tickled the scaly little creatures with very long branches till their giggling melted the ice and set the clearings ablaze. The fires burned for days. When it was over,

Gloamwoods was spattered with burned, blackened patches where soot drifted like dark mist.

"What a mess," said Kale, looking at the smoldering woodlands from the Mirkstone battlements.

"The ash will fertilize the soil, and next year we'll have wonderful plant growth," said Adele. "Food, habitat—this is a new start."

"I was hoping it would force Scream out of wherever he's hiding," said Kale.

"A number of leading magicologists are saying that with the throne gone he's probably greatly weakened."

"Still," said Casper. "He's out there somewhere."

"I wonder where," said Jasper.

"Let's try the mines," said Kale. "He has a thing about Black Ice."

They piled into the Colonel, who greeted them with an affectionate "Tally ho!" The count's insignia had been defaced with a rude picture, courtesy of Casper and Jasper. As Commander Brewski said, it was good for morale.

As they pulled up to the mine gates, a little blue figure leaped to meet them. Kale threw open the car door. "Herschel!"

They ran to each other's arms. Herschel sported a new coat, and the feather in his hat stood at a jaunty angle. *"Ach!* How you doin', eh?"

"Better now." Kale grinned. "What happened? Last time I saw you, you were soaring away on some crazy dragon."

"Oh, dat." Herschel tried to look modest and failed utterly. "She drop me here and take off again. Say she got to fine her boyfriend. His name Wessex an' he live in up north an' some stuff about true love."

"And you've been here ever since?"

"Yah. But guess what?" Herschel puffed out his chest. "I is no more Karetaker Eccentrikkus. Now everyone call me Herschel Dragonrider. I is de hero of *das Frözenshaften.*"

"Fantastic," said Kale. "Can we talk to them?"

The other kobolds greeted them with exuberance and took a break from restoring their ancestral home to its former glory. "I am telling you, it is almost like dat old *Drek-Spouter* was never here," said Hütchen happily. "My Starski, she is chust crazy happy to be home again."

"What does *'Drek-Spouter'* mean?" asked Casper.

"Oh, my, look at the time," said Adele, who had picked up some of the kobolds' language during her journey with them. "Let's go, boys."

"You mean the count?" said Kale. "Have you seen him?"

Hütchen shook his head. "No, sorry. But if he komen here, we gif you vaterver is left over vunce we are don wit him. Hokay?"

"Hokay," said Kale. And they drove back to Castle Mirkstone.

Each day presented a new challenge or triumph: tunnels had to be cleared, dungeons filled in, and, one particularly exasperating week, Brewski and the ARL held hearings for a committee of aggrieved werewolves complaining about their working conditions in the newly opened-up forest. But still no one had seen the count.

As the weeks stretched on, Kale and Adele found themselves thinking longingly of the broad, tree-lined roads and quirky shops of Middlemost. Casper and Jasper nightly dreamed of the Inglenook Bakery and Sweet Shop and their warm, cluttered room under the eaves. Plus, the letters from Becky and Zach had become more insistent of late. They went to Commander Brewski.

"We're going home," said Adele.

Commander Brewski looked up from the papers on his desk in the former throne room, which looked quite pleasant now that the ARL had punched windows in its walls. "We need you here."

"We'll be back," said Kale.

"But our other parents are worrying about us," said Casper.

"We were rather irresponsible on the way out," said Jasper.

"Didn't leave them a note," said Casper.

"Had no idea we'd be gone this long," said Jasper.

"Kids today," sighed Casper.

Not for nothing was Commander Brewski the most popular barkeep in Inglenook. He smiled. "We'll miss you, but if you need to go, so be it." He tore a piece of paper from a roll on his desk and jotted on it. "You'll need an escort. Been some saboteurs digging up the roads. Best to take the tunnel into the Troubadour. I'll have them get a couple rooms ready. You can wash up and have a bite before you go home." He whistled between his teeth. A pigeon fluttered through the open window and extended its leg. Brewski tied on the message and the bird flew back out. "On the house, obviously."

"Thanks," said Adele. "That's very kind."

60

The next morning found the Brandiwygns ready for their return. Even now, a trip through Gloamwoods was not to be undertaken lightly, and they were prepared, they hoped, for anything. They wore boots and warm clothes, and carried backpacks with roasted meat, bottles of spring water, fresh fruit, and sparkleberry preserves. Kale had a rapier; Adele had a saber and her billy club cane, which could double as a weapon if necessary. Daggers hung from Casper and Jasper's belts.

The Colonel pulled up, and the window rolled down. The driver tossed her long, blond hair. "All set?"

"Flora," gargled Jasper.

She smiled. "That's Lieutenant Flora to you. I wanted to be the one to escort you boys back home, seeing as how none of this would have happened without you."

"Aw, gee," said Casper, blushing.

"Haghhahaha," giggled Jasper.

"Great," said Adele, pulling the boys and her husband into the Colonel and dropping her cane into the back. "Any time you're ready."

To say the least, going down Mount Count was easier than going up. The family kept an eye out and weapons at the ready, but the balance of power had shifted so wrenchingly in the past few weeks that nowadays their enemies were more interested in hiding than attacking. The road was empty, and they sailed toward Inglenook.

"Halt!" roared the Colonel.

Flora stood on the brakes. "Dang."

"What?" said Casper.

She pointed. A heap of charred rubble blocked the road. Behind it they could hear baby wiggle-dragons giggling. Each time this happened, a puff of flame shot up.

"We'll have to go off-road. Hang on." Flora turned the wheel. "This way, Colonel, sir."

They bounded into the forest. The Colonel shot under massive trees and through burned patches, his wheels raising clouds of soot.

"Do you know the way?" shouted Kale.

"Yoiks!" bellowed the Colonel.

"Long as we keep heading downhill we should be fine," shouted Flora.

Adele blew soot out of her nose into a handkerchief. "Watch out for the swamp."

"Quite right," roared the Colonel. "Once more down to the beach!"

"No, I said—"

The Colonel lurched sideways. Flora wrenched the useless wheel. A squelching sound met their ears.

"—swamp," sighed Adele.

Flora turned off the engine and stepped out. Her feet sank to the tops of her boots. When she got back in her face was grim. "We're stuck."

Everyone climbed out and huddled on a hassock. Through the trees they could see sheets of water and marshmallow trunks waving in the breathless air. The Colonel was sunk up to his bumpers. "Bit of a soggysloshkins, what?" he burbled.

"We can head back and get a team to pull us out," began Flora.

"Good show," agreed the Colonel. "My kingdom for a horse!"

"Not with this bum leg," said Adele ruefully, leaning on her cane.

"We'd have to overnight in Gloamwoods," said Kale.

"No, thanks," said Adele.

"What's your plan then?" said Flora.

"Let's just keep going," said Adele. "We can't be too far from Inglenook, and we have food and weapons."

"What about the swamp?" said Flora.

"I've been through it dozens of times," said Adele.

"Let's skip the middle, though," said Casper.

"It's not all it's cracked up to be," agreed Jasper.

Flora scratched her chin and nodded. "I can make it to the first outpost before dark. So I guess this is goodbye."

They said farewell, the Colonel urging them to feats of glory and Jasper promising to write Flora every day. Bit by bit the Brandiwygns made their way through the bog. Sometimes they stepped on semi-submerged stones, sometimes they used crude bridges that Adele and her fellow mill workers had built in the bad old days. And although it was not, strictly speaking, easy—Kale fell into a pit of swamp mud and had to be scraped clean, and Casper was stung by a baby Venom Clutch, which hurt and left a tiny scar on his left hand—for the most part they proceeded steadily. By evening they were on dry land.

"How much further?" asked Kale.

"It can't be far," said Jasper. "I remember this stream."

"I think you're right," said Casper. "But wasn't there a pool? I remember thinking Captain Dwop looked better upside down."

"Reflection?"

"Exactly."

"Maybe the stream leads to it," said Jasper.

"Maybe it doesn't," said Casper. "But it's going downhill. Let's follow it."

"Right ho," said Jasper. They shouldered their backpacks, which they had taken off for a brief rest, and followed the freshet.

Afternoon was pushing hard against evening by the time they found the pool. It had been dark and mysterious the first time they saw it, shimmering with the reflections of angry men. Now it was lovely, almost perfectly round and ringed with stands of cattails and a willow or two. The water was greenish brown at the edges, and they could see rippled mud for a few feet. Then the bottom dropped away and the water deepened, becoming a rich violet the color of midnight secrets.

Kale set his pack down and knelt on a rock, splashing water over his head and neck. The others did the same.

"It's close now," said Casper.

"Good," said Adele. She had not complained, but the trek through the Slough had been difficult, and her leg felt weak and painful.

"We just have to circle the pond," said Jasper. "I can see part of the wall."

Kale stood up. "Then let's go."

"You will never reach Inglenook," said a voice like ice.

The Brandiwygns jumped. A pale figure staggered from the woods, lips parted in a snarl.

Count Wilhelm Scream's clothes were torn. His skin was scratched in a map of bloody lines. Some were weeks old and had healed; others were beaded with fresh scabs. His hair stood up in manic attitudes, and his hands were charred. "I knew you would come."

Casper cleared his throat. "Did you now?"

"We didn't know ourselves till recently," said Jasper.

"I burned the road with the dragons you set in the forest. I steered you here."

Kale felt his hands clench into fists. "Clever."

"Getting rid of our driver. So we'd go through Gloamwoods," said Adele. Gripping her cane, she eased between Casper and Jasper, shielding them.

"Good show," said Casper, trying not to look at the count's blackened hands.

"I never leave loose ends." The count rubbed his brow, smearing it with soot.

"That's a lot of planning, isn't it, for the sake of a few, um, ends?" said Jasper.

The count hissed. His teeth showed, jagged and yellow.

"Still, awfully inventive," said Jasper hastily.

"Absolutely crackerjack strategy," agreed Casper. They kept their hands at their daggers.

"You smashed my throne." The count hobbled forward, his eyes glittering like moonlit frost. Casper and Jasper and Kale and Adele backed up to the water's edge. Mud sucked their feet. Suddenly the count doubled over, hands on his knees. "And she—she—Princess. Why?" His face twisted. "Perfect. Obedient. Perfect. Obedient. Obedient."

"Egad," muttered Casper. "He's come unhinged."

"The state of his hinges was always rather dubious," pointed out Jasper in an undertone.

"Today I kill disobedience!" The count plunged a hand into his bedraggled robes and whipped out a gleaming shaft of Black Ice. His eyes fell on Adele, and he rushed at her.

Kale grabbed the count's wrist. His fingers froze in place. A dead whiteness shot up his arm. His face stiffened. The count shrieked with joy.

Adele struck the count's knees with her cane. He staggered. The spear of Black Ice fell into the water. Kale and Adele shoved him. He grabbed them with his blackened hands. With a splash, all three disappeared under the dark surface of the pond.

They sank, twisting and turning in a hideous dance. The count held on with a grip like pliers. The water was icy, bitter. His fingers tightened. Kale and Adele's skin burned where he touched them. Everything else was numb. They could not kick. They could not breathe. They stared in the murky water. They could not see the light above. Their eyes darkened. Their blood was gelid. They stopped fighting.

Count Wilhelm Scream had won.

A rocket of white bubbles hit him from above. His hands went slack. Adele and Kale floated free.

Adele's face broke the surface. She choked. Kale's head was underwater. She pulled him up by his hair. Black water spewed from his mouth. "Where are the boys?" he cried. "Where are the boys?"

Something writhed in the water. A lump of tattered cloth rose from the foam.

"No," said Adele. "No, no—"

Casper's head shot through the mass, then Jasper's. Kale and Adele grabbed them. Together they splashed to shore and stood, trembling. Adele's legs wobbled. Her eyes were so wide Jasper could see white all around the iris, and she embraced the boys with a fury they had never known. Kale's arms were wet and cold, but he too enveloped them with all his might.

It was astonishing to be held so fiercely and yet so tenderly.

"What happened?" gasped Adele.

Casper almost laughed. "He melted."

"What?"

"Melted." Jasper sat down, away from the water. He and Casper pulled off the black tatters that clung to their shirts. "We wanted to kill him," he went on conversationally. "But he just—dissolved."

"Dissolved?" said Kale. He sat down next to Jasper. Adele's injured leg gave way and she half-fell to the ground. Casper did the same. She touched him. His skin was chilly. Adele felt thick and cold inside. She blinked at the sky. White rays slanted through the leaves. They did not warm her.

Jasper showed them a handful of wet rags. "We were fighting an empty sack."

"Ice," mumbled Casper.

Adele opened her backpack, though the zipper seemed made of mud. She pulled out a blanket and put it over Casper's shoulders. She handed a second one to Kale, who draped it over Jasper. "What do you mean, Charles?"

Casper stared at the pond. Dead fish drifted to the surface. "He was made of ice."

For indeed, after all those years of sitting on his Throne of Black Ice and absorbing its powers, the count had frozen to his very core; so that as soon as he plunged into living waters, he simply melted.

Jasper coughed again. He had swallowed more water than his brother, and he felt wretched. "I thought you were dead," he said.

"We almost were," said Kale.

Adele looked at the boys. Their skin was still pale, and their hair was slicked back so they looked like redheaded seals. "Thank you," she said softly.

Casper wiped pondweed from his cheek. His grin was tired, but Adele thought it was the most beautiful thing she had ever seen. "It's not like we had much choice."

"No?"

"No," said Jasper. "We'd already lost you once."

"That's right," said Casper. "And we weren't going to do it again."

Epilogue

After a brief stop at the Tone-Deaf Troubadour to get washed and warmed, the family went straight to the Inglenook Sweet Shop. Aunt Becky and Uncle Zach welcomed the boys with hugs and tears and assurances that they were grounded until the next tyrant took power, which they hoped would be never.

Adele and Kale hung back awkwardly until Casper and Jasper pulled them over and made introductions.

"Thank you for saving them," said Adele.

"Thank you for throwing them," said Becky.

"It hasn't been dull," said Zach.

There was silence. Everyone looked anywhere but at each other.

"Now what?" said Becky finally.

"What do you mean?" said Adele.

"Do you...want them back?"

Kale ran a hand through his hair. "I think," he said, "we all need to consider how best to proceed."

"Perhaps over dinner?" said Becky.

"We would love to," said Adele.

So they stayed for dinner, which was fabulous and ended with some of the ice cream the boys had made before their adventure and which Becky and Zach had put aside for their return. Everyone tossed about plans. They decided that Kale and Adele should sell their old house in Middlemost and purchase a certain empty one across the square from the Sweet Shop. They loved it immediately: it was a great deal like their old one, with a bedroom for the boys under its slate-covered eaves. Casper and Jasper would stay there sometimes, and other times with the Zuckermans.

So that was settled. Now all that remained was everything else.

Now, it can be a tricksy bit of business to return to a place when your time away has changed both you and it. Perhaps you have experienced this: leaving home and coming back to find that the scent of twilight is somehow unfamiliar, and you see unexpected colors, as though with new eyes. This is especially true if everyone there sees you differently as well. As far as Inglenook was concerned, Casper and Jasper had left as delinquents and come back as heroes, and the citizens welcomed them in a delirium of gratitude. There was even talk of re-naming the school in their honor, but the twins refused as a point of honor. And after the first few parades, they found they were ready to get back to their old lives in their much-changed town.

The school's proctor system was abolished, the Thwacking Sticks were whittled into toothpicks, and the principal with the square, cement head was sent packing with all the clunky textbooks he could carry. Nowadays many of the classes were great fun, homework was a thing of the past, and the students were allowed to read anything they wanted.

Commander Brewski split his time between the Tone-Deaf Troubadour and his duties in the new government, and Flora and Till continued to play with the Merry Pranksters. Guthrum Danegeld, finding there was now scant demand for his skill set, became their drummer, said position having opened up with the departure of the count. The drums never lasted the night, but this cost was more than offset by patrons' marvelous generosity whenever he passed the hat.

The boys decided to take their original names for middle names, so Casper became Casper Charles, and Jasper became Jasper James. This pleased both sets of parents, which in turn pleased the twins. They continued to work in the bakery after school and on weekends, being already in the habit. The kobolds sent regular shipments of Rainbow Ice to the Inglenook Sweet Shop, cheerfully refusing payment, and Herschel often dropped by for visit and a frozen treat.

It turned out that Kale and Adele had much in common with Zach and Becky. They were entirely in agreement about things like attending school regularly and brushing one's teeth and not putting snakes in the toilet to see if they could swim clockwise. So in that sense, Casper and Jasper's worst fears were realized.

"It's not going to be easy, raising so many parents," sighed Jasper.

"No indeed," agreed Casper. "Still."

"Still what?"

"Still, I think the whole thing was worth it," said Casper. "Don't you?"

"You bet I do," said Jasper. "With all my heart."

THE END

Acknowledgements

Pilcrow and Inkhorn's Concise Dictionary, recently reestablished as the definitive repository of definitions in the Lands of Yonder, tells us that "gratitude" is "that funny feeling that merely saying 'Thank you' is not enough." Alas, the authors offer no instruction on how to proceed in the face of this insufficiency, so like many a grateful person in the past I shall now do what I know to be utterly inadequate, and salute those whose time, talents, and dedication helped me tell Casper and Jasper's story.

Mike Marano, my editor, told me what was missing from the story. It's not missing any more. Andy Bayiates read at least two different versions of the manuscript, and his comments helped me see what worked and what didn't. Plus, they made me laugh. Doug Jacobs read the book aloud to me and worked his many magicks on it. And Nate and Elwyn were always firmly convinced that this story was the most marvelous thing any child could ever read. They are smart kids, so I hope they are right.